RAVE REVIEWS FOR THE WORK OF DOUGLAS CLEGG!

"Every bit as good as the best works of Stephen King, Peter Straub, or Dan Simmons. What is most remarkable is not how well Clegg provides chills, but how quickly he is able to do so."

—*Hellnotes*

"Clegg's imagery is intense, horrific, but he paints with a poet's hand. Horror at its finest."

—*Publishers Weekly* (Starred Review)

"Unforgettable!"

—*The Washington Post*

"Doug Clegg is one of horror's most captivating voices."

—*BookLovers*

"Clegg possesses a master's unsparing touch for horror. [*You Come When I Call You* is] a brilliant achievement of occult fiction."

—*Rue Morgue*

"Douglas Clegg's short stories can chill the spine so effectively that the reader should keep paramedics on standby!"

—Dean Koontz

"*You Come When I Call You* is the first major literary event in the genre for the year. I've never had a work of fiction affect me more deeply. This is an absolute must read!"

—Garrett Peck, *Hellnotes*

"Douglas Clegg's writing is like a potent drink that goes down with deceptive smoothness—right before it knocks you on your derriere."

—*Horroronline*

MORE PRAISE FOR DOUGLAS CLEGG!

"Clegg has cooler ideas and is much more of a stylist than either Saul or Koontz."

—Dallas Morning News

"Clegg's gifts as a teller of grim tales are disconcerting and affecting."

—Locus

"Clegg is a wonderful writer. He knows how to deliver the goods."

—World of Fandom

"Parts of *The Halloween Man* bring back fond memories of both Straub's *Ghost Story* and McCammon's *Boy's Life,* but Clegg adds his own unique touches in this high-class horror novel. A memorable contribution to the genre."

—Masters of Terror

"Douglas Clegg has raised the stakes; for himself, as well as for the genre he writes in."

—FrightNet

"Doug Clegg has proved himself one of the masters of the supernatural thriller."

—Edward Lee, BarnesandNoble.com

"*The Halloween Man* is a stunning horror novel, written with a degree of conviction that is rare these days."

—Fiona Webster, *Amazon.com*

"Reminded me of King and McCammon at their best. I was awestruck."

—The Scream Factory

"Packed with vivid imagery; a broadly scoped, but fast-paced plot; powerful, evocative writing; superb characterizations; and facile intelligence, *The Halloween Man* is more than its blurbage could ever convey."

—Paula Guran, *DarkEcho*

THE FACE OF THE DEAD

I went about my day as though nothing were wrong.

I went down to the subway to catch the train to my ex-wife's place to pick up my daughter for the rest of the weekend.

I tried to keep from thinking about anything regarding Naomi. She was no more. Even my dream of who she was seemed to dissipate when I thought about Alan Cowper and his brutal way of telling me what he wanted me to know.

The platform was crowded with shoppers and tourists and those who move from one place to another, all asleep on their feet, all somewhere else in their minds. I felt I was the only one there, really there, really standing on the platform and knowing where I was.

And then I saw a familiar face, a face that I would recognize no matter what time did to it.

I saw her standing in a crowd, a crowd whose faces faded into blankness, I saw her there, I knew it was her.

I know it was her.

Shimmering like heat above a burning road.

Naomi.

Other *Leisure* books by Douglas Clegg:
MISCHIEF
YOU COME WHEN I CALL YOU
THE NIGHTMARE CHRONICLES
THE HALLOWEEN MAN

NAOMI

DOUGLAS CLEGG

LEISURE BOOKS   NEW YORK CITY

A LEISURE BOOK®

April 2001

Published by

Dorchester Publishing Co., Inc.
276 Fifth Avenue
New York, NY 10001

ISBN 0-8439-4857-4

The name "Leisure Books" and the stylized "L" with design are trademarks of Dorchester Publishing Co., Inc.

Printed in the United States of America.

Visit us on the web at www.dorchesterpub.com.

For Brooke Borneman—
With thanks to every subscriber of the List, as well as to
Dorchester Publishing and Subterranean Press.

Be sure to visit Douglas Clegg online at:
http://www.douglasclegg.com and www.ehaunting.com.
You can e-mail Doug at: dclegg@douglasclegg.com.

NAOMI

She knew that this was the last evening that she would see him for whose sake she had given away her lovely voice and left her home and family; and he would never know her sacrifice. It was the last night that she would breathe the same air as he, or look out over the deep sea and up into the star-blue heaven. A dreamless, eternal night awaited her, for she had no soul and had not been able to win one.

—Hans Christian Anderson, "The Little Mermaid"

Prologue

1

"Blood-red rose with thorns," someone whispered.

It was like the voice of a fairy tale. There should be a wolf and a maiden, and a small thatched cottage on the edge of a vast dark forest. There should be a field of roses growing wild in front of a castle with the tallest towers in all the world, and someone very evil would be whispering that, as a curse at the birth of a child of the kingdom, or perhaps it would be the Queen, dying, who would say it, the drops of blood upon her sewing as she named her daughter. "Blood-red rose with thorns," the voice whispered, and perhaps it was a dream, perhaps it was real, but it stayed with him for years, that voice.

The voice brought with it a strange sense of comfort, of warmth.

It was both the wolf and the maiden, the thorn and the rose.

He knew who it was. He just could not say her name. Not yet. Not until he'd been awakened from the dream of his life, into the dream of the world.

And the dream began the same for him, each time.

Once upon a time . . . it began. Once upon a time when you were young and the world was ancient and the caves were full of wonder and the girl you loved believed that you were everything.

So it began.

2

You never know what your destiny will be until you go through the darkness.

That's what Jake Richmond knew, when the darkness first hit.

Later, years had passed between the time he knew he loved her and the moment he knew he had lost her. [Naomi. Nawombi. Nayami. Nyomi.] All the names he'd called her, all the ways he'd stretched her name as if by tugging at it, he could somehow possess her. He could somehow hold on longer than she could fight to let go.

But they were children then. It was years ago.

Jake tried not think of that.

He could not think of Naomi. He could not imagine her as she was when he'd last seen her.

Or when he'd first seen her. Or when he imagined what she must look like now. She was the kind of woman that was remembered more in spirit than in form—he could not for the life of him, as he went about the daily grind of work and life and all the unfortunate choices he'd made (he told himself often), remember her face other than to remember that he could not conjure anything but her essence in his mind.

She had vanished from his life.

He had always had the feeling she would reappear again, like magic. It was his secret from everything and everyone else in the world. Naomi would come back in some unexpected way. He was sure that someone whose influence was so powerful could not completely disappear. He always had the sense that his connection with Naomi could never be lost. Jake, with his ragged dark hair, cut too short in the summer, too shaggy in the winter, who was too impatient to wait at crosswalks for green lights, who discovered early that he would never be a captain of industry or a star of anything or the best of what Manhattan had to offer, or anything other than the kid from Carthage, Virginia, who grew up and escaped and ran to the biggest city he could find; Jake, who still believed that neckties could strangle and that sneakers were still sneakers and not expensive pop-culture statements; Jake who fell in love once or twice in his life, but knew that love was something forged early, and that your first love was sometimes the only one you should never have left behind.

Jake, who believed himself ordinary in every way, had always hoped that the extraordinary would return in the form of the girl he had loved as a boy.

Sometimes, a man understands that the boy in him knows better how to love than the man he has become.

Sometimes, waking up early in the morning, a chilly dawn in New York City, with the sound of sirens or a dog barking or someone in the apartment above clomping in what could only be wooden shoes across the floor, he would lie there, half-dreaming, and remember it all. Remember Naomi. Remember himself, the little boy with the big crush.

3

Once upon a time, when he was just twelve and could barely understand why the world was the place it was, Jake Richmond held as tightly as he could to Naomi Faulkner's hands. He told her that he would never let go of her as long as he knew how to breathe.

"Blood-red rose with thorns," she said, her voice so small and yet so significant, it echoed within him even while he lived a different life. The torn crimson petals drifting, in her lap. She said it like it would mean something someday, as if she were taking a picture of the flower with her eyes and saying the words to record it.

He stared at the petals, and the scratches of thorns along her wrists. He didn't know why the rose's thorns had dug in her arms so deep. He had believed that she had gone running from what she called the Terrible Bad Place, and he had found her. He was a simple boy in those days. The Terrible Bad Place could be nothing other than their imaginary worlds, the Treasure Cave, the pirates within the Treasure Cave, and the people they created with their minds.

The babies were crying, that's what she said, the babies were crying in the Treasure Cave, and he knew they were the cats, but the game made them babies. The Cave was surely not a cave at all, nor was it a Terrible Bad Place, but simply a deep hole in the ground. And the blood-red rose with thorns lay in her lap, and they were both children, and he wished he could rewind the tape of life to that moment and start over.

It was all there, in those memory glimpses. The smell of mint and what they called spider grass, which had a scent like honeysuckle on some mornings, like in the tall grass. The taste of oncoming rain in the air, almost a sweet dampness. The feeling that summer was forever and ever, amen.

"Let me get some yarrow," he said. Then, after he'd pulled up the weeds, he took the soft, fuzzy leaves still heavy with morning dew, and patted them along the scratches. "There," he said, holding her arm in his hand, the dark green leaves across her wrist. His granny had taught him about the yarrow leaves, and about jewel weed and its juice that cured poison oak and could even help with snakebites. He knew this because once the snakes got him, and one bit him on the foot when he was eight or nine. Most of the grown-ups had yelled at him for going near the snakes, but his granny had just taken some jewel weed and pressed the juice against the marks the snake had left. Even though his left foot swelled up "like a sweet potato without the sweet," his granny commented, the swelling didn't last long, and he was walking again within two weeks. Since then, he'd wanted to learn everything he could about his granny's magic plants, which seemed to grow all over the roadsides of Virginia. He knew most of the herbs that grew in Carthage, and some that didn't. Over the year, he'd learned a lot about healing, and he'd even helped sometimes when his grandmother had brought babies into the world, so he knew all about the natural world of Carthage. His granny even told a story about how when he was a baby, she carried him with her to the Faulkners' the night Mrs. Faulkner had Naomi, so Jake could honestly say he was there at Naomi's birth, even though he was barely six months old himself. "Yarrow's for healing," he told her with some authority, feeling her pulse beneath his fingers.

"Your granny said it's for finding out true love," Naomi said, watching his fingers on the leaves as they gently rubbed her wrist.

"It's for a lot of things. Jewel weed's for stinging nettle and poison oak. But it's also for happiness."

"What are roses for?"

He thought a minute and said, "I guess they just are. Some things just are."

"You gonna be a doctor when you get older?"

"Naw," he said as if the idea of doctoring was one of the most unpleasant ideas in the world. "You got to go to school forever to be a doctor. Maybe I'm gonna be an astronaut. Or maybe I'll discover countries under the ocean. Or bring up something from down there. Something like a ship filled with gold or something." He mentioned this in all seriousness, a grave look upon his face, as if he'd thought long and hard about his future ambitions from the confines of the little town. "What are you gonna be?"

"A actress," Naomi said. Then she added, "Or maybe just someone special."

He looked up at her face. He almost couldn't see her sometimes because she was so perfect that it was a little like looking at an angel or a dream—he was afraid she'd vanish if he looked at her face too much. "You're special now."

"I am not," Naomi said. She kept her gaze on her wrist as his hands massaged her arm with the dark yarrow leaves. "I'm nobody. I'm awful. I'm worse than awful."

"You are not," he said, and then he let the leaves fall to her lap with the rose petals. He grasped her hand in his. She felt warm and tingly to him, and he realized the tingles were all on his side. Something else stirred, but his Better Nature, as his mother called it, seemed to press a beast of some sort back down into the back of his mind. The beast was that urge he had begun feeling lately. The urge that made him want to be alone with Naomi as often as possible. It was not his Better Nature, and he could fairly quickly talk himself out of it and put the beast back where it belonged for now. He was not yet ready to let go of childish things, and he preferred the sweetness of sitting with her, holding her soft hand, to the thoughts that sometimes threatened to come after him.

Then he told her the secret he'd kept inside him all the years he'd lived. It wasn't the one about how he was going to marry her. And it wasn't the secret about how he was going to get really rich and buy a huge house with a swimming pool and get on planes and go all over the world.

It was the secret of his twelve-year-old heart, which may just be the worst kind of secret a boy has to keep from himself and the world.

"I'm always going to be here for you whenever you need me. No matter what. I'm gonna make sure you never get scratched up by roses again. I don't care if you don't love me back. I don't care what else happens."

He felt his face turn to fire as the words came out. He prayed that she wouldn't laugh at him, but he was nearly convinced that she would laugh. That she would jump up and go running and even go tell the McCracken boys who drank rusty water out of an old coffee can, or tell the Jupiters up in Orchard Haven about it, the Jupiters who could not keep their fat mouths shut to save their lives and who sat in the first pews of church and acted all holy but really just were there to tell everyone about things like Jake's father and about the old woman's teeth that fell out at the [Krogers] in Sky Lark Village and how Belinda Frontiere was some kind of loose woman to wear those clothes on a Sunday. Jake's fears in that split second were endless.

But still, he said it, he allowed the vow out of his mouth, and he told her that he would always be there for her, and if she ever needed him, even if he were a thousand miles away on the moon, he would know and would find her.

Even then, some part of him knew it was probably a lie, just as so much of their small acreage of earth was a lie. He hoped she believed him. If she believed in him, the lie just might come true.

In those days of innocence, he had known a peculiar happiness, as of one who feels the presence of darkness but has not yet felt the shadow across his face.

4

One day, what he had been afraid of finally came to pass. He finally let go of her hand. Many years passed before he thought to grasp it again.

But forget the boy and the girl in the small town in the mountains; they've grown up now. Come to the city north—the landscape of giants and those who live beneath the earth.

Part One

The Haunt

Part One

The Hunt

Chapter One

The City

1

Destiny lurks, but when the time is ripe, it devours.

New York City, this year, right now, the world seems new as a century dawns, as winter surrounds the fingers of brick and marble.

Don't imagine for a moment the silver towers of Manhattan, shining in December with sweat and frost. Forget the postcard images in your mind of the city. The looming skyscrapers. The brown and gray apartment buildings obscuring any trace of morning sunlight. Lose your memory of the small grocery mart with its rows of oranges and apples and cheap flowers. The great clock over the Persian rug shop. The trattoria with ragged awning flapping, traces of soap on its windows. The smell of the street, of the stone, of the people, of the dogs, of the entity that can only be known as city, a thing both dead and alive.

Imagine instead a vast cavern of overgrown brownstone and gleaming pumice, frozen in spray up to the sky. Imagine the anthill and its inhabitants. Imagine anything but the buildings along Eighth Avenue, the yellow taxicabs, the young man in sweatpants and hooded jacket jogging, the gray-suited bald man with glasses, shivering, a steaming Starbucks coffee cup in hand, the handsome and the ugly; the elfin woman still drunk from the previous night, blown by an icy gust as she walks her Boston terrier on a short leash; the masks and the faces they reveal; the two shiny men with gym bags; the piles of trashbags; piles of kids as they wander with their Walkmans and cell phones; the overcoats fluttering; the hat pulled down over ears. Through it all, the serpent turns.

And it lurks.

And it will devour.

The message steams in the crisp, cold air, the breaths of fog that pour like smoke from the mouths of people wandering the chilly city streets. It's written in smoke from the exhaust of buses. The billboards, the walls, the wide boulevards, the narrow alleys, the scaffolding along Fourteenth Street, all of it is a warning to the one boy who understands the omen.

The citadel of stone could stand for a hundred more years, and still none will escape destiny as it waits, hungry.

Only you know it, because you are part of the Below. You are close to the pulse of how this island kingdom runs. You are one of the few who can journey from the Below to the Above and back. With only the fear to keep you going.

And you know that today, the serpent is loose.

Your destiny is tied up with the serpent, only you don't know why or how. You know, because it has been foretold. You know because destiny is a wicked thing.

But it is an ordinary winter's day. They call the city New York. They live within the belief that all is well for now.

Somewhere across this island, there are construction workers' jackhammers making the earth's crust tremble. Somewhere, between the Above and the Below, what should've stayed chained has been set free. They all dig down deep but never find the true Below, they never know all the wormholes that the serpent has, but you know. You and the others like you. You know the passages of the serpent. You always have understood the serpent and the darkness. You know that no matter how it looks in the Above, what has been loosed cannot be put back.

But it's business as usual here in the Above. Up where the sun burns and the city steams even in its frozen glory. Christmas is coming. The lights are up and dazzling, even early in the day. Shop windows are heavy with ornament and display. The snow from the week before has all but melted in the city. The trash bags roll and shift with wind, and rats scurry along the side streets as the Village bleeds into Chelsea into the Meatpacking District with its bones and the smell of the dead.

And she is there.

The woman who seems so familiar, perhaps because she resembles all the other women on the street, but she is their essence. She is determined. She is in focus and still a blur of movement. She is unstoppable in some way.

You watch her walk—no, you watch her *stride* toward her goal.

In her stride, her destiny.

She is the kind of woman that once seen, will never be forgotten. Not because of some ideal of beauty, but because of her very nature. She is the unmade bed. She is the lost unknown. She is the woman of whom other people speak but no one invites. She is unfathomable mystery. She is purity-in-chaos. Something makes you watch her. Something within you longs to follow her on her journey. Her eyes are brutally kind. Her face is pale without being sunless, a redness around her eyes and nose, a vulnerability.

She has the look of having been in the storm, droplets glistening on her skin, crystal snowflakes melting.

You read her thoughts in her hands as she gracelessly reaches in her coat for keys or some Kleenex or a good-luck charm or a memento from the past.

You see the childlike way she smiles at nothing, perhaps at the very air itself, perhaps at the folly of life.

She reminds you of the woman you'd want to meet someday; but she has darkness within her.

She has spent her life searching for the serpent. Now it will find her.

She is dangerous.

2

"Destiny lurks, it does, I tell you when your time's ripe, it devours, it surely does, it's a devourer, it opens its jaws and unlocks just to get you." That's what the teenaged boy on the corner of Fourteenth Street and Eighth said to the woman who had passed up his offer to allow her to give him change.

He shook the can that had once held Del Monte pineapple slices and now clanged with a few quarters and several pennies, and perhaps later on would carry water or soup if he could get some.

His stink was strong, a gust of foulness from the pit of some unwashed arm. His name was long forgotten, but those who called him friend also called him Romeo, for no other reason than the fact that he roamed.

"Listen, you give me change, lady, and I give you salvation. Nice bargain you was to ask me," he said, his voice like the squeal of brakes over shattering glass bottles.

He was too old to be young and too young to be old, and his red baseball cap had seen better gutters. He was probably no more than a teenager, but he still seemed ancient. His hair was yellow-brown straw beneath the cap. His eyes were dull and milky as if he suffered from some ailment a woman like this would never want to know about. His grin was infectious in all the unfortunate ways. "All right, lady, destiny lurks but it can devour any second, and just the price of a cup of coffee'll get you some relief. It's a—whoa—a huge mother of a snake, and it gets out, and it bites you where the sun don't shine. I said it's got a sting and a bite and then it just chows down like you don't even matter, and I seen it. I know what it can do."

He knew his words didn't sound as clear as he thought them in his head, but he said them anyway. Language was different in the Below. Words were used sparingly there. Words could not be wasted in darkness. (Scabber had told him once about speaking, and how words were like magic. "Magic don't get spent free," she had told him. "Gotta price. Like every damn thing. A big price. A great price.")

The woman with destiny glanced at him once. He was sure that she looked right through him before moving on.

She walked awkwardly toward the subway entrance, with her tan coat, her faded jeans, the way her hair wasn't quite combed, nor was it quite blond.

And something about the way she glanced back at him let him know that she was not one of the Above People even if she hadn't given him a quarter or the time of day.

She's one of us.

She had the darkness in her already. He could tell. Had she somehow escaped the Below of life and lived in the Above for so many years that she had forgotten the darkness? But the scent of it was still on her. She was meant for shadows.

The street, so alive with suits and skirts and rags and vendors and loafers, washed her image away like a sudden downpour.

Hunger wrestled with his fears. He kept shaking his cup and hoping that he'd get enough change to take care of his great burden. He didn't like the thought of the serpent or of the lady who wanted to find it, but there was no coming between what was and what was meant to be.

Chapter Two

The Woman in the Subway

1

Don't think, just do.

The words were like mosquitoes humming around the woman who stepped down into the urban underworld known as the subway. Within her mind, the world itself was a mass of mosquitoes all swirling in patterns around her. The past and present blurred into a mess in her brain, and her head ached with all of the images from childhood and from what she'd been hiding and what she'd been revealing—it was a storm within her flesh that had no calm center.

Just do, she thought, wiping at her nose with a Kleenex.

Quit thinking so much. Thinking too much about it is what screws everything up.

A cold, left over from Thanksgiving, lingered in her sinuses.

She fumbled with the nasal-spray bottle to get one last clear breath. She laughed at herself, wondering why she was so worried about her stupid cold, why she even cared anymore. Inhaling, she smelled the dust and piss of the subway and street. Then her head began pounding again. She'd had a Sudafed with a glass of wine at 6:00 A.M., hoping it would allow her to fall asleep. Instead, it just seemed to make the pain more intense.

She wanted to get the feeling out of her system. It manifested itself in a throbbing at the edges of her scalp and a constant hammering behind her eyes. Her head pounded with a thousand words left unsaid, conversations she'd wanted to have, arguments she wished she'd been brave enough to incite. But none of it added up to much, and so little was clear she just wished all thinking would stop.

Don't think. Don't let the voices and the words and the darkness come through. You know what must be done. What you must do. You can't go back to what never was. You can't make something gentle from a tangle of barbed wire. You can clean up what has already happened.

But one thought above all others pounded at her, the hammer of one thought, up and down, again and again, behind her eyes. One thought.

All she could think about as she went down the cold stone steps was that Alan would never have let her leave the apartment had he known that she intended to throw herself in front of the first train that came down the tunnel.

2

But he'd gone out for an hour, and she had her chance.

In under a minute she laughed, wept, and smiled. Then she closed her eyes and tried to pray but there were no more prayers in her. She glanced up at the sky before it disappeared from view as she went down the stairway into the bowels of the city.

A last glimpse of sky. White with clouds. The bare trees of winter.

She tried to picture the winter sky as she walked through the passageway. The walls comforted her to some extent; this was a safe enclosure, an antidote to the open, muddy fields and burned ruins of her childhood. The city was a cold but welcome embrace, and she never felt it more strongly than down in the subway.

She knew what he would say.

The Alien. His name was Alan. She liked to think of him as *Alien* because then it was easier to not let him touch her anymore, to not let him get under her skin in any way.

But still, she knew what he would say if he'd been there to stop her.

"Naomi," he'd say, "it's the winter blues, that's all. Have you been off your prescriptions again? That's not good. That's not sticking with the program."

Sticking with the program.

Learning to cope.
Making do.
Recovering.

All of them, Alien buzzwords. "When you have all your ducks in order, we can sit down and talk about the future," he'd say. Whenever he used this phrase, she wanted to get an Uzi and shoot all those ducks and watch the blood and feathers fly. Just in her mind. Just the imaginary ducks that the Alien talked about. She wanted to squeeze his voice out of her head. His voice, his metaphors, the sound of his footsteps.

She knew how he would suddenly be gentle with her. And how she would lash out at him. He would sit there and be gentle and even kind. Her thoughts would turn violent; his kindness would feel violent to her. Sometimes kindness was the worst sort of treatment.

She wanted to tell him she'd been seeing another doctor who suggested she'd been misdiagnosed. It was a lie, but she wanted to tell him that. She knew that the Alien would really find a way to twist that up so that she would begin to doubt her own sense of reality again. She didn't even blame him.

It was her. It was completely her. *"You need to pay for good medical care. These therapists, you know,"* he'd say, *his head shaking slowly, "bargain-basement prices, and no real training . . ."*

But none of that mattered.

She had to smile as she bought a subway token—a buck fifty. A subway ride was still a bargain, one of the last of the real bargains. *A real bargain basement*. You could go anywhere on the subways in Manhattan for a buck fifty. That was New York all over. Anywhere that didn't matter, you could get there cheap. She could go the length of the island and never get back to the place where she'd been happiest.

A child stared up at her as she dropped the token in the turnstile.

Dark hair, dark eyes, a wan look as if he had no expectations. His mother, a cool drink of water—that's what Jake would've said. (*Don't think of Jake. You can't undo all of it. He would know. He would find out. He would hate you.*)

The boy's mother was in a bad mood. Her eyes were fixed on the boy's hands, like a cat ready to pounce. "Where's your token?" the mother asked, and the boy's mouth dropped, drool on the edge of his lips. "Where the hell is it?"

The child watched her even while his mother clutched his hands, demanding his token.

Two men, tall and stocky, hair on one like a rock star, nonexistent on the other, businessmen in blue and gray uniforms, rushed past her. The earthquake rumbling of the approaching train grew louder. Catching a train was serious business. A crazy woman (she thought as she watched herself being watched) slowly walking to the platform was to be jostled and elbowed. A short redhead in a raincoat practically shoved her. Then the rain of people followed in her wake.

From all corners they shoved and slipped between one another, creating pockets of personal space. Black, white, a woman in furs, a teen in a leather jacket with purple hair, humanity as if one big ball of multicolored wax had melted together. They melted into one another as they rushed forward, grabbing their places along the platform.

To her, it was not a platform on the subway, but a precipice.

It was the Edge.

3

The Edge was everywhere.

The Edge was life, and she was always on the verge of discovering what lay beyond the Edge.

Her eyesight was all messed up: *Tears? No, not tears.* Tension. The headaches. The memory that she could never dredge up, no matter how hard she tried. All she could call it was the blank spot of her life. The yowling in the darkness; the feeling of rocks, the sense of what was there with her, hiding with her, breathing . . . But her vision sucked—she laughed thinking of it that way. The faces in the crowd, she remembered the poem, *the apparition of these faces in the crowd . . .*

We're all ghosts already. We reach adulthood, and we're already gone from the world that matters. We're just keeping things in order for the next crop of people. We go about our business. And why? We're ghosts. We repeat patterns without knowing that we have no effect. Our lives are determined before we're twenty. After that, we just repeat. It's already the future. These people are already ghosts. I am a ghost.

The apparition of these faces in a crowd . . .

I am no one.

My time has come and gone.

I am ruined, she thought, laughing to herself. It sounded so Victorian, so ancient, so melodramatic. *I am ruined. I will be no more.*

4

She stood there, her head throbbing.

Slowly, she walked to the edge of the platform, closing her eyes. Her steps seemed completely silent to her. Was she invisible? She could be. Maybe she had always been invisible. She barely noticed the murmurs as those she passed spoke about the lives they were leading, their victories that were really just defeats in disguise. Their eyes had not been opened.

Images bled in her mind:

Her mother, lying in the coffin; the things in the dark, moving like liquid; the Alien, his eyes flashing green, picking her up in the rain outside of Lincoln Center, his car so warm, his manner so smooth, her desperation so great; the blank spot, the blindness of moments in time, moments that were cut from her and had turned to yowling darkness; and Jake—*just his face, sixteen years old, sweat shining like smoldering ashes under his skin . . . Jake, if only Jake were here . . . If only I had the courage . . .*

Now, the other voice within her whispered. It was the voice of her highest self, she knew. The one who knew how to do things. The one who knew where she was going.

Now.

The sound of the train grew louder, and the tunnel windswept her hair—

One foot ventured into the air beyond the platform. The rumbling was loud.

She could feel the train's heat in the wind that gusted through the tunnel.

She could do it. She knew she could. Another step forward. Then she'd fall.

The train would reach her before she landed on the tracks.

5

She drew back her foot. She looked down at the track, and the train was suddenly there, its silver flash slowing to a blur and then it became solid, a train once more, doors opening.

The door opened in front of her, and a woman asked if she was going to stand there all day.

"Can you hear me?" the woman asked, her voice full of crust. "Hello? Move?"

She stepped aside for the crusty woman. The rain of people poured in, the doors closed, and then the blur of an impressionist painting as faces and train became one.

The train moved on.

6

The subway platform, empty, but for Naomi Faulkner.

She stood there looking wistfully at the flashing of the train as it moved through the tunnel. Naomi Faulkner, who had once had dreams like anyone else, but had reached the age where dreams no longer were enough to clean up a messy life. She had come to the realization that she was not special enough, that whatever magic she'd imagined life had, it was not for her. It was for other people who went on to bigger and better things. It was for people without blank spots. People who hadn't done terrible things when they were very young. People who had listened to their hearts and not the needs of others. People who had not given up control of their lives to the hostility of family.

It was for people that got on the train and had their minds on things other than themselves.

Selfish. That's what you are. Selfish and stupid and wasting your life chasing something that people like us don't ever get.

She heard her own voice in her mind saying those words, but she could not pinpoint from whom she'd first heard them. She hated the feeling of weakness.

I am not a victim. I will not be a victim.

She could say it a hundred times, but she would never be sure whether she meant it or not.

The platform seemed so lonesome a place now, with two empty benches. The wall bore smudges of washed-over graffiti (*She's all that*, one read; *I Moan Tiawai*, a spray-painted scrawl with an obscene sketch beneath of, she assumed, the girl named Tiawai).

40

She got the sense that she stood in the empty corridor of a windswept and icy school. It reminded her too much of waiting for the principal or the school nurse when she was thirteen, and expecting punishment. The Church of the Righteous, at the edge of Carthage, its ruined steeple, and the way they'd dragged her there like a dog . . . *Church, sins, the white chapel with the long aisle and the hardwood pews, and having to stand up in front of everyone on that day and confess sins . . .*

She went over and sat on the bench.

Glanced at her wristwatch. Eleven A.M., Saturday, December 14, and this would be her final decision.

And, as far as she could remember, the only important decision since she'd run off as a teenager too many years ago. That decision hadn't worked. This one would.

A man with a foolish grin walked by her. Perhaps he was thinking something funny. She liked that. The Alien had no sense of humor whatsoever. He was completely solid and sober. He needed to be like Foolish Grin a little.

"Damn you," she said aloud to no one. When she looked up, she realized Foolish Grin was still there at the platform, rocking back and forth, heel to toe.

He had prematurely gray hair and wore a houndstooth jacket over a bulky sweater. He glanced at her briefly, then looked away.

Let me tell you what I'm planning, she thought. *I'm planning on leaping off the platform into the path of the train. I'm planning on feeling*

41

every moment of this train bursting my bloody atoms apart. Then, with luck, I will be nothing.

She heard the hoofbeats of wild bulls—the sound of an oncoming train—she glanced down the track and saw two pinpoints of light. She glanced at her watch. It had only taken a few minutes for the next train.

She stood, smoothing her coat. Then, she giggled to herself at her own vanity. *Who cares if my clothes look like hell? Wait'll they see my apartment, then they'll really know I went the failed-diva route.*

The image of her messy bedroom floor with its piles of laundry and stacks of paperbacks brought to mind little Katie. She was sure that Maria or Soozan would come to Katie's rescue in a day or two. In the meantime, the cat had enough Friskies in her bowl and plenty of water in a shallow pan to last her till then.

Surely, one of her friends would remember the cat as soon as the news was out.

What if she was so obliterated that no one could identify her for weeks? What if Soozan was off on one of her last-minute trips to the Bahamas? What if Maria were so involved with her work that she forgot to give her the usual Saturday night phone call, let alone check in on Katie?

No, I'm sure they'll remember Katie; they love Katie. Maria was there when Katie got spayed and even loaned her money for the vet bills.

They'll think of Katie before they even think of the Alien.

The train drew near. She stepped up to the

edge of the platform. She could practically see her tabby cat mewling for food and water in a dark, forgotten studio apartment. *They'll find you, Katie, within two days, and Maria will probably let you come live with her.*

Naomi Faulkner, a struggling actress in Manhattan, threw herself to her death this morning at the Fourteenth Street subway beneath the express train going uptown. She is survived by her cat.

She imagined the words. It would be nice to have an obituary, no matter how brief.

Katie would be fine. She'd sent a note to both of her friends, and they'd be getting their copy by Tuesday at the latest. There were enough Friskies to last until Wednesday. Once they got their notes, they'd go get Katie and that would be that.

Foolish Grin stepped up to the platform, not so much beside her as behind her. She could sense him even if she couldn't see that grin. *Get a load of what you're about to see, Mr. Foolish Grin. Watch this swan dive. It's a once-in-a-lifetime experience.*

Now, she thought. *Now. Do it.*

The twin headlights of the train—only now they were dreadlights, eyes of spiraling fire—heading for her, zooming down the tracks . . .

And now, you have to jump. Just another second, and—

But I can't, she thought. *Oh, God, it's like willing yourself to drown. Can't do it, have to fight for air, have to survive.*

Damn it, I can't jump.

Yes, I can. I can. Damn it, just jump, real easy,

just step off the edge and walk on air for a second and then when the metal smacks you upside the head, you can get rid of that headache once and for all, and you'll never have to think again, and you'll just sleep forever and ever . . .

Just think of what you have to live through if you go back there.

Think of what's lying ahead down the road a few years, think about how the Alien's going to somehow make nice, and you'll be taking more Prozac and then you'll be secretly sneaking out, and how all you want to do is go back to a place you can never go, and twist time around and pull back to that one moment when you made a decision so monumental in less time than it takes to jump in front of a train, go back to that and then see if you can stop all the crying in your head, all that noise.

And then, it began.

The cats all yowling, the alley of her dreams, full of cats and snakes, the rattles and the cats, the cymbals all smashing together like windup toys, and the girl in the middle of the muddy field screaming louder than anyone could possibly scream . . .

"Shut up." She wasn't sure if she opened her mouth or if she was still living in her mind, but it all hurt, all tore at her—

There was something about knowing that this was it—this was her last chance—that forced the images in her mind: the friends; the lousy job; the apartment that was like a crate with a toilet attached; her cat; even him, the Alien; the painting on the wall that would not let her sleep; and then the memories of Carthage, hell-hole and heaven all at once; and Jake, Jake who was no longer there for her, but somehow, just the fact that he existed somewhere—in a place she would not go—was enough. Just knowing that he was there, that he might still be there for her.

That she had gotten so close . . .

Here come the lights. Close, closer, getting warm, feeling the warm, dusty breeze of the train against her skin, the silver blur . . .

7

Blood-red rose, cats are crying, snakes are coming, the roses are blooming, someone too familiar whispered.

Voices from the past erupted within her as she closed her eyes, willing herself to jump.

"It's not as bad as it seems."

"Oh, my God. It's the worst thing a human being can ever do."

"No. You're wrong."

"You know I'm right. You know this is the worst thing. It's a sin. That's what it is."

"There's no such thing as sin. And this is not your fault."

"You're wrong. This is a sin. What I did. What I never should've done. I can never be forgiven. This is the worst sin on earth."

She remembered those words at a distance of thirteen years, the girl who lived in Carthage, Virginia, the girl who had never really gotten out—

The girl who had become a woman at some point in time and had moved to New York only to make her life's ambition a leap from the platform of a subway station into the lights of a train.

The end of the line.

8

And she could not jump.

The life spark was there—it was like the voice of an old friend within her.

Life had importance. Life had substance. Life was everything she knew. Even something about church teachings was screwing with her and wouldn't allow her to give in and jump. Or maybe it was pure biology. Perhaps her whole body, its flesh and blood and bone, all refused to help her accomplish what should've been her greatest triumph.

It just felt like the nearly inaudible mumbled whisper of life asserting itself.

She wanted to live, after all. She took a deep breath. The train was speeding into the station, but she would remain on the platform.

Here it comes, but you won't be leaping. You're a coward at heart. You love life too much. You just need to get away from the Alien. You need to figure out this mess. You need to begin anew. So what if you become an alcoholic or a head-pounding freak? New York was a good place for all that and more. Other women reinvented themselves here, they couldn't all be together, hip, interesting, sexy, and brilliant, could they? There must be some mouse like you that just fell into the wrong maze and can't quite find the cheese. There's got to be a place for you.

She didn't need to kill herself just to get away from the Alien. She didn't need to prove anything to anyone. She needed to figure it all out; she needed to get her life back. That's what it was. She needed to grab the keys to the car and drive, which was something she'd given up doing. That was the problem. Life wasn't the problem.

Thank God, something within her whispered. *Thank God, because you didn't really want the pain. You didn't really want to find out what it would feel like to have all that metal and fire inside you, tearing your skin, bashing into you, breaking you. You didn't really want to find out— not yet—if all that preaching that had been branded into you as a kid was really true or not, to see if there could possibly be hellfire for an act as simple as jumping in front of a train. That was something you didn't need to know. Not yet. Maybe some other time.*

Maybe Alan wasn't so alien. Maybe the one person you need to break through to can be reached.

The name. Say it. Say it out loud, something within her whispered.

"Jake," she said, softly, the breeze of the train making her catch her breath.

And then she felt the hand pressed into the small of her back, almost a tickling sensation.

"Wait," she gasped, half-turning, but then he pushed—Foolish Grin? Was that who was pressing against her?—the rough hand making

Douglas Clegg

sure she went over the edge, into the path of the oncoming train.

But there was no one standing there, pushing.

But still, she fell and knew that this was her fate.

Chapter Three

Naomi

1

Destiny lurks.

2

Naomi stretched her arms out defensively as if this would stop her fall. She seemed to fly over the edge of the platform. The tracks came up fast. Her left knee went into broken glass. She glanced up and saw the train's lights growing from white spinning saucers into moonlike orbs with a dark tiger behind them. Her body knew before she did that in seconds, the metal would tear into her, and that thing in life that arrived for everyone would arrive too soon—the endless seconds of pain, the unimaginable rending of one's own life. Her body did what she herself could not believe.

She had seconds, she knew. Every instinct within her moved on that brief knowledge.

She stumbled across the track with the train bearing down upon her; another flash of the lights showed her scrambling like a rat toward the other side of the track—

Third rail, she remembered with fear. The two words zapped up almost before her eyes as she grasped for what she could—

She reached for what seemed like a hand, an arm reaching for her—someone was on the other side of the third rail, from above, and she took the arm and allowed it to pull her out of harm's way.

The train's lights, so close . . . the train screeching and scraping . . . she was nearly unaware of anything but her savior.

And then, breathing, heaving, and sobbing, she felt something like ice water trickle down the back of her neck. In the moment of her own salvation, she turned her head slightly, and saw her rescuer.

Something purely animal in her, a brute understanding, remained after her brain began scrambling.

Her mouth opened in a scream that would never seem loud enough. The part of her that still tingled with nerve endings knew that she was looking into the face of a devourer.

These are things that happened in New York
City that week: six policemen shot a man to
death in Central Park; although there was a
public outcry, the man who had been shot had
been a serial murderer and rapist, and in fact,
had just finished killing a young woman, his
sixth and last victim; it was announced that the
Senate race was heating up; a storm watch was
issued, with possible flash floods along the major highways and throughways around the city;
someone from the mayor's office announced a
new policy toward the homeless population;
social workers discovered that there were an es-
timated 2,000 people living completely underground in Manhattan, although the estimate
was called "wildly inaccurate" by those who had
researched the by then well-documented so-
called Mole People, who inhabited the tunnels
beneath the city, none of whom were moles, all
of whom were people who, for reasons known
mainly to themselves, chose to live beneath the
world rather than above it; a woman in Brooklyn was caught running a credit card fraud ring
and was arrested—she had already become
known as the Brooklyn Dodger, because of her
successful avoidance of the law for several
years; some archaeological discovery was made
behind a brownstone in Greenwich Village, and
at first it was thought to be a secret burial
ground from centuries before; there was at least
one heartwarming story on the nightly news
about a fireman who had rescued a family of

puppies from a burning tenement, and within four hours, all the puppies had found new, non-flammable homes; the protesters were already out to block the spraying of neighborhoods to kill mosquitoes to avoid the dreaded West Nile Virus, which had not yet made an appearance, but was due to make one as the weather continued warming up; a parade was set to go on the weekend, if the storm had passed; in Greenwich Village, a bar called One Man's Meat was evacuated because of a bomb scare, but in fact, no bomb was found; a school in Harlem had begun a program for young math scholars in conjunction with Columbia University; a doctor in Westchester County had appealed a famous malpractice case; a new face in overpriced designer pogo sticks had taken over Wall Street, with men and women in suits, leaping up and down along the famous street, reliving their childhoods; parents in the city had begun a movement called WebSafe to make sure there were safeguards in place for kids on the Internet; and a small bit of statue from the top of an apartment building on the Upper West Side broke off, nearly killing a man working below on some scaffolding.

Chapter Four

Metropolitan Life

1

A letter, at least thirteen years old, tucked in a copy of Catcher in the Rye *owned by Jake Richmond:*

Dear J,

I can't even begin to tell you what last night meant to me. You listening to me go on and get weepy and maybe a little dramatic practically all night, and being so sweet, and not treating me the way the other boys treated me, made all the difference.

I am sitting here in algebra, and all I'm thinking about is how I'd rather be out riding horses again with you, or stealing apples, or jumping into the quarry over in Goshen. I'd rather be with you doing just about anything. I wouldn't mind skipping fifth period (it's only bio, and since I can't seem to get better than a *C*+ in it, what's missing a class going to do? Who will notice? Not Mrs. McCarn, that's for sure). Do you think you could skip English? I know you like the class, but who's more fun, me or Chaucer or Steinbeck or whomever Massie's making you read now. I better finish this up. Owen said he'd take it to you in phys ed, and I think he's trustworthy, and if he's not what the hell. The bell's going to ring in two minutes. McCarn is giving me one of her many evil looks. If I ever play Lady Macbeth on the stage, I'll have to remember Roberta McCarn.

I can go out through the stairs in East Wing, and then maybe meet you by the old magnolia near the stone wall. See you?

And Jake? Do you forgive me? That insane outburst? I am chagrined. Positively chagrined. I don't know why I have these spells. I don't know why all that stuff keeps coming up. I don't know why the blank spot starts and stops like that and I end up having a temper tantrum like a little girl. Forgive me, Jake?

N

2

Jake had been raised in the Shenandoah Valley of Virginia, but had sworn that by the time he reached adulthood he would never look back.

His mind did not roam the beauty of that distant country, nor did he stare off into space while in a cab or on the subway and wish he were riding a brown mare or chasing a cottonmouth across the muddy grass by the river with a pole and noose. He didn't miss frog-gigging with the crazy kids from school. He didn't miss the fresh air of the country, nor the gentle feel of wild grass beneath his feet. He didn't think much about the church he'd been christened at with the spiderweb-cracked marble baptismal font or of the painful hardwood pews nor the interminable Christmas services where, at the altar, he would be responsible for snuffing out the candles. His family, he thought of even less, for they'd stopped answering his letters long ago. His grandmother was long dead, and she had been his main connection to that plot of earth. Whenever he thought of calling his mother or his brother, his phone calls home were never picked up on the other end.

He had learned too many times the truth to the phrases that "nothing lasts forever," and "you can't go home again."

New York City was about as far from Virginia as anyone could get—farther, it was said in the small town he'd been born in, than flying to the moon or exploring the depths of the Pacific. Carthage, Virginia, was green valleys and blue hills and people who clung to the earth and rituals and good families and bad people and all the things that reminded him that he was Snaky Jake, an epithet he'd never enjoyed. Now he was merely Jake, and proud of it.

He'd written a book about New York, a funny book that people seemed to buy in places like Ohio and even Norway, called *Eating the City*, presumably witty commentaries on life and restaurants and being an unemployed writer in Manhattan. It made him modestly famous in his twenties for exactly four months. People thought he was a New Yorker. He never said "y'all," anymore. He lost his vestigial accent. He had lived in New Jersey for a while, and even friends thought he was an exile from Hoboken, Jersey City, or Newark. He had been twenty-four when he wrote the book. It sold, people bought it, and he never wrote another book.

Instead, he began to write for magazines, and then worked for an Internet company that provided him with a comfortable existence. He knew even this would not last.

And then one night, things came back to him, and life would never be the same.

3

He sits now at a makeshift desk that is more table than desk, with a laptop balanced precariously on its wobbly surface. He tries to forget any place he's ever lived except for the place he lives now.

The trees along the street are in heavy blossom. The river smell fights the exhaust of cars and the breeze for first place. The blacktop of the park is covered with baseball teams and hoop shooters. The dogs bark at one another from across streets, and a man named Jake Richmond sits at the desk before the kitchen window that surveys all, feeling as if he owns nothing but the Compaq notebook computer and the wobbly table and the can of Dr Pepper. Spring has arrived, and he wishes that winter would've lasted just a few minutes longer.

His fingers graze the computer's keyboard.

His fingers remember the winter.

4

Jake's Journal

First entry in ten years. Spring. New York. Where else?

Beginning of a new century. What the hell does that mean? Is all this, rampant irony, this self-serving hipsterism of the last two decades going to finally die? Are we going to return to sentiment, to virtues long forgotten, or are we all just going to maintain distance from our own lives as if we have God inside us and are just playing along with the Human Joke? Jesus, what a mess. Who respects politicians? Who thinks they are anything but smoke screens? And popular music—it all sounds like it was made in 1973. And movies? Computer graphics substitute for acting, and sadly, it's compelling.

And this whole Internet thing, this communication that is so extreme I can talk to someone in Kalamazoo, Michigan, but I have no idea who lives in the apartment across from mine. And who the hell lives there?

I stare at the door across the hall sometimes. I really wonder who's behind it. The Silent One. Is he living a happy life or is he miserable? Is it some old shut-in who peeps through her peephole and shivers when she sees me? Maybe it's some rich jerk who's off in Europe for the winter and only returns for one week in the spring and one in the fall before going to places like Gstaad or Martinique.

And why do I care?

Why do I come in at night and look at that door and think: *Why is it I'm always here in the hall, and you're always in that apartment, but I'm the one who feels like I have no life?*

God, do I get another beer or a Dr Pepper? I was going to go to the movies to try and catch something good. No love stories. Maybe just to watch whatever was on the screen and forget all this b.s. Or go to Blockbuster and pick up some dumb movie or to the store for some confection that will make me feel all warm and fuzzy inside.

But I can't even bring myself to leave this building, let along my apartment, not tonight. I can't summon the energy to pick up the phone, and even going online depresses the hell out of me. I have just enough energy to tip-tap on this keyboard and try to get it all out of my head before I explode.

When I was sixteen I remember looking up at the stars and telling someone that when I was nearly thirty, the century would just be turning, and I thought that sounded so old—nearly thirty—and that it would be forever until I got there. But it was like lighting a match, a flare of light, a sniff of sulfur. Suddenly, I'm here, and sixteen looks like the day before yesterday. It's some celestial conspiracy, this whole aging thing, this whole time thing, this whole counting the years and how fast it begins to move at a certain point just when you wish you had a few more years to get a little smarter.

The world was never my vision of how life should be.

If I had been God—assuming there is a God—I would've taken more than seven days to create this.

I would've spent some time thinking it through. I would never have allowed so many mistakes, so many misfortunes, and so much sorrow into the world. Here's what I believe: I believe this is no evil beyond human evil, and I believe there is no happiness without sacrifice. Perhaps my puritanical parents drummed this into me. Perhaps the world showed me how it was; opened its skin like ripe fruit and showed me the seeds.

My full name is Jacob Fallows Richmond.

Jake will do. Call me J if you want, as Naomi did, the Naomi from my childhood. *Nay-womi, Nay-Wombi,* I used to say when I was four and couldn't pronounce her name correctly, *Nywami, Nomy, Namya,* I'd joke in grade school. She was the girl who used to play with me on the railroad tracks, used to listen to my dreams, used to sit with me at sunset out by the river and sing, when we were both too young to know why, *Playmate, come out and play with me, climb up my apple tree* . . .

I was then the Jake who felt wholly alive—in childhood. I am the same Jake who spent half his life in a coma. All right, it wasn't a real coma, but the kind of mental state where you are moving underwater, unaware of how a current toward some inevitable rapids is pulling you. I awoke to my own life when I was nearly thirty, and it's a shame that to wake up, you have to destroy a dream.

That's when you wake up. When the bad things happen.

Nothing bad ever happens on the Upper West Side of Manhattan. The crime, the criminals, the underbelly of the city, that's downtown, that's so far uptown it's not even town, that's somewhere other than in one of the gorgeous high-rises a few blocks off Central Park, that's elsewhere. You can go to Manhattan and never see crime; if you live there, you hear about it like myth, like brownstone, like the foundation of the great city that calls to anyone who has ever had ambition or dreams of making it in the world or anyone who has ever been dragged down into its chaotic beauty. I am Jake Richmond, and I know more about Manhattan and its crimes than I'd ever care to admit.

I was born in the Shenandoah Valley of Virginia—yes, something of a farm boy who hated dirt and cows and the bucolic acid of field and stream. I dreamed of this place, this shining

Emerald City to the East, this shrine to the human drive, this island city.

As a boy, I had gone to New York City on a spring trip with the high school band—I played the trombone badly and was quite proud of it. It had rained the whole three days we were there. Even so, I felt inspired by its brown and steel elegance, by the sheer weight of its buildings, by the wind as it whipped around the corners of the modern equivalent of the Pyramids of the Nile. By the time I was eighteen, New York University and Columbia had rejected me in one fell swoop.

Instead, I attended Rutgers in New Jersey, commuting to the city when I could to peruse bookstores in Greenwich Village, to watch movies up at the big movie palaces, to taste the reality of those who rushed through the blur of the city's fast-forward life.

I met Amy six months after I graduated from college. She had been standing in line for a movie at the Waverly—I think it was some German expressionist silent movie about an evil doctor, although I barely watched the movie. I guess I stalked her—that's what it seems like now. I recognized something in her, something I could not quite identify. She stood there, her shoulder bag slung over one shoulder, her tan skirt catching an October breeze, her glasses so out of place on that near-perfect face that she laughed when I told her I liked them because they gave her face character. "I hate them just for that reason alone," she told me, slipping them into her jacket.

"You go to movies by yourself a lot?" I asked, ever the stupid young man.

"I'm meeting someone," she said, and then proceeded to tell me that she was going for a cappuccino afterward, and specifically the location of the coffeehouse where she would get the cappuccino. I was there, right after the movie, and I waited, but Amy never showed. Then, I saw her—again, purely by chance—at a party that one of my former roommates from college was giving because he was shipping out with the Peace Corps. Amy had arrived with a couple of her girlfriends, one of whom knew the sister of my former roommate (the incestuousness of college graduates should never be underestimated). We laughed about the cappuccino, and then I took her out for a beer.

We ended up staying up all night and wandering the Lower East Side until dawn, and then we wandered over to the Hudson to watch the sunrise and nosh on bagels and coffee. We fell asleep that morning in her small single bed in the two-bedroom she shared with three other girls—Amy's room was the living room, so I felt strange when one of her roommates, a girl who worked in publishing, came through in her bathrobe at 8:00 A.M. and whispered something to her about money she owed her. Amy rolled over my still-clothed body, and grabbed her shoulder bag, handing it to the girl. "Rob me blind," Amy said groggily, as I was just half-falling asleep. "Just leave me alone so I can cuddle with my future husband."

And that was the beginning of it. We got married at city hall. Her parents didn't like me. My parents were clearly not interested in knowing me. We were orphans in the sea of orphans, and we were in love the way you can only be in your twenties.

When we had both turned twenty-four, the following year, we moved from our place in Jersey City to what I considered the beginning of a dream just off Broadway and Seventy-fifth. Amy came into some family money, which helped a lot on the rent, and also gave her the kind of independence in our relationship that she craved. I was happy to watch her invest in the stock market, and buy the things she really wanted, and do exactly as she pleased. When you care for someone, nothing makes you happier.

Life, I felt, could never return to the emotional and cultural squalor of my childhood.

In those days, I still had royalties coming in from my one book, and we both had jobs, and let's face it: The more money you make, the more you spend, and you still never have quite enough to do the things you really want to do with it. But we felt like we were on top of the world then.

And nothing bad ever happens on the Upper West Side. How many times can you say it before it seems true? How many times can the myths of your life become part of some great cathedral, overblown and spread upward and outward, and then eventually it stops growing and encloses you, and pretty soon you don't know which is the myth and which is the hard, cold reality.

Nothing bad ever happens here. It's the Nice World. It's the Comfort Zone.

That's what the real estate agent told us when we first moved into the tiny one-bedroom with an actual kitchen and part of a dining room as well as a pretty damn good view of Central Park, back when rents there were considered low at $1,700 a month, back when we were a double-income household. We had been married three months, and had saved a grand total of $5,000 which went directly to the real estate agent who had been, for five minutes, our best friend; soon, she was not returning our calls. I had 10,000 bucks in royalty money left over that soon enough went to taxes and furniture and future hospital bills. Amy was already pregnant with Laura, although we were calling our daughter James then because we had no idea he would become a she. Laury wouldn't like me to tell it that way. I can just hear her now, "I was never a James. I was Laury all the time."

By the time Amy was six months along, I changed jobs twice, landing at a dot-com company when the idea of dot-com was still in its infancy. Amy was still working nights at the printer's on Wall Street, but by her eighth month, she decided to take an indefinite leave of absence, which easily meant that we would be a single-income family for some time to come. Even though Amy had her money, it was always kept a little separate, and we both considered this a good thing, because we needed to have some security for the future for our up-coming kid. Unfortunately, the pressure on me felt enormous, and I took on moonlighting jobs to help cover the mounting bills as I waited for my health insurance to kick in.

Laura Amanda Richmond came into the world at a quarter to seven on a Thursday morning, and barely waited for me to get my shoes on before Amy was shouting in the hall that she didn't think she'd be able to make it to the elevator. But, in fact, we made it to the hospital, and now it seems like a blur—that moment when I held my only child in my hands—yes, my hands. I helped, and it was a messy and beautiful business, watching Laury come into the world. She was so tiny and delicate, like something that had yet to develop a hard shell around it, a fairy baby, a wisp. I looked at her squashed, mottled face and knew that despite it all, she was indeed the most beautiful child who had ever existed on the planet.

Were we happy? You'd have to ask Amy. I was too busy running back and forth, calling in freelance work from cheap employers, running in place as fast as I could to just make sure the telephone stayed on and the heat kept running all through that winter. By the time Laury had taken her first step, my wife was ready to go back to work—itching to go, in fact. Amy was the kind of person who compartmentalized everything, and she felt her Hausfrau-Mommy years were behind her when Laura was two, and by the time Laura was four, Amy already had hired a superb nanny from an agency in

Westport, Connecticut—Amy's family home. My energy began to wear down as I approached my twenty-eighth year, and by twenty-nine—with Laury in first grade—I thought we were settled, even in the little one-bedroom where Laury had a screen around her bed, the place we knew—as a family—that we would leave as soon as Amy got her next raise, as soon as we had the down payment for the condo in Connecticut.

Those words echoed: Nothing bad ever happens on the Upper West Side of Manhattan. I remember the real estate agent was lovely the day she said this, lovely when she showed us the apartment that would eventually be ours, lovely when we handed her that first check—the one that included her fee.

Nothing bad ever happens on the Upper West Side.

Of course not. All the lowlife crime, the street crime, the danger is downtown, or so far up on the Upper West Side that it is no longer referred to as the Upper West Side. Those are the crimes you can see—the crimes where someone pulls out a gun or a knife or demands money or lifts a wallet or runs someone down in the road.

But the unseen crimes can happen anywhere, and so it was that one afternoon. I was at the market picking up a stack of magazines for Amy, some flowers for the table, and a bottle of wine to go with the dinner we were planning. Laura, who I now called Laury, was at my side, her dark hair shining in the fluorescent light of the market, her face eager with expectation of a Snickers bar or perhaps just a handful of warm cashews from the vendor out in the frigid March air. She kept grabbing my hand and letting go in a playful game known only to her.

How was I to know this was a perfect moment, and that I should've held on to it for as long as possible?

Let me tell you about Laury. She looks a lot like Amy's mother, vaguely Italian with a creamy complexion from the British side of the ancestry, with small almost sad eyes that can disappear when she smiles. She's good at math, even at six, in a way I had never been, and she was verbal to the point of constantly making up stories. It was hard sometimes to have to tell her to pipe down as she told the tale of some beautiful pony named Rainbow and the three caterpillars named Rufus, Goofus, and Doofus.

"It was the most beautiful horse that ever lived," she said, slapping my hand playfully as I wheeled the small cart down the narrow aisles, hoping to find a good bottle of olive oil among all the myriad oils on the shelves. "Its name was—"

"Let me guess," I said. "Rainbow."

Laury shook her head. "No, its name was Rupert."

"Ah, a new story I see."

"Yes," she said, the childish lisp still clinging to her *s*'s, a hangover from a slight speech impediment that I wished would never disappear. There were times when I wanted to keep her small and childlike and even dependent just for that glimpse of innocence we all lose as we get older. "Its name was Rupert, and he lived in a castle by the sea."

"And he had a friend named Annabelle Lee," I added.

"How did you know? Daddy?" Laury looked very cross. "Did you read my mind again?"

I nodded. "You know mommies and daddies can read their children's minds."

Her eyebrows knit across her brow. "And what am I thinking now?"

I gave her a perplexed look, and then laughed. "You're thinking I should buy you something. Maybe some Juicy Juice."

"Amazing," Laury said, and grabbed my hand and heartstrings—assuming I had them—tugging, drawing me to the counters and bins where the lures all sparkle for children and their unsuspecting parents.

We finished our shopping.

She finished her story of Rupert and Annabelle Lee, two horses that bore a striking resemblance to the carousel horses from the Disney movie *Mary Poppins*.

She accidentally dropped her bottle of Juicy Juice on the sidewalk when we both saw my wife—Laury's mother—getting in a taxi across Broadway, going downtown rather than uptown. It was a Saturday afternoon. I certainly never spied on my wife's comings and goings, but given that it was my birthday, given that I had planned a rather extensive dinner for the three of us, given that Amy had said she'd be home all day doing some editing, and given that she rarely took cabs, I was slightly concerned.

Laury saw this, too, and turned to me. "I think Mommy's going to find you a big present."

"Ah," I said, winking. "A surprise for Dad. Smart thinkin', Berry." Berry was yet another of my nicknames for my daughter, short for Raspberry; sometimes I called her Princess Peachy and sometimes Helen Wheels, although she never quite understood the last one.

But when my daughter and I unlocked the door to the apartment we shared as a family, my world changed completely.

I should say, all our worlds.

5

A letter, written light-years before Jake ever moved to New York, still pressed in his high school yearbook, next to the picture of a pretty blond girl with an unremarkable face but with remarkable eyes, a radiance that came through the black-and-white image and the yellowing page:

Dear J,
   I can't see you again. You know why. Why even say it again? Why write it down? You know, and I know, and I feel like too many people know. I remember when I first saw you—or at least when I first can remember anything—and it was this crazy little four-year-old in a tree throwing mud bombs at me and my sisters and that kid got scared spitless when I lifted my skirt and started climbing the tree and then that

kid looked at me and said Nywomi like he had starch for brains, and I knew even then that this kid named Jake would be someone special in this world. So don't worry about the day after tomorrow for you. You'll do fine. I have to find something else. I just have to. Either that or kill myself. It's the roses blooming and it's the cats crying and it's the Terrible Bad Place, and they're all growing inside me again, just like they've done now and then, only this time, they're growing too big, and I can't seem to block them anymore. Sometimes I think I'm going mad and that this is just what I'm supposed to do, and I'll end my days like my mother taking those pills and nodding and having a drink or two at night and just staring out the tear in the screen door on the front porch like I'm waiting for something to come for me, something like angels or devils, coming for to carry me home, only not the home I want. I know you're going to understand this. I know you understand me like no one else ever has. In a just world, I'd get help for this, and you and I would get a little house over in Charlottesville or down in Roanoke, and we'd live a simple little life together, if I were capable of love—real love, the kind you always know about— but I don't think I am, and these visions come at me, the Terrible Bad Place and the cats and the snakes and the roses, and I don't know what they mean but I do know they mean that I can't be around people who I might hurt.

So I leave or I jump off the proverbial cliff. Those are my two options at the moment.

You will never hear from me again.

But know this. I love you.

N

Chapter Five

Romeo

1

Above, the city blasts and farts and backfires and roars, but beneath its tunnels, a hidden world of near-silence blossoms. The subways and holes lead to shafts and abandoned platforms. The avenues of shadows appear. The corridors within the walls that hold the city above leak into the vaults beneath vaults, the sidewalks beneath sidewalks—like the places under rocks and around the roots of trees that teem with life. Life begets within the hollow underworld of Manhattan. These are places that few go who do not stay. These are highways narrow and long, and fraught with danger. The people who live there have run from something in the world of daylight, or have not been able to survive in the Above, or were born to the lightless environment of the Below.

In a city the size of New York, there are thousands who live below street level, and all are called Outcast by those Above. Some are called Mole People by social workers. Some are called Homeless by the ignorant. Some are called Scary by any who encounter them as they emerge into the upper world. But they are people who have come to this subterranean system of sewers and tunnels in order to live their lives away from the harsh daylight world.

It is a world that seems unreal from the moment the daylight extinguishes, and all electric light fades.

It is a world of fire and stone and eternal night.

2

Under Fourteenth Street, in the darkness of the avenues of the Below, a boy named Romeo turned fifteen.

He lay down in the arms of the woman he considered his mother, ignoring her stench and the feeling of hunger in his gut. Her clothes were soft like eiderdown, and her arms, despite her small size, were strong. She was the mother to more than a few of those who lived in the Below. She sometimes called herself the Mother of All Rats, because she called those who lived down under the pipes and the streets and the buildings her tribe of Rats. He had dreamed of what his mother really looked like, but to him, the face was always Scabber—for that was what the woman called herself. Scabber, no doubt because of the scabs she'd acquired during a time when she had to crawl along some of the roughest terrain along the old tunnels.

Romeo had the bad dreams again, and it felt good to be with this woman. To be held. To be rocked as if he were a much younger boy. As if he were not a teenager at all, but a baby who needed care and affection.

He wished he were too young to know better about the world, and that he had never seen the face of the serpent as it raced after him down some dark dream—

In his hands, he clutched something cold and sharp. Even as he fell back into the dreams that terrified him most, he knew he would wake to an endless night and hear the cries of some denizen of the tunnels, caught in the jaws of that creature.

The Serpent was hunting, and it would be a terrible time for all that lived Below.

In his dreams, the boy was living in the suburbs of the Above in a pretty house with a pretty lawn and a sky above that threatened nothing, and he knew that somehow this was a vision of hell.

Chapter Six

Maddy

1

Madison Sparke was not a woman who would ever turn heads purely from her face or figure. She was stocky and forty-five and had the look of one who would hurt you should you trespass over the invisible magnetic field around her body.

But heads did turn when she passed, for people felt as if something truly grand had touched their lives.

She was short and broad and everything about her was contrived and overdone and yet perfect in some indefinable way. Her hair was a curious red and her eyes, a brilliant green. Her face looked sensibly British, which she was not, her family having come over from Italy in the

1800s, and having owned much of the Lower
East Side to say nothing of nearly all of Rose
Street and Bloofer Street in the Village by 1926.
They had lost all but the two Greenwich Village
properties by the time of the Crash. She still felt
that she owned the city, and believed that the
blood of her ancestors flowed through her body
(with poor circulation at times, too)—and that
all that had been accomplished by her forebears
was somehow inextricably linked to her own
achievements. She walked the sidewalks as if
she were on parade in her kingdom. Her shoes
were not sensible ones—pointed, cruel, and
heavily heeled, lifting her an extra foot or so off
the pavement. She had a bit of the Dutch trader
about her—another influence in the family, for
her grandfather Marini had married a teenaged
girl named van der Dien in 1902. Then her
mother, Lorena, had married Guy Sparke, an
all-American soap salesman who hailed from
Chicago and managed to spend much of her
mother's fortune and give little Madison—
named for the avenue—or Maddy as she was
best-known a sense of adventure even in the
heat of family rows.

Being an only child in a wealthy family, she
had been sent to nice girls' schools in Vermont
and Connecticut. At the schools, she'd been
whacked on the hands by nuns, been subjected
to nine-year-old girls who wore pearls and cash-
mere; been told, at the Catholic school where
she began, that every time she was bad, another
thorn went in Jesus's crown; been told, at the
secular preparatory school she attended, that

because she was Catholic, she worshipped statues; and then, when she turned around and told these pearl-laden girls a thing or two about how their fathers had really made their money, she became the most unpopular girl in the history of the school.

Still, she had rebelled by age fourteen and returned to the city to finish high school at the Dalton School without being thrown out more than twice. Her friends were all at the public schools, and she shed her fine clothes in the afternoon and put on dirty jeans and oversized T-shirts as a senior in high school, to hang out with her buddies and run wild around the city, shoplifting when the mood took her (for which her guilt made her return later with the items, an apology, and even a little something extra—often in the form of her father's soaps—to make the manager of the store feel better about himself). Then she'd studied at NYU just to be able to rush home from classes to relieve one of the visiting nurses that sat beside her mother, dying at the time. After her mother, her father followed, presumably of a broken heart although the nurses indicated it was the fifth of Scotch per night. By the time she was twenty-six years old, Maddy Sparke was alone and had money.

But it was not money that made her attractive—her wealth was tied up in property and stocks and was of a lesser sort than many of her neighbors' treasures. Money merely spotlighted her uniqueness, causing her own natural charms to become more noticeable. After her parents had died, she had reinvented herself in many ways as a Greenwich Village Tough for whom nothing was too wild. Then, pregnant at twenty-eight, she settled into a quieter life until her young son died at the age of three from the hard measles. During the subsequent mourning period, she lost six years of her life to her second love—alcohol. During that time, she never spoke of her dead child, and no one in her neighborhood saw her out of the house much.

Eventually, she dumped her overly clingy lover, alcohol; and then at the age of thirty-seven, began rehabilitating the old brownstones on Rose Street that her father had neglected for thirty years.

2

Maddy Sparke was on her seventh restoration, and it was the grandest of all the homes on the street. She was cash poor, but property rich, and she needed to get ahead of all that by selling the properties to the highest bidder—and during that particular year, Manhattan property values were at an all-time high.

She knew she could make millions from the house if she could just get it to shine the way it had when first built.

And there she was, her dream of this brownstone dashed because of something they'd discovered in December.

Those goddamn workmen.

Still, despite all of it, the curses, the snarls, the cold glances given them, the men at what they now called the dig thought she was devilishly attractive, but used other terms of endearment much less flattering. She wore a smock over her jeans and chambray shirt. Her hands were already muddy from sifting through the morning's treasures. She ignored the rain, as she ignored the workmen.

She could not forget the winter months, and how the discovery had pissed her off royally. At first, when the workmen found the bones, she was sure the previous tenant had been a serial killer—something she had suspected from the moment she'd met him. Then, she thought it might mean there was another African-American burial area, or a Native-American ceremonial plot, or something that was going to destroy her hopes of reconstructing the interior and basement of the brownstone. It took until nearly spring for the Museum of Early Manhattan to run all its expensive tests and come up with its exact findings.

"My damn luck," she said, practically cursing the skies for the light rain. "I want to rebuild a brownstone, and you want to give me a damn museum, you, you," and then the expletives flew like pigeons in Washington Square, and even some of the workmen had never before heard some of the words that flowed like rancid butter off her tongue. Maddy swore some more, but with a warm smile on her face. Affection came not from the tongues of men and angels for her, but from the most vulgar of profanities.

Maddy glanced over at Andreas Harris, the curator, with his shiny bald head and shiny eyes and said, "All right, all I care about is this. I want a cut of every goddamn museum these pieces go to, and if this gets declared a goddamn national landmark for some goddamn reason, I want my name carved in gold, and I want a major goddamn tax break from this city, understood? I've already lost two hundred thousand sitting on this since December, and pretty soon every penny I've ever inherited will be out the door, and I'll be working at goddamn Kmart."

Andreas nodded, clutching his umbrella. His voice was like damp velvet; she had not liked him on sight. He looked like the kind of man who would sell his brother for the right price, and would probably throw the rest of his family in to sweeten the bargain. "Yes, Maddy, of course. This is something we could never have anticipated when construction began."

Maddy lit a cigarette, spitting out smoke. She waved the cigarette, grabbing at the air with her other filthy hand. "And what have your people found so far? Indian pottery? Slave crap?"

Andreas half-grinned. "No, nothing like that. Something wholly unique for Manhattan. For Greenwich Village. Something we never thought had occurred here."

She snorted. "I've seen the bones. Don't tell me this is going to be a reservation or something. I don't want to hear that kind of crap. My great-grandfather didn't come to this country to lose his property to some goddamn historic landmark."

"More interesting. More wonderful," Andreas said. He went to the table and slowly uncovered the canvas.

3

Beneath the canvas, Maddy Sparke saw something that made the small hairs stand up on the back of her neck and produced a shiver that would have been exquisite and perhaps even sexual had it not filled her with an unnameable dread for what the workmen continued to uncover in the muddy earth on her Rose Street property.

4

The rain had stopped as quickly as it had begun. It was spring in New York. The weather was unpredictable. Maddy wished it would rain for a month. She wished it would flood the place on Rose Street that had been so recently dug up.

She wished she could get what she'd seen out of her head.

"I suspect," Andreas Harris said, his voice beginning to gurgle as would a fountain turned off too long, which yearned to spring to great heights, "that we've just found evidence of witch trials on Greenwich plantation. I suspect the four bodies we uncovered were hanged. Their hands were thrust between their jaws after death—we've seen something like this in New England when whole families were suspected of vampirism. So, after death, a bone would be lodged in their jaws to keep them from biting others. I suspect the witch trial and hanging preceded this, but human brutality being what it is . . ."

They were in the garden behind Maddy's house on Jane Street now, hands washed, all traces of dirt removed from them, and of course the shock of what Maddy herself had seen just beginning to wear off. Andreas Harris began to look less and less like a museum curator to her and more an more like an undertaker out of some Dickens novel. Of course he would spend his life playing with the dead, she thought as she poured out another cup of Irish Breakfast tea. It was a suitable profession for him.

Andreas raised his finger in the air to make a point, and began, "It has always been my pet theory that—" and then, shifting gears, "What's that smell?" He sniffed at the air.

Maddy inhaled deeply, trying to catch something other than the car exhaust or the river stink or the gentle stench of her dying gardenias that had barely lived for three days. "I don't smell anything."

"It's a . . . cat smell. Do you own cats?"

"Oh," Maddy nodded. "Yes, six of them," and she turned on the small garden chair, casting a glance up to the small balcony on the second floor. "My little mutty strays." She saw three of them—Caspar, Jabba, and Evian—sunning with their backs to the world. Then, Maddy returned her attentions to Andreas Harris. "It's hard not to smell of cats when you have six."

"Cats are filthy creatures, you know," Andreas said, sipping his tea, his eyes revealing nothing.

"Allergic?"

"Not at all, except perhaps to heart viruses and the kinds of parasites that can make someone very, very sick," Andreas said, setting his cup on the glass table, eyeing it, Maddy thought, as if there were cat germs on it. He glanced at the watch that wrapped snugly around his bony wrist, and then tossed his head back to look at the sky. "I should get back to the dig."

"My house, you mean," Maddy corrected him, closing her eyes for a minute, sending off a prayer to the cosmos to rid the world of museum curators. Opening her eyes again, she felt slightly refreshed with the thought. "The Rose Street house is not a dig. I'm not sure we've even worked out details of what—"

"Is what," he finished for her. "But imagine, Miss Sparke, imagine how what we've found will change the history books. A witch trial in the Village."

"People were burned here?" she said, gasping.

"Not burned. That was the old method in Europe—when witchcraft was considered a heresy. Here in the colonies, the practice of witchcraft was a felony. They were hanged. Justice subverted. The Devil in New York. Rituals. Brutality." Andreas Harris said it with a morbid glee. "Think of what a find this is."

"For God's sake, Andreas. Just get the goddamn bones out of there, and you can have them for your goddamn museum. And that . . . thing . . . that . . ." She set her cup down. Then she leaned back, crossing her arms behind her neck. "Get that out of there, too. And let me get back to fixing up that house so I can make a little money instead of watching all my cash go down the drain." A chilly breeze came off the river and sent a shiver through her for a moment. Again, she closed her eyes and tried to not picture what she had seen beneath the canvas . . . the thing in the box that Andreas had uncovered . . . the thing that she wished had not been found.

Chapter Seven

Jake

1

Jake's Journal

Nothing bad ever happens on the Upper West Side of Manhattan. Can I write it a thousand times and still believe it? Not in $1,700-a-month one-bedrooms with eat-in kitchens and happy families. The note was so much like Amy that I laughed at first, assuming it was a parody, a practical joke on my twenty-ninth birthday.

Dear Jake,
  I have been trying to work up the courage for this over the past six weeks. Here's the thing: I'm leaving you. Not for another man, and not for any reason I can name.

Strangely enough, not because I don't love you. I do love you. But there's something that's not right between us, and I can't name it. I will say this: You know better than I do what we've had to put ourselves through to stay together these past few years. And I just think we both need to find the life that's meant for us. I don't think this one is it. I think there's more for both of us. And I can't keep dealing with it. I'm spending the night at Trisha's, and then we'll figure out what we're going to do.

Love, Amy

2

That was pretty much it.

Like a truck slamming into me at 100 miles per hour.

Like the world itself had slammed into me, and suddenly I could feel its rotation. I could feel the winds of space as they swept by me.

That's what it was like.

I was trembling. Coughing. I dropped to the floor, lay on my back, knees bent, looking up at the ceiling, while my little girl—my Berry, my Helen Wheels, my Laury—stood still as if she'd done something terribly wrong and did not want to breathe for fear that if she did, the world would crash around her, as well.

I nearly laughed at my wife's letter. Not because I wasn't feeling nausea in the pit of my soul. Not because I didn't see my life, as I then knew it, melt like snow in July. Not because of the several reasons and feelings that threatened to obliterate my consciousness at that moment.

I nearly laughed at my wife's letter because I realized the inevitability of it.

Women I knew always said good-bye in a note. And not just good-bye, but "good-bye and let me explain to you why I'm leaving because you're not smart enough to figure it out on your own."

And yet, I knew.

I knew better than anyone.

My wife was leaving me for another man and was too chickenshit (*sorry, honey, but you were*) to actually say it outright. I had loved her for a lot of things over the years, and one of them was the way she'd shirk some responsibility—something that nearly endeared her to me most of the time. And now, she even wanted to withdraw from a good-bye. I felt denied some battle. Some upset. Some drama. Make no mistake, this kind of separation is violent, whether anyone raises voices or fists or not. It felt like violence inside me. I'm sure she felt it, too.

But now, she was going because it had come to that—no fights, no outbreaks of passion, no flare-ups of white-hot anger. It was quiet and nearly genteel, and was that much more like a knife in the gut because of it.

She was leaving me because she had probably left me a year or two earlier, only I was too dumb to notice, and too involved in my own world to watch how she had been doing her best to stay away from me whenever possible.

And I knew all this. I didn't know it consciously in my day-to-day life, but I knew it like there was this train on some track, and I'd been listening to it roar as it came down, only I was pretending the train wasn't due for another ten minutes.

And then it hit me.

Like I said, it was violence. Violence and icy pain and all the bad things that no medicine—no Valium, no beer, no chocolate, and no cigarette—could ever make better.

3

Weeks passed in a haze. Amy and I would meet to discuss things. Something truly dreadful entered my life: I would begin to entertain hopes. Hope that we could work it all out. Hope that if I apologized, or maybe if she apologized, or maybe if no one apologized, it could all be patched up. Hope that time would heal all wounds, and other less obvious clichés of the very needy. Hope can be a terrible thing. You hope too much, and you live in dreams, and when reality hits, it hits so hard you wished you never had dreams at all. Hope was like a smell for me. The world stank of it, briefly.

Amy would take Laury over to the Upper East Side where Amy had miraculously found an apartment for cheap within four days (liar that she had become. I can think of worst words than *liar* but I will be something of a gentleman and not write them here). I visited the new place. It was fairly snazzy. It had a bedroom for Laury and for Amy. It had a dining room, in addition to a living room. This was something that Amy and I could never have afforded. I didn't ask how much it cost, as most New Yorkers would have. I let some things just be. I pretended maybe we'd get back together, that love was stronger than whatever bug had gotten into Amy's rear end. I pretended that I was fine, that I was in fact the best man in the world, taking it all so well, and I'd even go out to dinner with Amy and Laury and play nice. All of it, part of that dream and stink of hope, until Laury mentioned Daniel, and then I knew I was screwed.

He had a name now. Even to my little girl. He had a name, and he was real, and he wasn't just some guy who helped her feel beautiful or in lust. He was marked with a name: Daniel. I had even been over to his place once or twice. I used to call it, jokingly—I could kick myself—"Daniel's Lion's Den" when Amy and I would come back from a visit. That was back when we were dating. Yes, that long ago. Before we'd even finished dating, they'd known each other.

My friends, it was that bad.

He was your basic nightmare: handsome, tall, dark hair that was shockingly thick, and his forearms were strong, and he worked out at the gym (good executive that he was) and liked to see Fellini movies by himself (that should've been the clue, since Amy loved Fellini far too much). Daniel also could never have been a Danny—he was formal and minimalist all at once, like a flower arrangement that costs a hundred bucks but only has three flowers in it and a couple of stones. But still looks good. But still stinks of smashed dreams.

Daniel was Amy's best friend's ex-husband, an investment banker with whom I'd shared a cab on the way to my own wedding. Daniel had told me then that I was the luckiest man in the world. Mysteriously, after the wedding, I had never heard hide nor hair from him.

Now I knew.

I knew in my heart that Amy had stayed in touch with him, perhaps not in some damning way. She protested to me that I was prematurely jealous of Daniel since they were still just friends, even now, even after I saw the book of poetry he gave her sitting on the back of the toilet in her new apartment. Even after I opened the book and saw the little scrawled dedication. *To Amy, She of the dancing smile, who was always there. Daniel.* She had stayed in touch with him—no doubt—because she knew that someday our marriage would end.

Rage was a delicious lunch, but came far too cheaply. I raged. I stomped. I threw things at the wall. Books, pillows, pencils. Mainly unbreakable things, because I am nobody's fool. I was tempted to throw this notebook computer, but I wasn't sure I could afford another one anytime soon.

Of course, I raged in my own little place where no one but the Silent One across the hall might hear me.

I would've preferred that my heart had been ripped out rather than what Amy told me next. What she told me and what I should've known

from nights of cold sleep and lazy Sunday af-
ternoons when all went unspoken between us.
But I sat there at her place, thinking on some
stupid troglodyte level that she might realize
her mistake and beg my forgiveness and ask if
I'd take her back (my fantasies were endless),
fork raised mid-air, as Amy told me that she
didn't think she had ever really loved me the
way a wife is supposed to love a husband.

I kind of wanted to laugh and make a feeble
joke like: "Baby, you loved me just the way most
wives love their husbands," but I didn't think it
was the right time, and I doubt even now she
would've seen the humor in it.

And what she said kept pinging off my innards: "I don't think I've ever really loved you
the way a wife is supposed to love a husband."
For just a second, I remembered the last time
we'd made love, and it made me ache, not for
sex or for pleasure, but for that feeling of security when we were together like that, pressed
as close as two people could get. The little boy
in me (no, not my inner child, that kid that
never leaves you, and you wish he would, that
kid who doesn't feel all socialized and polite and
knowledgeable, the one who still has impulses)
wanted to cry, but I shut up that kid.

Instead, I just got pissed off. Sorry to say, I
didn't keep my trap shut. I started doing all the
things you know you're not supposed to do. I let
it all rip. I started in on her with, "You know,
you're right, you never really loved me the way
a wife is supposed to—but who the hell wants
that? I thought we were special. Christ, we have

Laury: We have a life. We have a future. How can you not remember the night we had Laury, and how I was right there, and you screamed all the words Laury isn't supposed to hear, about fifty times, and you know what, Amy? Not once did I mind. Not once did I stand there while our little girl was taking her first breaths and think, *Wow she's telling me to fuck off, she must really mean it,* and then when you got mad at me for—what?—for nothing, you would fly into these rages because I wanted to go with you to the movies. To Fellini movies. *Juliet of the Spirits. Amarcord. Orchestra Rehearsal.* The goddamn *Orchestra Rehearsal,* Amy. And you threw fits because you wanted to go alone. Well, I guess we know you weren't alone. I guess we know there was someone else at the Fellini festival down at the Waverly or the Angelika or wherever you went. Oh yeah, baby, that's right, I guess you outwitted me," and I thought: *Jake Richmond, can you hear yourself? What you're saying to her? How you're saying it?* but that thing inside me that I'd been keeping under lock and key needed to get out, and now was the only chance. "I guess all the days and nights when I was here for you through anything you had to deal with, you were somewhere else, and I guess maybe it's because I'm just one of those stupid people who don't see the writing on the wall and hang on to things just because I believe in hanging on—"

I probably said more than this, but this is all I can remember before my mouth became the quickest route of vomiting up my soul all over the place. Words came out of me that I had held in far too long—about our sex life, which had gone out the window, about our daughter, about how I had been a martyr, and it got worse from there. Something within me wanted to sew my lips shut, but it was like opening Pandora's box, and I wasn't about to keep in all the ills of the world. Especially not when she just sat there and took it.

All right, that was the worst part of all.

She remained across the table, her eyes so large it was like one of those God-awful velvet paintings of waifs and clowns, the big, sad wise eyes, the *ojos de Dios*, the all-seeing eyes of Dr. T. J. Eckleberg, looking out from Amy's face. She was too calm, and it was awful having to be there and watch her be so calm and even dispirited.

She let me have my yell and my spit, and then she just watched me, waiting for me to settle down into the routine of our separation. It felt like I had just given her some small bit of happiness within the darkness of our tragedy.

I had given her the real reason why we could not stay together, and its name was not Daniel, nor was it about Amy at all.

4

After a weekend binge in which I drank every kind of beer that the bars on Hudson Street could produce, I took a week off work and just stared at the walls of our old apartment. I had begun to feel that all human evil began on the

Upper West Side, all crime to humanity, all bad things buzzed like trash can flies there, but it was all hidden. Lower East Side, Harlem, the Village, nothing could hide there, for there were no hiding places; but the Upper West Side was full of the silence of plots, manipulations, and scheming; corporate terror was there as was marital ice, as was the separation between two human beings—that vast canyon, greater than the Grand Canyon, greater than the space between the earth and the stars—the distance between two human beings who could not connect.

I went to see a Truffaut film, and then a Three Stooges festival, and in the same night found a little movie theater that played *Breakfast at Tiffany's* and I actually cried when Holly Golightly lost her cat. Leaving the theater, I knew that something was wrong with the world, and I had to make my end of it right.

I decided to get on with life, whatever that would mean.

5

My new home was less than spacious. In fact, it was less than pretty much everything, but I liked the 'hood and the local taverns and coffeehouses, and I was completely ready to live in a hole-in-the-wall at this point.

I had found a place in the Village, off Horatio, across from a grassless park—it had been completely covered with blacktop, and was generally used for local basketball and informal baseball games. I'd been to this park several times, when I'd felt low, and wanted to hang out in a less intimidating place than our apartment (I can say "our" but it was always hers). This part of the Village felt like a neighborhood. I'd be able to jog around the streets, down to the river. I'd be able to wander the bookstores and cafes. I counted six Jack Russell terriers chasing balls in it the first day I went to see the apartment. Then, I saw two very happy people walking hand in hand through the park—this annoyed me, but romantic love had become a disturbance to me. It made me remember my early days with Amy. It made me remember something within myself that I would've preferred to just forget.

It was an unassuming building, sandwiched between two very assuming brownstones. My window was angled in such a way that I got a view of the park below as well as a bit of the rooftop patio of one of the brownstones. I could watch this guy walk around in his boxers on his patio, and ogle his wife who was hardly worth the ogle. They had a little garden, frozen solid in the winter. The wife would sometimes step out in little more than her panties, even on an icy winter morning, and do her yoga stretches. Why her ass never stuck to the patio, I don't know—you'd think she'd be blue in the face, but she had that sort of Nordic look that was like a placid lake that never froze over. No doubt, she thought she was invisible, owing to the frost-covered roof garden, but my place was slightly above them. I had a perfect vantage point to watch her body go into its contortions. I wondered what it would be like to be rich enough to own an entire brownstone and to have a half-naked wife on my roof. (I stopped watching her one day when her husband came out in his boxers and happened to glance up right into my window. He didn't wave his fist or look angry. Worse: He just shrugged, and went to put some clothes on. For some reason, I had no desire to spy on them again. But on my first day in the apartment, I saw her there, and thought: *not a bad view from a dingy little flat.*)

The place was within walking distance of work, a one-bedroom that hovered at the outer edges of my price range. The stairway up—like all walk-ups I'd seen—was fit only for a demolition crew. The corridor held three apartments. The one at the end of the hallway contained the person I came to call the Creeper, mainly because he always seemed to skulk around, furtive in his movements, as if he had chopped someone up and hidden them in the walls of his place. Probably, it was just another one of the city's lonely souls, but I didn't let that stop me from mythologizing him. As with the Creeper, I also never saw the Silent One—whoever lived in the apartment directly across from mine. It was the quietest building I'd ever encountered—and I wondered where all the noise of the city had gone.

Standing in front of the door to my new place for the first time was awkward. I had not lived alone in years. I felt like a clumsy student with poor social skills who now had to conquer the world in some small and terribly insignificant way.

I almost wanted a roommate.

Once inside the apartment, things got a little better, although the shower was a little too close to the kitchen sink, and the bathroom was so small that I could actually sit and shave at the same time.

It was perfect.

I sublet it from a Dutch artist who would not be back in the States again for three years, so I had the bargain apartment of the Manhattan universe, $900 a month for a four-flight walk-up one-bedroom with roof access.

I took the news of my divorce in stride as I poured myself into work. I sat in a cube from nine to seven, tapping away at some new e-commerce notion, writing something that was now called "content" rather than "article"; my little girl slept over on weekends while her mother got ready for her next wedding. I taught Laury how to play catch, and inline skate. We played Mario Kart with the Nintendo 64 her grandmother had bought for her the previous Christmas. Sometimes we played until mid-night, when Laury would be jumping up and down as her Peachy character slaughtered my Yoshi. Without meaning to, I taught her the first serious cuss words she had ever heard, and then had to unteach her in a delicate but firm man-ner: "Daddy was very, very bad to say those things," I said, speaking in the third person as I always seemed to do when I was very, very bad.

"Mommy says you're a hippocrotamouse," Laury said. "She says that's when you say one thing and do something different."

Hippocrotamouse. What an adorable word! But I knew that what Mommy had really said is that Daddy is a hypocrite, and Laury confused this with, first, a hippopotamus, and then a mouse.

There was truth to all three accusations.

But it made me say some more very, very bad things, and finally I told Laury. "Look, you know how you can't drink beer?"

She nodded.

"Well, just like that, you can't use these words that sometimes slip out from me. Not yet."

"When can I?"

"When you can drive. Everyone can use those words when they drive," I told her, and there was some truth to that.

6

Spring arrived, and spring in New York is unlike anything anywhere in the world—it is as if the world were born, just that morning.

The Village was alive and pulsing with its own urgency. Urgency was the word. I felt urges I hadn't in years and hadn't even realized how much I'd been repressing stuff, not just my libido, but my urge to have fun, to celebrate, to have dinner at midnight at a diner or to walk the rain-swept streets of springtime with a hot cup of java from Starbucks, or just to sit on a rooftop and listen to the night and its honks and sirens and shouts and screeches and barking dogs. I felt an urge, I went with it. I dated women who were either too young for me (twenty-three) or too angry (thirty-four) or too wise (any age). I woke up in strange apartments and felt the taste of sour beer in the back of my throat. I did foolish things that at twenty-nine I probably should've stopped doing at twenty. I lived, basically, as if there were no tomorrow, and I went with whatever urge came at me. It was a mindless, brief sublease of my spring-time, and it felt like a cure for something that had no name.

And then, I got the urge to call up my old girl-friend.

Naomi, Nywombi, Nyomi.

7

Naomi and I ran away together at sixteen, but we only made it to Baltimore before we were gathered by the cops and returned fairly quickly to both our folks. Naomi was not pregnant; I was not a thief; neither of us had set fire to anything. These were all the things we'd been accused of. It was the summer after my band trip to New York, and I knew she and I could be happy in Manhattan. Manhattan was like the Golden Arches or the Emerald City for us, it was the place that we'd dreamed about, it was where people made it or got stepped on, it was trash or treasure, it was junk food piled forty stories high and shining like, well, the top of the Chrys-ler building. Once, I saw a big trash bag stuffed with rat bait sitting in front of the Plaza Hotel. This said it all for me—New York was both of those things, and both were equally appealing at times.

In our own time, we both managed to scrape it together to get to the city that never sleeps or apparently dreams—once you've been here long enough, you feel that someone else is dreaming about your life, someone in the sub-urbs or out in hayseed territory. You are living the dream, which is never quite as much fun as dreaming the dream. Of course, she and I ar-rived separately, not even knowing where the other lived anymore.

Naomi got to New York City first when she was seventeen—she went to study acting at Cir-cle in the Square, at least that was the story she told her father. Truth was, she arrived at Port Authority on a Greyhound, she shared a one-bedroom with three other young women, and I never even knew what part of town she was in. By the time I was eighteen, I wasn't even sure she was still in Manhattan. While I commuted up to the city from Rutgers, I never saw her, I never ran into her, I never met anyone who had ever seen her. When I met Amy, I put Naomi into the past, into my childhood—which was, after all, a place where some of my worst night-mares as well as happiest moments lived—like a box of old photographs, I'd closed it, thinking that one day I'd get around to sorting through the past.

I worked up the nerve to call the old number

I had—her father's house—and I did everything I could not to imagine that place.

"Mr. Faulkner?" The line buzzed and spat, and I could just imagine Naomi's father with his pipe hanging halfway out of his hound-dog face, and a housefly perpetually spinning in the air around his bald scalp.

"Speaking."

"This is Jake Richmond."

"Alma Richmond's son," he said, his tone never changing, as if he were consulting the annual crop-yield chart.

"Yes, sir. I'm trying to track down Naomi."

He was silent for a bit, and I thought that perhaps the line had gone dead, or he had hung up. Just as I was about to slam the phone down, he said, "You probably didn't know about her accident."

Again, very little fluctuation in his voice.

I could picture him existing in that perpetual state of boredom I associated with all things Carthage—the zombies on Main Street; the farm boys in the 4-H, all dead to anything other than the filth of the sheep or the next dance or the next beer. The women who got old too fast. The men who had never been young.

"She died. There in New York. It was all over the papers. Surprised you didn't read it. They report all kinds of garbage." Then, before he hung up, as if he had merely reported his daughter's death for the umpteenth time and had no more details to add, he crowned the conversation with, "She killed herself because of you. Because of what you did to her. How you ruined her. She jumped in front of a train. Those damn subway trains."

So I have begun writing all of this.

8

I began seeing Naomi in my dreams almost immediately, she had already begun haunting me, and then one day in the subway, I saw, on a wall behind a column, the most curious graffiti. In red paint, someone had written NAOMI LOVES JAKE TO DEATH, and these words—having no obvious association with me or with the Naomi I had once known—sent me to my knees, weeping like either a madman or a baby, weeping and sobbing and wishing that I were God so that I could turn back the years and become a boy again who would make things right for this girl I had once loved who had died here in this hole in the ground, had gone down the rabbit hole of death, when a boy named Jake should've never let go of her hand, should never have let the night come to her—and should have still been holding her hand when she had come down to this subway platform so that a subway train would not have carried her to the underworld.

And then, I think, I began to go a little mad.

Chapter Eight

Blood-Red Rose with Thorns

1

Jake awoke in the dead of night, his mouth dry, his head pounding.

For a second, he was sure that someone was standing outside his apartment, someone was out there, saying nonsensical words over and over.

He looked through the vague darkness, his vision fuzzy while waiting for the ambient light to define the room for him. He saw the shapes of his place, the shadows of tables and chairs and book piles in corners. The man outside the door—he was sure it was a man's voice, although a young man, a very young man, perhaps a sixteen-year-old boy, was saying it—those words all running together.

Chanting.

Then, as he sat up, feeling the sweat-damp of his back (*you give me fever,* the song went), the voice was a young boy's, a kid's—all right, some juvy case was outside his apartment standing right in front of the door saying the words.

And then, Jake realized that the voice was from within.

He said it again, and then stopped.

"Blood-red rose with thorns," he'd been saying.

He flicked on a lamp by the bed.

Christ.

Written on the wall in his daughter Laury's bright red Crayola: BLOOD-RED ROSE WITH THORNS.

In his hands, the stub end of the crayon. His fingers smeared with the waxy color.

Jake Richmond went to get a glass of water, checked the clock (it was 4:00 A.M.) and decided to go for a pre-dawn jog rather than sit on his bed and wonder if he were losing all his marbles.

2

After a run through the Village in the literate darkness of signs and portents hanging from storefronts, the cabs of dawn moving like mist, Jake hopped in the tiny shower in the kitchen and washed off the sweat and anger. He had that low-level anger now, anger at life, anger at God, and some anger at his ex. He scrubbed the red crayon smudges from his hands with Ivory and some Lux, and took a sponge to the wall by his bed. He managed to get all but a trace of the writing off the wall. His muscles felt sore in all the right ways, and he returned to bed as if he were welcoming quicksand.

Back in bed at 5:00 A.M., Jake began hearing the voice again as sleep seeped into the back of his head and beneath his eyelids. He let it prattle on—*It's in your head, it's a nervous dream, you are headed for an asylum, that's okay, just get some rest first*—but it was only darkness awaiting him in dreamland, and the voice grew softer.

It was her voice, not his.

"Blood-red rose with thorns," Naomi said, her little-girl arms impossibly covered with barbwire scratches from the roses; her face scratched up, too. She had been running in thorn bushes, she said, and had gotten caught.

She stood there, her bare feet covered with mud, her dress torn and ragged, and behind her, the concrete pipe that led to one end of their playground.

The cats were at the edge of the Treasure Cave, and all of them were crying like babies. Naomi said, "Stop it from crying, Jake. Stop it from crying," and one little yellow ball of fluff kitten was under her arm, and it was wailing. Jake went to take it, and Naomi said, "They're not really babies, they're cats," and Jake said, "I know, Nyombi," and she got mad just like she always did when he went out of his way to say her name the wrong way.

Then someone said, "You kids're too old to

play like that. Get outta there, I told you, get outta there!"

Finally, a forgetful sleep descended upon Jake Richmond.

3

Jake's Journal

And now, I find that even leaving my apartment takes enormous effort, and when I hear a key turn in the hall, even as I type this, I wonder who are all these strangers in this city, who are all these people who live on top of and under one another and don't care and exist within separate walled kingdoms, and will they—we—all one day catch the same train that Naomi caught?

My daughter comes this weekend. My ex-wife will meet with me for coffee. My job is doomed because I don't see the point, but I do it regardless. Yes, I'm alive. Yes, I've awakened to my life.

And awakening, I'm in a world of sleepers.

Life goes on in its own unimaginable way, but now I haunt a subway platform, waiting for a train.

Wherever I am in this city, I'm waiting for that train.

Chapter Nine

Within the Box

1

What Maddy Sparke had seen when Andreas Harris had unrolled the canvas earlier in the day, and had shown her what was in the box:

What looked at first like a small round sponge, completely desiccated, and of a curious pale red hue like a faded rose.

Before the museum curator opened his mouth to tell her what it was, Maddy knew.

2

It was a human heart.

Dried and misshapen, and a pale rose-red. Parched and crumbling, a curled sponge of brown-crimson stain. There was so little of the human about it now, after all these years when it had remained in its box. So little of what had once been a beating organ that pumped blood to a living human being.

Now, it was an object.

A curiosity.

Someone had taken thirteen slender white needles—no, they were carved splinters of bone—and had pressed them into the heart as if to keep it from beating.

Part Two

Naomi Loves Jake
to Death

Chapter Ten

Mourning and Memory

1

Jake's Journal

I will not write about my grief over Naomi's death. I had become disconnected from her by life, but hearing from her father about her death—her suicide—was like having someone kick me in the gut several times. I will not go on and on about how my head and heart both ached, thinking about her, about the last time I had seen her, about how, in my mind, she would always be a young girl with a tear in her eye and a gardenia in her hair and her feet spattered with mud from the stream.

But I needed to know more than her father had been willing to tell me. For all I began to think about was Naomi, Naomi, Naomi.

I spent a day trying to track down my mother, but she was no longer listed in Carthage, and my father was not worth talking with about this.

It's a long and boring story with my family, and what happened when I was a boy is something for which there is apparently no forgiveness.

Perhaps if my father had not had his own form of darkness within his fifty-four-year-old form—and yes, I imagined him with a glass of Jack Daniels in his fist and a gun in the other, or out back by the shed, cleaning his guns, or off in the woods, alone, shooting at life as often as he could; and my mother, whose long-suffering nature had led her to be canonized and then ex-communicated from the little church we had attended and who now, also in her fifties, was, like all former saints, waiting for some special day to be named just for her. I imagined that she'd be sitting up in bed like some Victorian dowager, pillows piled in back of her head, lap dogs all around her bosom, and a copy of the family Bible laid open between her knees. She would no doubt like to be depicted this way in a carving of soft stone or Ivory soap.

If I seem cruel in my description of them, then let it be known: I am a keenly ungrateful son who was so accused of youthful crime as a child, so implicated in any barn burning, any hedge slaughter, any missing jewelry, any stolen trucks, any poisoned rabbits, that even my own parents were known to call the local sheriff if they once caught a look from me that seemed vaguely defiant. The anger of childhood may be insurmountable. It feels that way. It feels as if childhood is a country of fire and ice, and the only respite is the rest of nightly sleep and the escape into books or movies or, for some, drugs and drink. For me, my escape was of a different sort—a place there in Carthage that seemed a secret between me and Naomi, our Treasure Cave, and the imaginings we took to it. But it was sealed when I was in my teens, and we could no longer play there.

There were times when I wished that I could erase all my memories from that time. Naomi said she had erased most of hers, back when we were kids. She told me that she couldn't remember all the things she knew were better off forgotten.

Just before she left me.

Just before I graduated from high school.

My father, gun in hand, had told me, "She wasn't no good, that gal. She saved you some trouble just by disappearing."

Then he raised his gun that day and shot at a bird that sat defiantly on the telephone wire near our house. Missed the bird completely.

My father blew out half the phone lines in Carthage that day. And blamed it on me.

2

Why were my folks so against their own son? You may well ask.

I have many thoughts about this, but no real answer.

Perhaps it was my one great crime, which I had committed in utero; perhaps it was the then-infamous show-and-tell I performed on the steps of our little church in the vale when I was fifteen; perhaps it was just that, being the son of my father, I was marked. Perhaps I was just too damn sensitive and bookish and not part of the country-boy life I should've been leading. Perhaps my father was—as some said—an unrepentant sadist, and my mother was, at times, part of that mean puritanical tradition that holds that anything natural and human has to be snuffed like a candle or burned eternally, and anything icy and unfeeling must be encouraged because it meant control. And life, to my mother, was all about control. But who really knows why they always seemed to treat me like I was a hostile alien from another planet?

Why does anyone end up in New York City? It is an island of orphans and outcasts and escapists and speculators and re-inventors and nonconformists and the abandoned and those who abandon. All of us here in one way or another came from a Carthage.

My grandmother was in heaven before I could grab her and hold her back. She was the one sane person in our household. But she left as soon as she could—at the age of sixty-two and no amount of yarrow or jewel weed was going to bring her back. My parents remained behind, and my life at home, while not a complete torment, was out of whack.

The mystery of our lives is often the mystery of those who were there before us, who in creating us, felt they were not making a child between them, but burying secrets in earth. Had they but known that the buried would rise from the mother's body and bear witness to their secrets of guilt and human frailty and cruelty, they would never have united.

In a small southern town in the shadow of the great Blue Ridge, it all gets very biblical very quickly.

3

With these grandiose thoughts swelling within my brain, calling my own family was out.

But I wanted to find out more. I wanted to know more than Naomi's father would tell me. I wanted to know where Naomi had lived. How she had come to die in the subway. Why she had never found me, also living in this city.

When I remembered the name of the man that Naomi's sister, Rachel, had married, I called information in Carthage hoping that there was a listing. Turns out they lived down in Covington, a much more civilized place, and even the operator for the listing seemed more sophisticated, her voice less tinged with the regret of backwoods thought. After leaving two messages, Rachel finally called back when it was nearly midnight, and I was half-asleep. "Who is it?" I asked, looking up at the shadows on the ceiling, then focusing on the red digital numbers of the alarm by my bed.

4

"Jake, it's Rachel Evers. I got your message. Did I wake you?" Her southern accent was still twangy as only Carthaginians could twang—the surrounding towns and hill retreats had called us Picts because there was still too much Scots-Irish in us, and lest this be seen as a badge of pride, it was a way of referring to trash and low-lifes all over the valley—said with a snort of derision and a knowing glance. Virginians can be ever so cruel, as my mother used to say. "They are the cruelest," she would say, "to their own."

And as a kid, I'd think: *No, in fact, you, Mom, are cruelest to your own.*

But then, she was a Virginian.

But back to the phone call with Naomi's sister:

I said, "Rachel. I'm so glad—"

"It's good to hear your voice," she interrupted, and then her voice dropped to a whisper. "I don't miss many people back there. But you were one of the good ones."

"I need to know. When did it happen?"

Rachel hesitated. Then she whispered, "This past December."

I felt my mind reel as if it were disconnected from my body. Just a few months ago, just last December! Naomi had died. Naomi had been close to me. I would've had my chance had I only gotten beyond my stupid problems and tried to find her sooner. I might've kept her from jumping. I might've . . .

The might'ves all slapped at me as Rachel

116

continued telling me the small, unimportant details, having no idea how I was screaming within myself at God and Life and the Idiot Cosmos for being so unfair.

Then, she told me how Naomi had been working as a waitress in the Village. "She did some acting, I guess, too. I guess you could call it acting. I never really understood it. She would have what she called showcases. She was in a class maybe. I never thought she was very good. I told her she should come back and settle down, but . . ." Rachel paused, and whispered something—probably to her husband. "Sorry. Jake?"

"Still here."

"It was an unforgiving place," she said. "I'm glad you got out. I'm glad she did, too. For what it's worth. I know you were innocent."

I did not respond.

This was my blind spot in life. Everyone has blind spots I guess. When it comes down to it, it might've been part of the human animal. Memory is terrible sometimes—it's a curse to live in the past and the present at the same moment. Memory is the home of the migraine. Memory is like icy water that you drink all at once and your head aches and your chest clutches. My blind spot of memory had to do with something I haven't really considered over the past several years. I knew I was innocent of what I'd been accused of in that armpit of the Shenandoah, that worm-fodder hole of a place, that pit that was both beautiful and hideous at the same time, where nature had covered over the face of corruption and the stink of rot by making the trees sing and the hills echo and the sky lacquer it all in sunlight and a sense of heaven when in fact it was the entryway to another destination.

Timidly, I asked, "Where did she live in the Village. Do you know?"

"I have my address book, hang on," she said, and then a few seconds later she came back to the phone. "She was in three different places. Somewhere near Hell's Kitchen, first. And then a studio down on a street called Paulus something. And then, what was it? She made some joke about Shakespeare and Hamlet. I've got it here, hold on. Oh, right. Here it is. Horatio is all I have."

"Horatio?"

"That's what I have written down."

I remained silent, my head throbbing.

It was too much. I should not be thinking any of it—that's what kept going through my head— this is something that seems true but can't be.

I lived on Horatio Street now.

Naomi, too, had lived somewhere nearby.

5

Before we got off the phone, Rachel added, "She was always trying to kill herself. She may just be the only one of us who ever succeeded at anything." Then that sweet laugh. I didn't blame Rachel. The laugh didn't seem as chilly then as it does now when I write it. It was warm the way she said it; warm the way she laughed, and Rachel had managed to muster some gallows humor for what must've been devastating to her. She had been so close to Naomi.

The phone went silent, and then a dial tone followed. She had hung up without saying good-bye.

I rose from my bed, pulling on a pair of sweat-pants. I opened my door. The hallways to the apartments always smelled like a musty, damp attic, with a scent of curry and cooking eggs somewhere nearby. I went out into the hallway and stared at the apartment across from mine.

Naomi had lived in the apartment across from the one I now occupied.

She had been there.

Her warmth had existed within these walls.

Her perfume had smothered the damp and curry and eggs.

I can't write this down enough. I'm not the smartest person in the world, but if I were to venture a guess on the pattern I felt existed in the madness of the world—of the spiderweb strands that reached across years and miles and memory—then, it would be that there was something to the notion of predestination.

What is destiny but a series of mishaps that form a pattern in retrospect?

6

The apartment across from mine had been Na-omi Faulkner's up until the time of her death.

She was there, waiting for me.

Somehow.

She and I were meant to be together.

Chapter Eleven

Below

1

If you were standing on the corner looking down one of the alleys that pop like small veins from the main artery of Fourteenth Street as it crosses Eighth Avenue, and you glance down the half-street that dead-ends in rows of Dumpsters, you might have seen something unusual on this particular day:

The sight of a hand pushing up the construction-cracked storm drain.

The passersby out on the sidewalk swept like dust before the rain, too fast and scattered to notice anything other than the world before them of routine and reliability.

But up came the hand, and then another, and then a face that was covered with filth. Finally, an entire creature emerged like a frog from a pond.

A teenager, small for his age, scruffy, muddy, and pale as a worm where the clinging scum had not painted him, emerged.

He looked every bit like an escaped convict from an underground reform school, his brow severely twisted in thought, his eyes wild and glassy. Somewhere within the muck of features, he possessed that spit of life that only the young possess. It was a spit and shine that overcame the general sense that this boy was both insane and possibly corrupt.

But for the boy, coming up into the city was always a painful and unnatural birth.

2

The cavern called Manhattan burst with light as it always did, but it never fooled him; no, it never fooled Romeo who knew that there were places on earth that looked like light but were in fact dark. There were places that seemed to others to be night but were truly day. The darkness was not always where there was no light, and sometimes the deepest cave of the Below was the easiest to comprehend.

Romeo had that sense since the caverns of his childhood. Back in that place he thought of as his past life. It wasn't this big city—it was a smaller place, where even the underground was small. But all the wormholes were the same, and all the serpents seemed to know the labyrinths beneath the ground better than he ever could.

He scraped his stomach raw getting through the storm drain by the construction. When the rain had begun, he'd welcomed it. He shook off the mud and blood along the fresh wounds. He took off his ragged shirt and wiped it across his stomach before putting it on over his head again.

The hunger had grown in him, as it always seemed to when he was awake. Too hungry sometimes. Scabber always told him it was because his mama had never fed him enough. He knew that was crazy. He knew that his mother was night, and she always fed him.

And now, hungry and more than a little scared, Romeo knew that he needed to find someone to give him what he needed.

His mind was a jumble, for in the Below his thoughts seemed clear and lucid, but Above, where this city fumed, words and images got all messed up. The sea of cars and trucks and the larger stream of people robbed him of any clarity he could muster.

Scabber needed meat, or she'd get very sick. Ro and See had cravings for sugar, and they never had enough sugar in the Below. Romeo himself would not mind some oranges, and then there was the Forbidden that he had to feed as well, for if he didn't, it would die, he was sure of it, and in the Below death was always waiting along the tunnels; death and the Serpent.

All the Forbidden in the past had died, they

couldn't just live on the water that ran down from the Above, and if they ate the slugs they'd be fine, but they didn't seem to want to, and then the Serpent would get them, and he never wanted to be around when the Serpent was around so he could never help them then.

He could only run down the tunnel to the fire where Scabber kept the soup boiling and cover his ears so he wouldn't hear the Serpent howl when the Forbidden was finished.

3

"Change?" he shouted as he ran into the street, his hands cupped before him.

A man older than time passed by, raising his umbrella to the water pouring down. Romeo noticed the fat pockets in the gray coat and the fat face and the fat jinglies in his hand, and knew the man had money to spare. The jinglies were always the sign, and Romeo could hear them in pockets and hands and purses.

He cupped his hand, letting the rain run down his arms.

"How old are you? Fourteen? Fifteen?" the man asked, disgust growing in his voice like a cloud of exhaust. "You should be in school. Jesus. Where the hell are the authorities? This world. This world."

"Change," Romeo said ever mournfully, knowing that it was just a matter of sounding like wind through the cracks of a cave to get fat-pocketed men like this to give him some of their jinglies and cracklies.

"Cha-a-ange," he chewed and pulled on the word until it was painful to hear. Let the man say what he wanted. Romeo needed money. That's all—just the jinglies and cracklies, and if he entertained someone with his Below stink, so be it. After Romeo endured a brief lecture on how he should be in school, Mr. Fat Pockets tossed him three quarters.

With that, Romeo knew his day was made.

He caught a lady who looked as if she was sure he'd slit her throat. He gave her a little blessing of salvation when she dropped three crispy cracklies on him. Never had he made so much money on such short notice.

Stealing meat was easier. The stores themselves invited him to do so by leaving it all in a row. Meat was so perfect for slipping into his shirt. Then, some butter, even simpler as he slipped it down in his oversized pants. The hard part was parting with the jinglies and cracklies, the coins and paper money, that he had gathered within two hours. There were some things that could not just be harvested from stores or hunted down an aisle of a market.

He caught sight of Opal and Weasel standing outside the Chelsea Market jostling and terrifying all the businesspeople who went in to buy their lunches and coffees.

Opal held up a small broken locket she'd retrieved from the pavement. Weasel laughed and told Romeo that Scabber had stolen matches from all of them while they'd slept. Romeo was too busy to hang out with them. He had to do his hunting before the day wore too thin and while the rain poured, for he could not stand the thought of the sun coming out again and burning him.

As he scurried ratlike back down into the night of the Below, he heard the keening wail of the Forbidden even above the rumbling of the trains. He covered his ears, but still the sound gnawed at him.

When he finally found Scabber, she was already angry.

4

"Shut up," she said, and he always obeyed since she was the only mother he could remember. She was mother to them all as far as he knew. She was old and tough as the beef jerky he tossed to her, which she gnawed at greedily. "The demons went dancing all night and now she goes in the daylight. The dead get too damn hungry."

"Hungry as you?" he joked.

"Shut up," Scabber snapped. She often said this with a great deal of affection, as one might say "I love you" to a favored child. She tore ferociously at the thin strip of meat.

He knew her form better than her face, but in the humming firelight, her face was like a beautiful potato with a roundness and the pockmarks of a troubled life pressed into it. Romeo could not tell if she was a hundred years old as she claimed, or just a few years older than the others. Scabber was the wise woman. She had taught many of them the pathways between the subway tunnels, how to identify the wormholes of the Serpent, and how to cross them.

Scabber could not move her legs, but she was the keeper of the fire and the warmer of the Below People, her Rats, as she often called them.

Without her, there would be no knowledge of the Below, and of the Forbidden City on the other side of the dark river. She knew how to speak to the Mole People, too, and how to make sure they never spoke of the Below or who lived there.

She knew it all and could spit farther than anyone Romeo had ever known.

After she'd taken her fill, and he saw a rosy flush to her cheek, he nestled against her and said, "Tell about the City and where it grows."

"Shut up," she snapped and then began telling it all in her scratchy and grumbly voice. He watched the dancing fire and forgot, for a while, about the cave he'd grown up in that had its own kinds of serpents.

5

*Scabber Chants the History of the Below
and the Forbidden City, Translated*

This is the knowledge! This is the terrible truth! This is the portent of things to come, mirrored in the broken glass of the past! Ages ago, back when no one remembered and no one knew and those who could speak had their tongues cut out for telling, before there was even a Serpent and before there was even a fire, the Forbidden

City grew from the bones of those who were born of the earth.

The people of the earth were mud and clay. When they died, their bodies dried and cracked and returned to the earth. Their bones settled beneath the Below. Their blood created the river that runs between the Below and the Forbidden City, and only those who know the secrets of the City and possesses the Keys can cross the river and enter therein, for it is written—and here, as always, Scabber, when asked, would say that it is written on the wind or in the soul or somewhere down one of the great tunnels leading to the Forbidden City and Shut up anyway—that a great Serpent guards the Forbidden City, and will devour any and all who try to enter through its ancient gateway. Upon its towers sit the twenty-four skulls of the Kings of the First People. Its walls, all of bone, contain the souls of those First People, as well, and to get beyond them would be torture, for the bones will suck out the blood and flesh of all that try to pass. And the Serpent owns the Forbidden City. It is the Kingdom of the Dead and the Damned, and no human has ventured within the City without paying a price beyond measure—and here, she points to her legs, and says, "I crossed into the Forbidden City once, and I knew the three secrets, but I forgot one of them when I was leaving, and the bones tore at me like the devil's pincers and shredded my once-beautiful legs. But I got out with my life and my soul, and that's more than most can say, if they could say it at all!"—and so, we are the guardians of the Below, making sure that no human enters what is the land of Death and Pestilence and the Terror of the world. From the souls and spirits of all who came before us, guardians of the Below, the city above us grew. The stones flew to the sky, the brick met pavement, the land was coated with dark rivers of street and boulevard and trees took root, and our minds sprouted a cavernous city above our darkness to cover over this spot of earth, this tainted ground that is the entrance to the Forbidden City! Those in the Above believed they built that place, but it was from the dreams of the Below that the Above grew! And one will come, it is foretold, one will come who will have the Keys and the Secrets and will rise up against the Serpent, and it will be in my time, it will be the one I shall see! So it is written! Though the Serpent spills innocent blood to renew its vow with darkness, we are keepers of the fire that holds the Serpent in its lair.

At this point, the boy named Romeo begins laughing. Scabber gets furious at him. He says, "I can't help it, I can't, I don't believe you got there, not all the way to the Serpent's Lair." Scabber says, almost too quietly, "I ask you to shut up a thousand times, and all you do is talk. Now, let me show you the Secrets in their boxes. You cannot see what they are here, for they will only be revealed truly in the Forbidden City." Then, Scabber reaches into a small pouch—the container of all her valuable possessions—and withdraws what seems, at first, like nothing at all, and within her hand a sharp piece of glass.

Chapter Twelve

The Headless Statue

1

Maddy Sparke had no time left for unimportant details. Her money was running low, and none of her properties were selling for the kind of cash she needed—but she didn't intend to lower her prices. She didn't intend to become anything less than a multimillionaire in this life, and she didn't intend to spend her old age in poverty. The thought loomed large in her mind, the image of watching herself in a nursing home drinking puree and wishing she could've afforded a better nursing home, or even one at all. She had what she called "the bag lady fear"—that she would end up in the street as she got older, crazy and mumbling to herself and sleeping in the alleys, having lost all her property to debt and bad business decisions. It was a ridiculous fear, she knew, but one she could not shake.

She had to face it. She didn't know how to be poor. It would be devastating.

And that's where Andreas Harris had her by the horns. She had begun to understand that she needed the dig at her property to start paying for itself.

"Let's talk turkey, Harris. I want to know how much someone would be willing to pay for this kind of crap." She had begun dressing like one of the workmen, in boots and Levi's and an oversized T-shirt. Andreas, as usual, wore a light suit and a mask of self-interest. "You want me to take care with all this crap, but we haven't mentioned a dollar amount, and the damn clock is ticking."

He looked at her with a mixture of wisdom and pity. His eyes were little squints, and his teeth were so white it was like seeing the pale underbelly of a lizard. The Weasel still lurked within him, too. "Well, given that every day we find something special, some indication of ritual and perhaps murder or even the possibility of witchcraft trials, I'd hazard that we'd be able to find someone to take the property and its contents off your hands for . . . "

She held her hands up. "You can dream but it don't mean someone won't slap you awake, Harris, I ain't selling this place. But if your cheap-ass museum wants something on it, then maybe . . . "

"One million dollars," he said.

"Not for this house you don't. I know a condo

on the corner that starts at a million. My brown-stone's worth five, if you're lucky."

"Not for your house," Andreas shook his head as if he were in the presence of a moron. "For the dig. The contents of the dig. The rights to continue exploring this property for six months."

"A million?" she tilted her head to the side to take him out. "I don't think so, Andreas. Chump change. It'll cost me most of that just to keep paying bills and make sure I pay the goddamn city for all the damage to the pipes that's been going on."

"I could," he said, and then hesitated. He had a way of holding his hands together as if praying. Or preying. "I mean, perhaps it's possible to find investors, of course, who . . . might just be able to make the terms more favorable."

"Could ain't the word. You will," Maddy said, and then barked at the workman who kept spitting. She stomped over to him and thumped his chest lightly. "Nobody pays you to spit on my property. Just take your spit and go to the curb. That's a disgusting habit!"

When she marched back over to Andreas, he was already looking at the new finds, all of them laid out in a row.

"Just think," Andreas said, sighing. Something was human within him after all. Maddy thought he sounded like a kid in Disneyland for the first time. "All my life I've wanted to discover something like this. I would never have imagined this. This. Here." Maddy wasn't convinced the pearly tears in his eyes were genuine, but she admired his dramatic abilities. "Four bodies. Brutalized. Buried on unhallowed ground."

"Witchcraft trials, damn it," Maddy said, laughing. "Hot to kill women and take their property without having to marry them. What a world."

"And then, there's the fifth body," Andreas said.

"Fifth? I didn't hear about no fifth," Maddy said. "Christ almighty, this is going to turn into one of those protected burial grounds, ain't it? And every damn Wiccan and ACLU lawyer is going to be camping at my door making sure I lose this property, and it gets called some kind of Human Rights arena. Damn it. Damn it. Damn it. We find anymore bodies, I'm gonna throw them next door and let that old fart deal with them."

Andreas Harris gave her a sad look. Maddy knew that she sounded pathetic, but she was exhausted. She just could not help it. Her year had not been going as planned. She thought of her mother and her grandmother and suddenly felt as if all the things they'd worked so hard for would be lost.

"The fifth coffin is special. Here." He stepped aside, and Maddy strode forward, heels clicking the planks they'd laid down along the mud and pipes. She peered over Andreas's shoulder to look at the rotted wood that had once been a coffin barely large enough for a child.

"Just don't show me no more hearts, all right?"

"An angel," Andreas said.

Inside the coffin, a small statue, its head severed and missing. It was crude, made of some slime-covered stone, and if the statue had not had wings, Maddy would not have guessed it was an angel but just a piece of sculptured crap, a rock with a bit of form. There was beauty, perhaps, beneath the muck and filth, but she was not one to care about it. The inside of the statue had a small hollow opening, where the neck would be.

How the hell did Andreas know so damn much?

"Given that the year was somewhere between 1690 and 1710, we can assume this statue is from a chapel. Perhaps a baptismal font, although it's a bit large for that. Most churches wouldn't have this kind of sculpture—not here, not at that time. So, it's unusual for that alone. And this," Andreas reached into the inside breast pocket of his tweed jacket and withdrew a small tattered leather book. "Was tucked away, right here." He pressed his fingers against the rim around the neck of the angel.

"What is it?"

"A diary. Presumably, the diary of a witch. The woman meant for this coffin was given a special fate. These other women were hanged. But the woman who kept this diary was buried somewhere else here, in a special way." Andreas could not lose his grin. Maddy wished sometimes that she had never met him.

His grin was enough of a weasel snarl to make her want to sic the dogs on him; and his museum, for all its cachet and getting written up in the *Times* and its impressive Board of Directors, had yet to have much to offer the community other than some photographs and a few beads robbed from graves. He wanted her brownstone big time, and she knew it. She wished the witch graveyard had just stayed buried. She wished her stupid workmen had never gone running with their mouths open. She wished she could just sell the damn property and be done with it.

"Someone," Andreas Harris began, his voice all misty and soft, "believed very strongly that she had great power. This is all very ritualistic."

"You wasting my time with nothing again, Harris?" Maddy asked. "I don't want those—those TV people sniffing around here like they did in December, looking to dig up all my other properties on this street. And where the hell would she be buried, this witch?"

Maddy did not want to ask the question that had plagued her since she'd first seen the dried heart pierced by several bone splinters. The mess that was like a sponge with slender white toothpicks pressed into it.

She did not want to know why someone had done that, nor did she need to trouble herself with wondering who owned the heart. *Owned? Or held it inside their bodies until someone, some horrible person, cut it out and set it aside. Pierced it with those bone pieces.* She had been trying to wipe the image of it from her mind for days. Instead, she tried to imagine her dwindling bank account and how she had once been a child of wealthy parents but was soon going to be a woman with too much property on her hands and too little income. "If she's buried on my land, I want her out."

"She's somewhere on this lot. Don't worry. I don't think we'll have to go into the house next door. This one is buried deeper. And if my suspicions are correct," Andreas said, patting the small book. "They did something terrible to her."

Maddy Sparke looked down through the planks, to the holes gouged into the ground where once the lovely if slightly unloved garden and basement had existed to a brownstone built ages ago, and said, "Let the witch stay buried. I don't want no more jackhammers in this place or the damn utility company digging up the sidewalk out front or—"

But even as she spoke, she felt a twinge of curiosity.

Beneath her feet, somewhere, a terrible thing had taken place. It was ancient history. But someone hated a woman enough to cut out her heart and to possibly commit worse atrocities. Who was the killer? And this woman?

Who was she?

Chapter Thirteen

The Three

1

Jake's Journal

The night I discovered that I had chosen an apartment directly across from where Naomi had lived, I knew I had to go there. I had to see what was in it. I had to know something about her without even being sure exactly what it was I sought.

I had less trouble than I would've expected in breaking into the apartment. Growing up, Naomi had always left a key for me on a ledge above her window. As if anticipating that I would one day be near her, I found a small key tucked away above her door. She hadn't changed in all those years. She still trusted people. She still left a key. She still knew, somehow, that I might be right around the corner.

It took a few turns of the key to get the door to budge—and when it did, it seemed to open of its own accord (my imagination, I know, but it felt like a magic moment to me). I stood there, staring into the dark room, half expecting someone to be there.

Maybe a new tenant.

Maybe Naomi herself.

I glanced along the hall, in case anyone was coming. After all, I was breaking into someone's home. I had no right to do this. I just felt that I had to do it.

I tried to switch on a light, but the electricity had been turned off. Went back to my place and got a candle; my flashlight batteries were dead. The candle was a fat, short one, and smelled like vanilla. It was something I managed to swipe from our old apartment (*our* was a funny word when I thought of my ex-wife). I struck a match and lit it, and carried the candle in front of me like I was a monk headed for vespers. Within Naomi's small apartment again, I realized that, unless I was hallucinating in the candlelight, nothing had been touched.

Everything had remained as she had left it. That was my guess. It was as if she'd just walked out that morning.

Tried not to think the rest of that thought. Tried not to imagine her state of mind, as she went to the subway.

Tried not to imagine that unimaginable point between the moment she was standing on the platform, and the moment when the train hit her.

I took a deep breath, thinking just such awful thoughts. The apartment was solid. I could cling to that. It was what was left of Naomi. It was somehow hers, still, without having her there.

First, there was the smell. It wasn't a stink. It was not even unpleasant. It was as if a woman had just washed her hair and brushed it out—perhaps there was a touch of cologne in it, perhaps it was a clean soap smell. I closed my eyes, and I tried to remember if this was the way Naomi's hair had smelled. The last time I'd pressed my face into her hair was the night before she left me forever, back when I was too young to understand what "forever" might mean. But I couldn't place this scent. Then, there were others in the apartment: the mustiness of a closed room. The slight smell of a pilot light that might've been out, the gas turned off, but still, the smell of it lingering. The barely noticeable—but unavoidable—swamp stink of old laundry.

Her bed was a twisted mess of comforter, sheets, and pillows. The kitchenette—hardly more than a shelf, a sink, and a small refrigerator—was piled high with pots and pans and dirty dishes. The shadows of the apartment began to strike a slow kind of dread within me. I felt a cold finger along the back of my neck. I felt the draft from an open window. It was like walking into a dream. Somehow, I knew it would look like this. Somehow, I knew it the way I still knew Naomi. This was all her. She was still there, that's what it felt like.

I did not know what to expect or what I thought I would discover as I went through an apartment that seemed too small for any human being to live within.

But I found what I believe I was meant to find.

There, on her dresser, along with a picture of her sister and a picture of a man I'd never before seen, a phone number, written in her careless hand, with the words *Alan, go to hell* beside it.

I finally fell asleep at dawn, on her bed, smelling her hair and her perfume, or imagining I did.

I slept that day until three in the afternoon as if I'd never known how to sleep before. I dreamed we were back in Carthage again, and our families were happy, and we were in love, and no one in the great wide world had ever done to a girl of thirteen what her father had done to her.

2

Romeo reached up to Scabber's face and felt along the knobs and impressions and craterous skin of that great wise woman. He read her face in the firelight with his fingers as she finished the tale of the Below and the Forbidden City. "Tell me. About my destiny," he said, only his words were garbled as they sprouted from his lips. He was tired. He just wanted to hear her voice. It would calm him.

Scabber nodded, happy to keep telling for as long as she was asked. She began it as she always did. Her words were haphazard and struck like small flashes of light in his brain. But he understood it. She said, "Nobody comes here because he's lost. This is the found place. This is the war zone. This is where the boy who knows the dark and the caverns comes to us and finds the three secrets and stops the Serpent. And you may just be that boy," she said, stroking his matted hair. "I saw it in one of my dreams. You may just be that boy."

"Ain't no boy. I'm a man," he whispered, and she cackled at this. Others, who had gathered around the fire, also laughed, and someone said something else funny. Romeo laughed at himself and at the jokes they all began telling.

3

Across town, Maddy Sparke sat up in bed and gasped for air, her face shiny with a fever sweat.

She glanced around, seeing the murky shadows of her own bedroom, and then lay back among her multicolored pillows. Her cats rearranged themselves around her form. Their warmth was a small comfort. She tried to forget the nightmare in which a woman beat against the lid of a coffin as a man stood over her and tossed dirt into the grave.

Maddy was there, both within and without. The dream had its logic, and she could be in two places at once in it. She watched the man cover the coffin with dirt and then she was inside the coffin with the struggling, screaming woman. The woman's breath was like a subway tunnel in midsummer, a blast of impure heat. The woman's mouth, mid-scream, opened impossibly wide.

But the only sound was the beating of a heart, a loud hammering, a rhythmic pulse that was more terrifying than the words forming on the woman's lips.

4

Jake's Journal

That first morning, I awoke to hear a bird singing from just beyond the windowsill. Or perhaps it was just someone whistling for a cab. It was getting hard to tell the difference, the longer I lived in the city.

The sun melted beneath the ragged white blinds and shot spears of brilliant light into the room where I had only seen shadows before. I could smell her hair—her scent—there in the bed. I looked up at the ceiling and saw small stars—she had painted them there, and clouds, too.

When I got a better look at her apartment in the daylight, beneath the mess, I saw a mural at the far wall, around the door. Some artist—Naomi herself?—had re-created Carthage there, or else it had never left her. Someone had done a beautiful job of painting the purple slopes of the Blue Ridge mountains on the wall. When the morning light fully covered it, I

could see what might or might not have been
the church, the graveyard, the trees, the way
blue and green mist seemed to cover the ground
on spring days—and a figure of a young girl, a
girl that might've been Naomi, walking there
among the willows and magnolias.

Naomi had done this, somehow. It was like a
message to me. It was as if she'd known that at
some point I'd find her, somehow, some way.
And here she was—a messy apartment, and a
beautiful landscape, a way of both remaining
trapped in Carthage and a re-creation so lovely
that it seemed like paradise.

As I sat up in bed, I pulled the blinds all the
way up. Something warm—a small blanket?—
had wrapped itself around my feet in the night.

I glanced down and saw an orange tabby cat
that did not startle me in the least. Somehow,
it felt right to have it there and of course, I knew
it was Naomi's cat, as she had always been taking in strays as a young girl: The starling with
the broken wing, the cat that was missing both
an eye and a tail from some fight, the rats that
my father had wanted to kill with slow poison,
but that Naomi gathered up with their young
and had brought to a specially made nest in the
shed in the woods behind her home. And all
those cats she took care of, all of the yowling
along the Treasure Caves, having kittens for
generations, living wild there.

I reached down to pet the cat, and it purred
as I lifted it into my arms. It was a scraggly little
soul, and one of its ears had been bitten off. No
doubt it was an alley warrior, and had survived

its share of scrapes and near-accidents.

The birds continued their early calls and tunes outside the window; yes, even in an alley of Manhattan, there were chickadee and sparrows and jays and mockingbirds. And sirens. And people shouting. I felt almost sentimental about it all. It was a symphony of the Village, and this is something one has to experience to know. It's as if, within the maze of the city, nature and human warmth could still not be bricked over and paved across. It was there, always.

The painting of our hated Carthage on the wall, the birds, and the warm cat, all conspired against me. What I wanted to feel, what I wanted to think, all of it sad and even dreadful— thoughts of Naomi's death, thoughts of tragic lives, of all that happened in Carthage in a short span of years that could affect our lives (mine and Naomi's) until the end of our days—but you can't really think terrible thoughts when a cat is purring, and birds are singing. I almost believed that Naomi would walk through the door any minute. She'd come sit beside me and make tea. We'd sit there and just laugh about how good it was to have gotten out of that town and how good it was to stay friends for so long.

Then, reality set in.

I got up in a clumsy way, nearly tripping over a pillow that had fallen to the floor, and went to get the cat some food.

I found some cans of sardines above the sink, and figured that for now this would have to do. I fed the cat, and it gobbled down the fish greedily. It was healthy. If this was Naomi's cat, someone had been caring for it. The grateful feline came over and rubbed her body against my ankles. Then it went back up to the bed to lie in the sunlight that streamed through the open window.

Naomi was here. She is still somehow alive. I know it. This apartment, with the paperback books in the corner, with the funny magnets on the refrigerator, with the stars on the ceiling and the painting on the wall—I know she's still here.

She can't be dead.

But, of course, it kicked me in the gut again: life. Real life. She was dead. People died. Trains could kill.

I called the number on the dresser, the one by her picture. I left a message for someone named Alan. I told him who I was, where I lived, and asked him to call me back.

When he called that evening, I learned more about the woman that Naomi had become.

Chapter Fourteen

The Haunted

1

"Hello. This Jake?"

"Hi—who's this?"

"Alan Cowper."

"Jesus, I'm glad you called back."

"Well, I had to. I can imagine what you're feeling."

A pause on the line.

Jake hesitated. "I thought perhaps you could tell me about Naomi. About what happened to her here."

Another one of those pauses. It was the most uncomfortable silence Jake had endured since his last call to his ex. Maybe worse. He wanted the man at the other end of the line to say something. To give him something. To jump in with some wonderful story about Naomi. About her life in New York.

Anything but this silence.

"Because you were close to her," Jake added.

Pause.

"Yes, Jake, I was. I know you better than you'd guess. I was extremely close to her. You could say we were each other's better halves. But I know you were important to her. I'm sorry she's not here to see you. She would've liked that."

"Me, too."

"You've been in the apartment?"

"Yes."

"Good."

"Good?"

"I knew you'd get there eventually. She left the key for you. She always told me that. I warned her about break-ins, but you know what? She had no boundaries. She didn't feel that it was really her place." Then, the man took a breath. It was more like a smoker's cough. "Did you snoop?"

Pause.

Alan laughed on the other end. "Sorry to sound so aggressive. The apartment is in my name. It is my apartment. I let her live there while she pursued her dreams. I was supporting her, you know. I loved her more than anything. I still love her. In memory."

The pauses in the conversation were getting annoying.

"Have you met Katy?"

Jake thought for a second. "The cat? Yes."

"She always comes back there. She was adopted by one of Naomi's girlfriends, but she always comes back. I shut the window, and someone—maybe Soozan, Naomi's friend—opens it again, and the cat goes in there. I really can't stand that cat. Some cats I like. Katy is not my favorite. Are you a cat person?"

"Not in particular," Jake said. Then, "Yeah, I am."

"Take the cat. She's yours. And I need to meet with you about something else. Something that was very important to Naomi. Something that she left for you. What's your schedule like?"

"Open."

"Do you know the White Horse Tavern?"

"Sure. Right around the corner."

"Right. Let's meet at ten tonight for a beer, all right? You'll want to know this."

"All right. Ten. I'll tell you, this seems so much like fate, that I've been trying to find out about her and now I—"

"And Jake—"

"What—"

"I had the electricity turned back on in her place today. Not that it matters, but I know you'll be going there a lot. It's no coincidence that you're living across from her apartment."

Then, silence on the line.

The dial tone.

Jake's Journal

So, we met that night.

My first thought—my immediate one—was that I had no doubt seen Alan Cowper before. I knew it as soon as I walked into the White Horse. He was handsome and burly and the first words out of his mouth were that he had a doctorate in psychology as well as a real estate license. "You live in New York, you see business opportunities everywhere. I own some condos that I rent. I have a management company handling some buildings. You're subletting—illegally, I might add—from my friend Kaspar."

"The artist," I said as if I knew exactly what was going on. "So what are you saying? You set this all up?"

"You need a beer," he said, grinning, and flagged the waitress down. After I had sipped from the mug that arrived a few minutes later, he laughed a little too loud. "It's not that I set anything up. It's that I knew you were here in New York, and I heard through friends that you were looking for a place."

"We have friends in common?" I asked, utterly befuddled. In fact, I don't think I'd ever been able to use the word *befuddled* before, and was happy to feel it. "I know you?"

"We've seen each other, only, I have to report, I had the advantage. I understood who you were, but you had no idea that the man Naomi was in love with was perhaps across a table from you, or at the theater with your wife's friends when you ran into them at the opera or at the Museum of Modern Art or any number of places. We've crossed paths a few times. All right, five or six times to be precise. In many ways, this is a smaller town than most people think. Six degrees of separation is becoming three degrees these days. I know Daniel, your ex's friend."

I watched him watch me. He must've been in psychologist mode, the bastard. All right, I will admit to this: I tend to play an annoying game of one-upsmanship when I'm around another guy. Particularly another guy who in some sleazy way was laying claim to Naomi. It was the troglodyte in me, but I wanted to clobber him and beat my chest. Or something equally goofy. He was beginning to piss me off. He had already begun, actually, just by the fact that he knew Daniel. Daniel, as in my ex-wife Amy's Daniel. Daniel, who, in my opinion, was a snake. And no friend of my ex, either. She was sleeping with him, in love with him, and Daniel, that S.O.B., probably knew all along that this Alan person had wanted to know a lot about me. Alan's eyes were intense, his lips half-curled, as if this were all a good joke.

"And who are you, anyway?" I finally asked.

He had a bemused expression on his face. "Alan Cowper. Naomi and I were together for seven years."

"No, I mean who are you. What is it you want. Why would you engineer this. All this. My getting a place across from Naomi's. Why do you—"

"Oh, damn," he said, the half-smile gone. He looked down into his glass of ale. "You're angry. I understand. Sorry. It's all a bit much, I'd guess."

"Not pissed off. Confused. You can straighten it out. You hold the cards, right?"

"I guess I hold some of them," he said. He took another drink, and then leaned back in his chair. "Here's the thing. You're the only connection I have to her. And I loved her. I loved her."

I didn't want to see that blurry shining tear in his eye, but I did. This may have pissed me off more than anything because—and as childish as this seems, forgive me—but she was mine.

I loved her.

I alone loved her.

I had always loved her, and she had loved me, and I knew it in my heart as well as I had known anything in life. Even when I had loved my wife dearly. Hell, maybe my wife knew it wasn't that kind of complete love where you always put the other one first, where you would do anything for the other one, where you would lay down your life for her. I would lay down my life for my daughter, and for Naomi. I guess I would never have done that for my ex. Maybe she was smart to bolt.

But I loved Naomi. I truly did.

This Alan person was here to ruin all that.

Life sucks.

Perhaps he was pathologically shy when it came
to his own life even if pathologically aggressive
in his business life, but I had to admit—shining
tear in his eye and all—Alan Cowper was a man
who had truly been touched by Naomi.

As we walked back to the apartment on Horatio Street, I felt very nearly brotherly toward
him. There was that brotherhood between us,
with Naomi, the bridge. We were two guys who
had loved, who knew it, and had even spoken
of it—something I'd rarely seen men do. I certainly had never spoken to other men of my love
for a woman. We laughed about some of our
own foibles. We both nearly shed tears over the
remembrance of the way she took off her shoes
on hot days and got her feet filthy.

He spun a tale about meeting Naomi down
by the river on a summer afternoon and sharing
his lunch with her, and then happening to run
into her at Lincoln Center. She had scraped together enough money to go to the opera without
having enough for subway fare home. It had
been raining. He had his car. He pulled over to
the curb and rolled down the window.

"Need a lift?"

It had been that simple.

Damn him.

I heard it in my head like a bad joke. "Need a
lift?"

When he'd heard her tale of woe about being
fired at the restaurant and then having to eat
macaroni and cheese for six nights running, he

had taken her to Le Madri, a restaurant known for its amazing meals and high prices. He had lavished one of the most expensive meals that existed on the planet on her (at least in my opinion, for the chic restaurants of New York were out of my range unless they had takeout; yes, even me, the man who had once penned a book called *Eating the City*). Then, after their dinner, Alan Cowper had made a mental note to call her landlord in the morning and pay off her back rent.

He had been smitten. Even in the lower depths of my jealousy, I could not blame him.

He told me how she had resisted at first. She had pretended that she could never be interested in him. How it had turned to love and warmth and a deep friendship as well. In her old apartment, I sat on the bed, and he in a chair. We broke out a couple more beers. He alternately laughed and wept and told me that they'd had ups and downs. He completely blamed himself for her death. He said, "She and I had been fighting all week. She had a prescription she refused to take—just to keep her balanced. She had so many extremes. But you'd know that."

I nodded.

"She had gone through so much down in that awful place," he said, referring of course to Carthage, Virginia. "Her moods were better if she'd just keep taking what the doctor prescribed. She threw it all out. She would just go on this rampage . . ." I almost laughed at the way he said it, his drunkenness changing it to a rolling *r* of "rrrrampage."

He softened. He must never have held his anger too long. He remembered her, and how he loved her. Damn him. "Even like that, she was magnificent. Look, even this mess. The way she never cleaned up her place—the kitchen—it all made me love her more. She only cared about the important things, and this—"

He waved a hand behind him at the wall painting. "This, she even hated, she wanted to kill me for this."

"You painted it?" I asked.

"No, the guy who you're subletting from, Kaspar. He's an artist. I commissioned him to do it as an early Christmas present. Thanksgiving weekend, she stayed with me. I had a photo of that place, and he painted this, God, so beautifully. I knew even though she hated it I knew she'd love this because you have to go home again sometimes. You have to remember the good things, and I thought, if she did, if she could just remember . . . the good things . . . but . . . it infuriated her. I didn't understand. And then within two weeks, she was gone. Just gone."

He wept openly. I felt sorry for him. I would've spent my life feeling sorry for this guy until he said, "But then I found this."

He reached into his breast pocket and drew out a small lavender square of paper, which he unfolded.

4

Dear J,

If you ever get this I want you to know that I did this for you. I saw you last week with your wife and little girl, and you looked so happy. I knew it would never be the same for us. There are other reasons. But I knew I couldn't ever have what I wanted. Not in this life.

I've known you were here in this city for years.

I just could never work up the courage to interrupt your life. I would never want to remind you of what you'd left behind. I wish I had never found you. I wish I had never been born.

You ruined me. You destroyed me.

I know what I did was the most terrible thing in the world. I need to make it right. He won't stay dead, Jake. He won't. I've seen him. I pretend it's not him, but I know it is.

It's like that day you told me you'd always be there for me, Jake. Remember the roses? The thorns? I was a little girl, but I knew what I should've done, even then. I should've let those thorns open my veins and pour my life out. If I'd done it then, maybe things wouldn't seem so complicated now.

You saved me once, Jake. But you can't save me all the time. I can't even save myself.

There's no way around it. I've see him all the time, and it's insane, and I know I have to stop whatever it is that my life has become.

N

5

Jake's Journal

I would rather have gone to my grave having never read that note, that last note from Naomi Faulkner.

That she was so messed up, in so much pain before her death, and that she would write those words. It all meant too much. It all meant that I had, indeed, destroyed someone I loved and cherished and whose memory will never leave me.

Alan left, drunkenly wobbling down the hall, big bear that he was; I leaned back on the bed and reread the note a hundred or more times. I wanted to find new and different meanings in it. I guess I kept hoping there would be a code I could break and come out on the other side with some message of hope.

Katy, the cat, returned at daybreak. I managed to get up without spraining an ankle, the beer still knocking out brain cells in my head, and my footing less than sure. I brought her to my apartment for a can of Fancy Feast before I went out and bought a litter box. Somewhere in there, I drank a shitload of coffee and scarfed down a bran muffin before I keeled over and slept for another few hours. When I awoke, feeling only barely refreshed, I went about my day as if nothing were wrong.

I went down to the subway to catch the train to my ex-wife's new place to pick up my daughter for the rest of the weekend.

I tried to keep from thinking about anything regarding Naomi. She was no more. Even my dream of who she was seemed to dissipate when I thought about Alan Cowper and his brutal way of telling me what he wanted me to know.

The platform was crowded with shoppers and tourists and those who move from one place to another, all asleep on their feet, all somewhere else in their minds. I felt I was the only one there, really there, really standing on the platform and knowing where I was.

And then, I saw a familiar face, a face that I would recognize no matter what time did to it.

6

I saw her standing in a crowd, a crowd whose faces faded into blankness, I saw her there. I knew it was her.

I know it was her.

Shimmering like heat above a burning road. Naomi.

Chapter Fifteen

The Book

1

It had taken Maddy less than a day to retrieve the tattered, leatherbound book from that weasel of a museum curator, Andreas Harris, but she'd managed to threaten to withhold further contents of the dig if he didn't at least let her see some of the booty from his treasure hunt. "And you've given me nothing but nightmares since this began, and I have yet to see a check from the museum," she added, listening to his measured breathing on the other end of the phone line.

By mid-afternoon, she had it in her possession.

2

Pressed into the leather by some sharp tool, the words: THE DIARY OF N. CROSS.

Maddy opened the diary, and took a deep breath.

She began reading. Words were misspelled, *s*'s looked more like *f*'s, but she was able to get around all of it, for the voice within the diary seemed as if it were whispering in her ear rather than embedded within the words on the page.

3

From the Diary of N. Cross

I cannot write about my childhood, for I remember so little of it, but in the Year of Our Lord 1685, my family came first to the colony in Massachusetts before my father died, and my mother had to come down to the plantation here alongside the Wall of New Amsterdam.

But later, when I was nearly a woman of ten and four years, I first met the Lord of Darkness, out beyond the fields, near the river. It was not yet summer, and I had taken to wandering so that I might avoid the chores of a servant. My mother had worn her fingers to the bone, running the kitchen at the Great House for the Great Man who I had come to despise with all my heart and soul.

He had tried to take liberties with me before I had even given up dolls, and I have my beliefs that he fathered my mother's bastards. So I would often wander down among the high grass by the water and watch the Dutch traders out on their ships, and some of the other servants doing the washing late into the evening.

My mother would call for me, but with seven little brothers and sisters, she would give up her call for the one or two missing to table. One night I saw a man there. This was not unusual, but he was the most amazing man I had ever seen. He looked as if he had been living with the Savages, for his hair was dark and wild and fell past his shoulders.

His eyes lit with a blue flame as he watched me watch him. I was transfixed, bewitched.

I could not take my sight from him. His shirt was torn and his breeches filthy. He wore no boots, but was bare of foot. One moment I watched him from a distance and the next, I was by his side. I know not whether I had traveled to greet him or him to me, but we were close.

"Little one," he spoke words in a deep and almost musical tone. "You are not like these others, these sheep in the fold. You are the wild one. I have seen you before." I grew afraid at his words, for how could he know me? And why had I strayed from my household duties to hide among the reeds and grasses by the river? Strangers were dangerous, even in such an orderly and godly world as the plantation, but I had heard stories along with the other serving women of men who had destroyed girls and had taken their souls to the Devil. They whispered tales of dances in the forest in Massachusetts, where Savages and vile girls would meet to worship the Dark One and rain curses and magical incantations down upon the innocent and godly. I began shivering, remembering these tales, and I asked the man if he was the Devil come to take me.

"Only," he told me, "if you desire to be taken. Perhaps I am the Devil. Perhaps I am just a stranger. Perhaps I am all those things that you have been taught are of the gravest sin. But first, all I desire is one thing and then I will leave you."

I asked him what that was, and before I could answer he took me in his arms and kissed me.

He kissed me and threw me down in the grass.

He laughed as he tore at my dress, and my terror grew great for I could feel the fires of Hell all around me, tearing at me with pincers and tongues of poison.

And then I saw, as if I had an inner sight, who he was and why I had not recognized him.

He was no stranger.

I had not known him because of the wildness and desperation of his features. Nor had I recognized the long hair without it being tied back and tucked beneath his collar. For when I encountered him there by the river, he looked like a wild man, more wolf than man, his teeth a sharp snarl, his eyes burning, his form thrusting . . .

I had seen him before. Each Sabbath.

His face clean, his hair neat, his aspect grave and solemn.

Experience the Ultimate in Fear
Every Other Month...
From Leisure Books!

As a member of the Leisure Horror Book Club,
you'll enjoy the best new horror by the best writers
in the genre, writers who know how to chill your
blood. Upcoming book club releases include
First-Time-in-Paperback novels by such acclaimed
authors as:

Douglas Clegg   Ed Gorman
John Shirley   Elizabeth Massie
J.N. Williamson   Richard Laymon
Graham Masterton   Bill Pronzini
Mary Ann Mitchell   Tom Piccirilli
Barry Hoffman

SAVE BETWEEN $3.72 AND $6.72
EACH TIME YOU BUY.
THAT'S A SAVINGS OF UP TO NEARLY 40%!

Every other month Leisure Horror Book Club brings
you three terrifying titles from Leisure Books,
America's leading publisher of horror fiction.
EACH PACKAGE SAVES YOU MONEY.
And you'll never miss a new title.

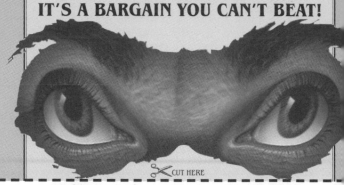

He was a minister of the cloth. As he ruined me, as he stole from me the only treasure I had been taught that I had to offer in this world, I looked the Reverend John Cotton in the eyes and knew him.

I concealed my shame for nearly six months before it began to show itself in the change in my form.

My mother must have been aware but she said nothing for her own shame was known far and wide. When we went to market I held several baskets in front of my body to keep others from noticing the way the bastard within me showed. I stopped going to the Sabbath. I used fever as an excuse to stay abed those days. The entire plantation and the small village surrounding it began to shun me, and I could only imagine the sermons about scarlet women and whores of Babylon as I suffered within the shame of my sex.

And then I noticed that a few other women, and some men, also remained behind during the Sabbath, feigning ailments or having to work despite the injunction to remain faithful to the Lord's Day. One of them, Goody Carrier, came to me and asked if I'd be needing her services. "Services?" said I.

"Yes," she said. And then she gave me what looked like a sign of the Devil, but which I have learned is a guild sign of the midwives. When I discovered her calling, I began sobbing uncontrollably and fell into her arms. "I am ruined!" I cried out, and others came, too, and all of them held me and told me that it was not I that had been ruined, but the Evil One who had done this to me.

He is no Evil One, I protested. He is the Ordained of the Lord.

And they laughed, at first slowly, and then more loudly until I felt the roof of our humble quarters would shatter and fall upon us.

"Take this," Goody Carrier said, offering me a small vial made of shell.

"What is it?" I asked.

"It is something to take care of thy pain," she said.

"Poison?" I asked.

She laughed and shook her head. "No, and thou best not drink it, child. Rub it along your belly and breasts and beneath your arms and where your maidenhood begins." She said this without shame and the others nodded. "At night," she said, "after all are asleep, ye shall see."

And when I heard the snores of my brothers and sisters, I went outside and stood beneath the stars.

I took the vial and poured out some of its grease into my hands. I thought of all the places she had told me to rub the ointment into me, but it frightened me to even touch those places, unholy as they were.

But finally, I did, and I found myself feeling light-headed, and I felt my breath as if I had never breathed before. A warmth spread over my body, from my breasts to my knees and then to my face, and soon I had shed my night-clothes.

I ran among the trees at the edge of the plantation, faster than I ever thought possible, with no fear of being caught, no fear of being discovered, no fear at all.

I began to understand words and meanings that I could barely comprehend previous to this, and I had visions of enormous houses built all around the plantation and carriages and stone roads. And through this, I still saw the Great House and all the quarters and beyond them the village, and then my feet seemed to feel different.

I looked down at them, worried that this ointment had somehow caused my feet to go numb.

When I looked down, I saw that I had already begun to rise from the grass, into the air, into the night.

Chapter Sixteen

The Apparition

Jake's Journal

In a moment, the face I was sure I had seen in the subway tunnel had receded.

Had it been Naomi?

I fought through the crowd to find her, but she was not there, and then I saw a woman—she was too far from me to identify clearly—down at the end of the platform, almost into the tunnel itself.

She leaped down into the track, but in a way that seemed less like a jump than a blur of motion.

I knew that it must be her. I felt it.

She turned for a moment. I saw nothing but a woman's face with blurred features, but I felt that she wanted me to follow her. I felt that it was Naomi, in my heart. I stood there frozen, not following, not knowing what to do, not understanding if this were some madness and a trick of my own mind, or if she wanted me to follow her. . . .

I am a sane man.

I really believe I am.

I had seen crackheads and bums and others wander down the tunnels before—knowing that they probably had openings or alcoves where they peed or shot up or fell asleep or escaped whomever was chasing them. But I had no desire to go to those places. I lived in the ordinary world, the world of sky and offices and coffee and meeting friends for drinks, not the world of those who know the ins and outs of the subway tunnels of New York. That was a world for the outcasts and the freaks and the people who had no part of the earth I recognized. I was a human snob, I admit it. I didn't want to be with the Forgotten of the world, I wanted to be part of the Remembered, the Good People, the Ones Who Led Productive Lives.

I don't care what anyone else thinks, I know that our hold is tenuous at best in this world of light and smiles and rent paid on time. I know we're all only a paycheck or two away from lying drunk in a gutter or sleeping all night on a park bench or of getting to know people who survive day by day and sleep in the tiled and pissed-upon corridors of the Thirty-third Street PATH Station and if our relatives disappeared, if our friends could not loan us cash, if our bosses decide that we're replaceable, we know somehow that we will be riding the subway just to have a place to lay our heads.

I don't fool myself in this. The curtain is thin. It can be seen through. And like others of my kind—all right, cowards, privileged, mythmakers all—even though I can see through that curtain to the other side every day, I pretend it's all destiny that I'm here and they are there, and none of it can mix.

I could not bring myself to follow this woman.

This woman who—and how, I asked myself, could this be Naomi at all?—walked so boldly into the dark tunnel. Naomi was dead. Enough people had told me that. The dead don't walk.

I slowly went to the end of the platform, where it dipped down into the seemingly endless tunnel. I laughed at myself as I stood there, and no doubt the teenagers who stood not far from me thought I was one of the crazed of the city. I laughed at myself for even thinking, for one moment, that a dead woman could be in a subway tunnel, that a ghost could be there, or that Naomi would've survived a train smashing into her—for after all, she was dead, she must be buried somewhere, she could not exist in a grave and in a subway tunnel. Life didn't work that way. Life could not work that way.

And then, I heard someone call my name, "Jake? Jake!" a woman; I turned back to the people on the platform, but they had not heard.

It echoed, this voice, it called and echoed, and I had wondered what a descent into madness would be like, I had always wondered—remembering my aunt who had, in the end, lost her marbles—what it felt like, how it came, whether it arrived with a series of slow plinks as the marbles fall from the head, or whether it just arrives suddenly, like a rush of wind.

And here it was. I had begun to decode the mysteries of Life and Death, apparently, for I knew it was her voice, and I knew that she was down that tunnel, and I knew that if I pursued her, I would be the Lost, the Forgotten, the Outcast. I would have moved to the other side of that thin, thin curtain.

I stood there, the hairs on the back of my neck rising, my left hand beginning to shake in an elaborate nervous twitch, for her voice grew louder, and it rumbled and soon a train had come into the station and with its wind, the smell of her hair as if she'd just brushed by me.

I can't keep writing, tap-tapping on this laptop, I can't just run home every time, I have to do something.

I have to face this, this madness, this screwup in the cosmos, this disconnection of my mind from reality.

I have to find out where her body is. What happened. Where they buried her.

Why I keep feeling that she is not dead.

Chapter Seventeen

Romeo

Romeo pressed himself into the concrete pipe. It was just large enough for him, and he was one of the scrawnier ones of the Below, so it was never a big problem to get across it. He moved slowly on his elbows, shifting from one to the other, knowing that if he just kept quiet, he'd get across fine.

He tried to put the thought of the Serpent out of his mind.

In his mouth, a knife.

He could see the flashing lights ahead.

The Forbidden City.

He didn't have all the keys, but he could get there, he could find them, he knew that all he needed to do was get there.

All the others were scared, and Scabber had been there once but had no desire to go back.

"It cost me my legs," she'd told him, but Romeo knew that he'd be different. He had always known that even if Destiny devoured him, it was something he could not escape.

The Serpent had left one of its meals in the Seventy-third Street tunnel of the Below, and it had been a warning to all of them.

Even Scabber had been frightened when she saw how the man had been mutilated. "We have to stay on our side of the Down," she'd told him. "No more trips to the Other Side, Romeo. I forbid it. Don't even try to enter the Forbidden City, you hear me? Don't even try. Just by going there, I may have opened the door for It. I may have been the one to let It out."

But he had to. He had to stop the Serpent somehow. Before it was too late. The blood had scared him. The way the man's throat was ripped, the way his innards had been torn at as if by a pack of wild dogs.

The Serpent had kept that man with It for a long while before finishing him off. That was the Serpent's way.

It was a Devourer.

Moving forward, Romeo felt the heat at the core of the Below, and the rumble of the trains not far from him.

Then, he felt something—

A touch along his ankle.

He held his breath.

Chapter Eighteen

The Initiate

Diary of a Witch

I flew not in the manner of birds, but as if my body and my heart and mind were separate. Even my eyes were not part of the body I had known, but seemed to have been pecked by ravens, which had then flown up into the night.

My body, like a husk, remained below. I still felt something of a body around me, but it was of different cloth, like the difference between wool and gossamer. I looked below and saw my own self falling to the grass as if dead. The bottoms of my feet brushed the outer branches of trees as I moved, and I was afraid.

In vain, I grabbed at the twigs and leaves, but they all came off in my hands. I feared this dream that felt more like waking life. Finally, I was able to tear at a slender branch, and this seemed to guide me as I moved more swiftly over the low trees.

I looked out at the world and saw the plantation houses, and our quarters, and the river beyond them. All of Greenwich Plantation glowed with green and blue hues, and I could see the birds nesting and even the worms crawling across the wild grass.

I saw all of life, all that moved in the night, the rat and the dog and the skunk as it fled to the forest. I, too, fled to the forest on a carpet of air, and felt the burning fever of the witch grease that I had spread about my body. I looked down upon my fallen form and had no sorrow over what I assumed was my death, for now, I was an angel and felt freer and cleaner than ever before.

As if my wings were suddenly shorn, I began dropping to the earth, called back, not into my body, but into the forest, the woods they call Forbidden Wood, beyond the bogs and pond, the place where the Savages still hide.

The Great Man has always spoken of burning the Forbidden Wood as being of the Devil, so I was afraid for my immortal soul as I felt myself pulled down into the hungry branches.

When next I opened my eyes, I was again in my own body, naked, in the woods.

A fire burned around a deep pit. I saw others of the English, the Dutch, and even the Savages gathered around the fire, and slaves, too, in colorful dress, and some naked as was I but clothed by tattoos and markings across their bodies.

What dream is this? I wondered, but knew it was no dream. Goody Carrier was there, as was Goodman Falmouth, and the six children I knew from the river were also there. More than thirty people in all. Perhaps more. No one felt shame for the nakedness, least of all I. For this was some sort of dream, or a life like a dream, as if all the rest of life had been a burden of silence and ignorance. Now we all were together in the truth of life; in the truth of the night; even the darkness would not hide us.

I knew this was the Devil's dance, this was the witch place, but I cared not. Soon, I drank honey mead and chewed upon dried grasses and felt light and free of all cares as we danced to music that came not from some instrument but from our own instruments within us. Our voices brought forth song and the music of nightbirds. The night itself kept us in motion.

These are the mysteries, Goody Carrier told me when the dance was over. She looked sweeter and warmer than I had ever known her.

She said, "We have been taught and have taught others for years beyond number. We know our true names, and we know what the Devilmakers have done to our forefathers. Our world is secret but it is a true world, and you are a true wise woman though you are too young to know it yet. We will teach you the old wisdom, we will bring you the stories of the forest and of the Beneath. We each have talents and arts for your tutelage."

"Mine is the art of speaking with the dead," said one man.

A woman cried out, "And I will show you where lie the treasures of the earth."

Three little girls no older than one of my sisters all told me that they had memorized most of the tells of the crones and would be happy to let me understand the history of our past.

A Savage as dark as night and as tall as a birch said to me, "Little bird, I can teach you the language of the wild animals, of how they speak one to the other, and how we can understand their own prophecies."

A slave woman, wizened and wide, grasped my hand, drawing me to the bread. "This must seem a strange sight, child, for at the plantation all is different and we are not known to each other. But here, in the Wood, we are all the same. There is no knowledge of Good and Evil. All is Good, all is meant to be, and even the serpent underfoot has both poison and kindness. We either step upon the serpent and invoke its wrath, or offer it a blessing and allow it to show us the way to water and the source of all secrets. This is the first lesson you must learn."

"But what of Our Lord?" I asked her, wanting to understand. "Is this not the place of Satan?"

They laughed, all of them, and I blushed with embarrassment.

The slave woman said to me, "The Lord may yet be Lord. We are not here to steal gods or to destroy them. We are here to break free of the lies of the world and see through to the truth of all that exists. I can see the future, child, and what I see both terrifies me and inspires me. But you, you have it, too. You hold the future in your eyes, and the power of magic in your heart, and in your hand."

She took up my hand, and looked upon it most curious. "In your hand, I see that you will rise up to strike the enemy."

"But the Devil? Is this not worship of the Enemy of Christ?" I asked.

The woman hugged me close to her bosom and whispered in my ear, "So they who would harm us say. But child, what is the Devil but what cannot be controlled? What is goodness but a mask for those who wish to control others?"

"He is here!" someone called.

"Yes, her consort has come! We have invoked him!" another cried.

The woman let go of me. I turned, and there at the center of the great flame in the pit, a form emerged as if from the fire itself.

A man stood there, a man like no man, a headdress of deer antlers upon his head, and night-black hair falling down his shoulders, and a body so slender and yet full of muscle like a field hand. His manhood was also engorged, and shall I write here the terror I felt because he was the most beautiful man I had ever seen?

"All eyes down!" someone shouted, and I glanced around the circle. All had dropped to the earth, their faces pressed into the dust. The slave woman grabbed my wrist and tugged me down.

"We cannot look upon the gods," she said,

"for they will destroy us with a glance. We are beneath them always."

"Is this the greatest of gods?" I asked, and she smiled and told me that no, the goddess was the greatest of all, but this was an image of the eternal, a spirit of what was male, not the most powerful nor the most just, but the incarnation of the male in the dust of eternity.

I fell to my knees, but I could not take my eyes from him, from his beauty, or the eyes that seemed to be as an owl's, or his lips, which curved in a smile as if he would in a moment laugh at his congregation.

I knew I would be destroyed in a moment, but still I kept watch upon him as he moved toward me.

"Are you a dream?" I asked as he stood before me, his skin shining, his thickly corded arm stretched out.

"Take my hand and see," he said in a voice that was familiar.

I touched him, and he was like a flame itself. I watched the tips of my fingers blacken with the fire.

"You are not afraid of what destroys you," he said.

"I am deathly afraid," said I, "that you are the Devil and that my soul is damned to Eternal Torment. This be a dream, I shall wake. This be true, then I shall die righteously."

"My daughter," said the god, "even now, a child grows within your womb. Its very creation has blessed you, for all new life blesses those who shepherd it into the world. But a bitter cup will be passed to you. Still, you must drink from it. Keep our worship of the great mother holy. Keep our sabbat blessed. Do not turn in thy sisters or brothers. I shall come to you and take you as my beloved when thy torment is greatest, so have no fear. You shall be the greatest of the wise, and a sacred protector of all that is below as above. You must promise thy child to me, in sacrifice, for this will show faith and loyalty to me."

I felt a pain in my womb, and clutched myself there. "My child?" I cried. "My child? Sacrifice? I do not understand. That is evil. That is of the Devil! You are the Devil!"

I held my hands up to the god in supplication. "Anything but my child! Anything but my child!"

"Then," the god said, "your life for your child's life. If you would live, thy child must die. If thy child would live, then you have promised yourself to leave the flesh and enter the world beyond this one. At the harvest moon, daughter, it shall come to pass. This is not a decree of the goddess or of the one whom I represent, but of the Fate to which you are bound by an understanding greater than thine own. Find thy peace, for life and death are mere doorways, and not to be mourned or dreaded. Thy child will find peace in Arcady, and shall become my own son, for whom I've searched thousands of years as he was born into the flesh and lost again at the threshold. He shall return and sit with the Eternal Mother here, and what was

Forbidden shall be Knowledge and what was Hidden shall be made Light."

The others all began writhing and moaning and singing of another world, and it reminded me of the dances we had been told were Evil and of the Devil, although there was great beauty in it and wonderful happiness. I fell to the ground. I kissed the soft moss of the earth and prayed that what I had been told would not come to pass. Once I could, I would escape these witches and tell of them to the whole plantation, and on the night of another evil sabbat I would take the Goodmen to this spot and burn all who had gathered so that their souls might be consigned to the fires of Hell.

I awoke suddenly, for it had been a dream, after all, but one sent by the emissaries of the most Unholy.

I lay in the grass as the sun came up, and bits of the dreaming came to me then. Of the dance, of the meeting with the Devil, of the spirits of the dead that had been raised in the circle of women, of the men wearing the masks of animals who mounted the women of all kinds, slave, Savage, English, Dutch, old, and of marriageable age. The herbs and flowers that we ate and the wild mushrooms that tasted of bitter copper. All of it spun in a nightmare in my head, and I tasted something rough in my throat and mouth. I felt in my mouth and found a small pebble beneath my tongue. When I spat it out, it was not a pebble at all but a tiny toad that hopped off into the grass. I had been bewitched. The whole day I could not speak, but did my chores, silent and weary. Finally, after dark when I knelt to say my prayers, I decided I must go to the one man who had both destroyed me and would be able to save me.

The father of my child, the minister of Our Lord. Only he held the key to the salvation of my tortured soul.

Chapter Nineteen

Maddy, Bewitched

1

Maddy Sparke set the diary down for a moment.

She had been reading at home in bed, and then downstairs in her living room, surrounded by cats; finally, she had to get out, so she sat at Starbucks, double almond latte in one hand, small leather-bound diary in the other. She would not have stopped her reading were it not for the desperate need she felt for a cigarette. It was almost a shock to come back to the end of the twentieth century after being so long in the diary. She smoked a cigarette outside, returned to Starbucks and grabbed another latte, and then sank into a big plush overstuffed chair and opened the small book again.

Diary of a Witch

I met with him a few days later.

My voice had returned. Still, I could tell no one about my meeting with the witches and the Devil, for they were all around me. How would I know if anyone I spoke with might be in the coven itself?

James Cotton, who had so terrified me when he had come and forced his body upon mine, now was clean and neatly attired, his face the aspect of an angel and his hand warm when he touched my own hand. He offered me milk and honey and bread spread thick with sweet butter.

"Thou art lost," he told me when I revealed what I knew, careful not to mention the names of those I had seen dancing. I told him of the witches' feast without once suggesting that witches lived within our midst. "Thou art but a lamb among wolves," he said, blessing me with a prayer against the valley of the shadow.

And then, as if forgetting all I had just told him, he professed his love for me and his longing for us to be together again among the mud and reeds.

He whispered that I must be a witch for I had so bewitched his flesh and occupied his every hour with the memory of my touch. I drew back in horror from him, but soon he was upon me again, whispering of love all the while he felt to me like a knife thrusting against my body. I will speak no more of my shame and the shame of my sex at the hands of such men as this. I will only say that my thoughts were turned toward protection of my child, be it bastard or saint, I wanted no harm to come to him. Whosoever reads this will forgive me for what I did next, for despite the power of this man, John Cotton, I held within me a child who would either be damned or saved, and I desired nothing but salvation for this child.

"Marry me," I begged. "I am ruined unless thou would take me as thy wife."

He swore then, to God and Jesus and all the angels of the firmament, that I would be his wife, and all my shame would be gone, and our child would grow beneath the name of Cotton.

"Nathaniel Cotton," I said, "we shall name him Nathaniel Cotton," and the minister of God nodded, and I felt my duty toward him change. I gave myself to him without shame or fear despite his rough brutality.

Nothing mattered, not my hurt or pain, for now my child would have a place in the world, and the Devil could take me if my child was protected.

I knew that all would be well, and that Our Lord would protect me from the seduction of the wilderness and its minions and the strangely beautiful but dark horned god who had been born of fire.

But soon enough, I found myself again at the gathering in the Forbidden Wood.

181

"I can almost see her," Maddy told Andreas Harris on the cell phone as she lit up her Camel on the sidewalk in front of Starbucks.

She'd spent half the day reading through the diary, getting used to the mess of handwriting, deciphering the squiggles and unusual penmanship as best she could. "How far did you get in this?"

"Far enough to know it's the genuine article," he said, his voice unnaturally cautious. "I would like the diary for the museum, you know."

"Of course," Maddy said. "Once a check has cleared my account from you and your investors, it's all yours. Did you ever find her?"

"Who?"

"This girl or woman. This N. Cross who wrote this. Someone put the small statue of the angel in the coffin in her place, with this diary. She is buried somewhere else?"

"Oh, we really can't assume any of this," he said. "And you haven't gotten all the way through, have you? The girl's fate is within that diary. All that and more."

"What do you mean?"

"She knew their secrets," Andreas said.

"Whose?"

"The witches. No doubt, in that kind of cult, the one who threatens them will be silenced."

Maddy glanced over at the cabs going by, the sun in the sky above the brownstones, the smell of exhaust and the touch of humidity in the air. Once, she thought, this was a plantation. Once this was grass and water and trees and a girl named N had lived and danced with witches in a circle. She puffed on the cigarette. "No, wait. The heart can't be hers, can it? You said you believed she was buried alive. Didn't you?"

"Yes," he said. "You must read more of the diary. It is all there. There is more to that little book than just Naomi."

"Naomi?"

"Yes, the N. She was one of six children of a servant on the plantation. You haven't read as far as you think."

"I'm a bit in," Maddy said, tossing the cigarette onto the pavement. A passerby gave her a dirty look. "It's absolutely enthralling."

"Yes," Andreas said. "A diary from the early eighteenth century of a coven of real witches, a diary that was not the result of torture or coercion, but from the imagination of a young girl who was more literate than her years."

"I was wondering about that."

"She writes with a curiously modern sensibility, doesn't she? She mentions this later on. She mentions how the women taught her writing and showed her books that she swore had not yet been printed, and that she even heard voices from a rock that told of the future."

"Do you believe in them?"

"In what? Witches?"

"Yes," Maddy said.

"Well, many people do. I've known some Wiccans. Some anthropologists have validated the existence of a witch cult in Europe. Some have argued quite successfully against its existence.

Perhaps this diary will be something of a bridge. Or perhaps it's all true. Who can say?" he said. "And Maddy, I need to meet with you— I hope tomorrow at three? In my office. I've found other artifacts that will intrigue you. And I will have a check for you then."

"Well, a check. Finally. Sure, I'll be there." Maddy hung up the phone, and lit another cigarette. She knew that one day she would have to kick this habit, but for now, she was a happy addict. She watched a good-looking man in tight pants walk by and decided that she needed a brisk walk to shake the feeling of dread she had from reading the witch's diary.

The diary . . . it had her now. She wanted to know more.

She walked several blocks over to Washington Square Park and sat down on a bench. She opened the diary and began reading again, her new addiction, all the while thinking that if there really were witches, why hadn't this teen-aged girl named Naomi just flown away from those who wished to destroy her? It was preposterous, of course, pure superstition from a superstitious age. There was no magic. There was no Forbidden Wood. There was no sabbat where the young were initiated into an ancient cult. Then, she glanced up, and saw a fortune-teller laying out tarot cards to three girls sitting around a fountain, and she remembered arguing with friends in her youth about Christ and God and virgin births and all the beliefs people had, and praying to a higher power, which she often did at her darkest moments.

If I can do that, who's to say others can't, and in their own ways? And who's to say that the disenfranchised of another time—slaves, servants, women, men, children—would not connect secretly back to a religion that would be considered evil by the social world around them? My own ancestors had times of persecution, and in turn, they persecuted. Why wouldn't a religion or cult go underground? It made perfect sense.

The diary called. She had to read. Had to. It was no longer a question of curiosity. Maddy wanted to know everything about this girl, Naomi Cross.

And what had happened to her.

4

Diary of a Witch

He had lied to me.

The minister of Our Lord.

He had promised to marry me and give a name to our child. Instead, he drew me to the steps of the stocks and called all manner of shame down upon my head. "She is fallen," he cried to them, and I, silent, stood by his side, unbelieving, not understanding why this man of God would so shame me to all. I was still very much a child myself and although I tried to tell my mother what had truly happened, she would have none of it, and neither playmate nor goodwife would hear my entreaties as anything other than the pitiful delusions of another fallen woman.

Good women did not become with child before God married her to a man.

Good women did not accuse righteous men of such base behavior.

Good women did not take the name of the Lord in vain as I did on more than one occasion.

I stood in stocks for two days, the shame of the village and the plantation. The boys threw stones and mud at me, and only the witchfolk were kind. They brought water and bread and a salve so that my wrists and neck would not hurt so much from the yoke. They rubbed my ankles and my back when I complained of pain. After my days of humiliation, Goody Carrier took me into her own home to make me well again. My own mother refused to let me sleep in the same quarters as my sisters for the shame I had brought down upon them.

Goody Carrier brewed teas and stews for me. I had never known such kindness as she bestowed upon me then. She believed what I told her about Reverend James Cotton. She knew he was the father.

She told me, "If there is a Devil on the plantation, it is that man. For he hath bewitched all into believing in his goodness and his understanding of the Book of God."

"But witches are of the Devil, are they not?" I asked.

"Oh, child, you have so much to learn. Witches are of an ancient art, a craft as old as time. We know the earth and its treasures, and the only magic we have is the magic of truth. Do you recall flying to our meeting?"

I nodded, for in truth I did fly there.

She said to me, "You rubbed an ointment on your body that freed you from how you thought of the world. You did not fly. You believed. We call it the astra, the movement of the soul from the flesh. That is worth more than wings. You believed, and you came to us, but your body lay behind in the grass, sleeping."

"Did I dream it?" I asked of her.

"Do you believe you dreamed it?" she asked with some mirth. Then, she told me about how our bodies are like ships on the sea and how we, like the captain, believe that if we leave them, we will surely drown in the sea and never return. "The sea is life itself. How can one drown in life?" she asked me, laughing gently. "What you rubbed upon yourself freed you from your ship, and you came to us, as each of us slept in our beds and still were there in the Wood."

I did not understand her, but she was of such comfort to me that I grew to trust her.

I decided then that rather than live as the plantation's scarlet woman, I would become one of them.

A witch.

It came time for my initiation, which I had both dreaded and wanted. For in truth, my life on the plantation had become one of torment. My shame had already begun to show to the others. Servants laughed at me, and the good-wives avoided me, pulling their husbands and sons from any path upon which I had recently trod. The goodmen at night would come by, offering me food and drink if I would promise to go with them into the tall grass by the river. They terrified me more than the fires of hell with their glances and their rough talk.

I began to care less for the plantation life and more for my time in the Forbidden Wood.

I had already decided. My child would go to the Lord of the Forest, the King of the Witches, who came to me as a father would, caressing me, and promising that my son would be the greatest of our kind, once I sacrificed the child in exchange for power beyond my own imagining.

I had been spurned by my lover, and had been loved by those whom others would spurn.

My child would be theirs.

Chapter Twenty

Jake

1

Jake's Journal

All right, I don't believe in them.

In ghosts.

I really don't.

Maybe I didn't see her in the subway. Maybe I just want to see her so badly now, that I will conjure her up in any face. Maybe I'm going mad. Maybe I just need to figure out my life.

Maybe I'm just hallucinating. Need to go pick up Laury. Need to quit writing every day and night on the laptop. Need to get a life.

Here's what I know:

1. Naomi is dead.
2. I am alive.

3. I live across from Naomi's apartment and practically sleep there now.

4. Naomi's old boyfriend is a jerk.

5. When she was alive, Naomi watched me from a distance in Manhattan.

6. I am a divorced man who is getting too old to obsess on past loves.

7. I just don't believe in my heart that she's dead.

8. Life is for the living. Take your daughter out somewhere fun. Forget all this. Let the dead be dead. See a shrink. Eat much ice cream.

9. Don't believe.

10. Believing means opening doors that should just stay closed.

2

He looked his age: just about thirty. He was the best and the least of the men who sat reading *The New York Times*, sitting at an outside table at the Bus Stop Café on Hudson, drinking his coffee, occasionally taking a bite from his plate of scrambled eggs and toast. Jake Richmond blended in easily with his environment—something about him looked absolutely New York, and he was only given away as a Southerner by his chestnut hair, which fell in a lazy slide across his left eyebrow, and by the way he sometimes forgot and said "y'all" and then apologized for it, and in the way he consumed Manhattan just by inhaling its air—his eyes were still bright. He had been in this city much too long to have bright eyes. His friends had left the

table moments before—two people he had
worked with for years who were moving on to
other positions—and when he checked his
watch, he saw it was time to go pick up his
daughter.

But there was something about him. Something
that might've been in the paleness of his skin
that had once been ruddy, and in the curve to
his shoulders, as if defeat had been passed to
him in some game; call it, haunted, for he was,
his eyes bright, his face clean-shaven, his
clothes wrinkled but ordinary, and his step as
quick as the next man's. Any that saw him on
the street would feel it, that word: *haunted.*

3

Jake took a cab and avoided the subway completely. While his thoughts of both work and
Naomi had occupied him on the ride to the Upper East Side, once the cab stopped outside the
building, he was thrown back into the present:
He had to see his ex like this every weekend for
the rest of his life. He had to forge a friendship,
despite all the anger he felt, the sense of be-
trayal, and the knowledge that Amy had probably been right to leave him. That was the worst
part. She was right to find love in someone else's
arms. He had only played the part of a husband
and lover to her. He had always been with
someone else in his mind. Somewhere else. No
matter how he had tried to escape it.

He got off the elevator on the fifth floor and

went down the hallway. Halfway to the door, he realized he had not brought a present for his daughter. He returned to the elevator, taking it down to street level. It had begun to rain slightly, just drips and drabs. The rain felt dirty—the air, dusty. He found a drugstore a few blocks away and bought a small keychain. That was enough for openers. It had become a ritual for him to buy Laury something every time he saw her. It was a cheap trick, he knew. It was a skunk ex-husband kind of trick, but he just could not come to her empty-handed. He never felt he could give her enough.

Riding back up on the elevator, he felt a slight tug at his heart—a minor pain. Too much coffee. Too much coffee and maybe too much beer at night, and maybe too much anxiety.

The door opened on the fifth floor. When he rounded the corner of the hall, he saw that his daughter had already opened the door to the apartment, knowing he'd be there.

"Berry," Jake said, his arms already out. She ran down the hall and leaped into them; he carried her back to Amy's apartment.

"Daddy! I had so much happen to me, you wouldn't believe!" Laury said. He kissed her ear, and she laughed because it tickled. He looked up and saw Amy standing by the living room window, her face both beautiful and vexed.

"Who's this woman who has been calling?" Amy asked.

Jake ignored her for a moment. He let Laury slide down from his arms, back to the parquet floor. He looked into his daughter's eyes and wished she didn't look so lovable. "All right, do we want to Central Park it?"

"It's rainy. I don't like rainy days," Laury said, and then looked at her father's hands. "You bring me anything?"

He looked back at Laury. He opened his hand to her. "Brought you this."

She grabbed the keychain out of his hand. "Pikachu! I love Pokemon!" She held the plastic yellow animal up for her mother to see. "Mommy, look."

"That's lovely," Amy said, without even glancing at the keychain. She glanced up at Jake accusingly. "She calls at night. It really pisses me off. You shouldn't have given her this number."

Jake couldn't meet her eyes. He always felt like they had lied to each other. He didn't want to look at her eyes again. "Who?"

"That old girlfriend of yours," she said. "The one from Virginia. Don't pretend you don't see her anymore. I know you do."

He stood there, his daughter running off to get an umbrella, his ex-wife turning away from him.

The back of Amy's long beige cotton sweater sagged. Her hair was shiny and just-brushed. She looked comfortable. It was almost like being home.

Jake saw the rain outside the living room window. The sky turned shadowy with clouds. He could see the tips of the trees in Central Park.

"Why are you telling me this," he said, and it was not a question.

"You still love her, don't you?" Amy said, not bothering to turn around again. She always had her back to him. "I don't even care. Just tell her to stop calling."

Chapter Twenty-one

Romeo in the Below

1

Romeo remained within the tunnel for nearly nine hours, sipping the water that trickled from the pipes above him. He tried not to move a muscle. Ever since the Serpent had touched his ankle, he had been sure that his time was up. The Serpent had stayed there, its cold skin against the calf of his leg, and then, even when he was sure it was gone, he still felt it upon him. The Serpent was blind to the dark, and it was only the heat of life that allowed it to see at all.

Finally, It had moved on. It was not interested in those who lived Below. It could not pick up their scent, and so long as they were still as It passed, it let them be.

Weak with hunger, Romeo pressed on. He

could find a rat or a slug for sustenance. He would not starve. He told himself that the bread of air was enough, that the dark water of the tunnels of the Beneath was enough.

Destiny would protect him. If he was meant to die, he would die. He had survived worse than this. He had been born to darkness. He had known the caverns of the whole world.

His home was this darkness, and Destiny was his only knowledge.

Scabber's words went through his head— "Nobody comes here because he's lost. This is the found place. This is the war zone. This is where the boy who knows the dark and the caverns comes to us and finds the three secrets and stops the Serpent. And you may just be that boy," she said, stroking his matted hair. "I saw it in one of my dreams. You may just be that boy."

2

It was time for Destiny because of what the Serpent was doing now. Because something had happened that had let It out. Some part of Its power had grown.

Something had freed It and Its children.

Its thousands of slithering children, all freed.

The thoughts in his mind:

Reach the Forbidden City.

Reveal the secrets.

Stop up the entrance to Hell.

Days later, still crawling through the tunnels—for they went on for miles into the earth, criss-crossing, spinning around one way or another, forking and then reuniting, all the while the blasts of the city and its trains around him, and the steam, he saw something that looked like—one of the keys.

One of the secrets within the keys.

It was cold and hard, and he clutched it as if for dear life and knew that he was nearly there.

It was a human skull.

Part Three

The Witch

Chapter Twenty-two

Maddy and Andreas

1

Maddy skipped reading *The New York Times* whenever possible, but this particular day, something looked too familiar on the front page.

She tripped over herself shoving her way into the newsstand, dropping down her sixty cents, and pressing the paper to her face.

A picture of her brownstone—*her brownstone!*

On the front page of *The New York Times* with the caption: WITCH HOLOCAUST IN THE VILLAGE?

2

She was on her cell phone before the newspaper hit the trash can on the street corner. Andreas Harris practically wept when he heard her voice.

"What's this?"

"Maddy?"

"As if you didn't know who'd be calling you today. What is this? I am reading this trashy article about a goddamn witch holocaust in my house, and you're the son of a bitch they interviewed, and you're going to tell me that you knew nothing about this?"

"It's . . ."

"I'll tell you what it goddamn is," she said, reaching into her breast pocket for a cigarette. She popped it into her mouth and then lit it almost in one stroke as she scraped a match against a brick wall. "It is a goddamn invasion of privacy, that's what it is."

Andreas Harris was silent.

After a minute or two of letting him stew, and after she'd smoked the cigarette almost to a thimbleful of ash, Maddy said, "I have the IRS threatening to freeze my accounts, and I owe many thousands to many people. Christ, all my cash right now is tied up into that house—and it's practically in ruins and here—what is it I'm reading? Twenty-one bodies found in a mass grave under one house—how is this? How did we go from goddamn four bodies to goddamn twenty-one bodies?"

"I couldn't be sure," Andreas blurted. "Before . . ."

Now it was Maddy's turn to remain silent.

"My people," he said, and she imagined the little weasel on the other end of the phone. "They just dug down and around a little more. And there was a shaft."

"A shaft?"

"Almost like a mine shaft. There were bones all around. It was like . . . like . . . catacombs . . . Stacked on top of one another. All around."

"And you called a goddamn reporter from the *Times*?"

"Well . . . no."

"Well what?"

"I called CBS News, actually. A friend. Only a friend. He works with one of the shows."

"Please tell me it ain't *60 Minutes*."

"If that's what you want to hear. . . ."

"It's goddamn *60 Minutes*? Harris, you are the dumbest most moronic son of a bitch I have ever come across. You called *60 Minutes*?"

"Once the Wiccans heard, and the Human Rights Foundation—"

Maddy spat profanities like a dragon spitting fire. "And just what are the Wiccans and the Human Rights people—no, don't tell me, they want it, don't they? They want my house."

"We don't know that yet."

"*60 Minutes*, Harris," She said it with defeat and disgust.

"You want your money, don't you? You want all that's owed you?" Andreas said, less nervously. "I'll be at my office. Let's talk this over. You have nothing to lose."

Then he hung up the phone.

3

Andreas Harris's private office was toward the back of the Museum of Early Manhattan, and Maddy had to walk through a few small rooms full of Native-American and early American artifacts, painting, display cases full of manuscripts and even small fossils. She knocked twice. A young, pretty woman who looked as if she were barely out of high school answered the door. The young woman was nervous. Her hands were shaking.

She's scared of me, Maddy thought. *Good.*

"He makes you work weekends?" she asked with a snort.

"Dr. Harris is extremely important," the girl whispered. Maddy suddenly felt as if she had walked into a school library and had regressed to age three. "His work often keeps him here late and on Saturdays."

"And he has no life, I bet," Maddy said, winking. "Which door?" She pointed to the narrow doors to the left and right of them.

"Please," the girl said. "Keep your voice down. He's very sensitive. He's so focused that any little disturbance can—"

"Miss Cannell," Maddy read the name off the girl's desk, "I have no doubt that Harris is disturbed, but I very much think he will not mind my booming voice. Now, which door?"

"Let me buzz him first," the girl said, but Maddy walked by her and opened the one door to which Ms. Cannell had been glancing toward.

Inside Andreas's office (first thing Maddy noticed: it smelled foul, like cigars. Second thing she noticed: there were no windows. Third thing she noticed: Andreas was as weaselly as ever), she said, "Christ, Harris, you have that poor thing out there scared as a mouse in a cat box."

Andreas Harris, his small face pinched and his scalp positively glowing with sweat, glanced up from his papers. He neither smiled nor frowned. His mouth was a small flat line. "Come over and sit down, Maddy. I don't want to waste your time."

"Good," said, nodding, and sat in the swivel chair opposite him. "Now, tell me how you've been screwing me over in the past twenty-four hours."

"You should've picked up your phone this morning," he said. "I tried calling."

"I never answer my phone on weekends if I can help it."

"Well," Andreas said, an awful grin spreading across his face—as much a grimace as anything she had ever seen. "You may have more than a few messages on your answering machine by now. Every historic and human rights group in the city and many from around the country are probably trying to reach you. You're going to be famous." He said *famous* as if it were the beginning of a disease.

"Famous and poor," she said, huffing. "Get to the bottom line, Harris. What are you going to do to clean this up?"

"Do?" he asked. "Why should I do anything?"

"Well, there's the small matter of my check. At least a million, but now, wouldn't you think this might be worth more like two?"

"I'm not so sure," Andreas Harris said, folding his hands in front of him, staring right at her with his deranged little eyes. "If your property on Rose Street is found to be a historic landmark, perhaps the city will pay you several thousand for it. With all those poor people executed by law, buried on that property, well, one would hesitate to say that it belongs more to the city than it does to you. This is after all, history, Maddy, not just your sad little money problem. Perhaps no one will pay you anything. Perhaps the city and state will dig up your land and in about a year, you will be able to fill it in and make it look moderately valuable. Perhaps in a year, the collection agencies after you will take the house. I think there will be a lien against the place shortly, if memory serves." Then, one last blow: "At least, that's what my lawyer said."

She sat in silence while he spoke. When he was done, she whispered, "You did this just to take it, didn't you? Your foundation never had the money to pay for it. You're going to somehow get this without ever paying a penny, aren't you?"

"My intentions have been entirely honorable," Andreas said. "But unlike you, I'm not in it for the money. I'm not some money-grubber who inherited wealth the lazy way and now wants to milk every last cent from money she's never earned, am I?"

Maddy felt rage about to burst from beneath her skin, and she imagined for a few seconds tearing his eyes out and setting his museum on fire.

She almost grinned like a well-fed cat when another thought came to her. Her voice was calm when she spoke. "Ah, but Andreas, there is one consideration, isn't there?"

He never lost his smile, but she could tell that something within him was beginning to stir. Some fear. He was afraid of her. He had plotted all this out, and now that he had found many more bodies, he thought he had her.

But he didn't have her yet.

"I have the book. The diary."

"I've made transcripts already," he said.

"No, you haven't. You would've given me the transcript if you had it, instead of the real thing. You know, I even wonder if you really want my property for your museum. You gave me the book. You didn't have to. You . . . gave . . . me. . . . You wanted me to see your wonderful find. The one document that can prove this theory of the witch holocaust right or wrong. After all, what if those bodies are nothing more than dead people? What if Greenwich plantation had a serial killer, and in fact, those people had no hate crime attached to them? They were just victims of a vicious murderer. Then all these Wiccan protestors and Human Rights people will lose interest. It won't be like Salem. There won't be a national monument on Rose Street. There will just be an embarrassing cleanup at the city's expense. I'll rent the place out or sell it cheap. It's just another property."

"There will be court documents. Perhaps they're buried in some wall or in a customshouse. We will find them," Andreas said. "And you will turn that diary over to me. You will." He slammed his fist on his desk like a little dictator.

"Diary?" Maddy laughed, rising from her chair as if she owned the world. "What diary?"

Then, she turned and left the office.

For just a second she was sure she heard what might have been a shoe hit the door after she'd shut it.

Chapter Twenty-three

Jake and Amy and Laury

1

At his ex-wife's apartment, Jake went to get a cup of coffee in the kitchen.

Amy sat down on the plush leather chair near the stereo. She looked good, and it bothered him that he thought it. Part of him wanted to hate her. But he couldn't. He knew if he hated her, he would have to hate their shared memories, and he might have to hate the part of her that was in Laury. Jake knew he could never do that.

Laury followed after her father like it was the grandest adventure in the world just to go in the kitchen with him.

"It's Naomi whatshername," Amy called out. "Make mine with extra cream," she added.

"I'm telling you it can't be, honey." He fell back into that familiarity. *Sweetheart. Honey. Darling. Baby.* All the words they had once said to each other. He reached over into the cookie jar and brought out a large gingerbread cookie, which he split with his daughter.

Jake poured some coffee into two large mugs, from a set of three that he'd given Amy when they were together—villain mugs from a trip they'd taken to Disney World the year before Laury was born. It had been a three-day weekend of feeling like kids, and truly being in love, and he'd bought her the Cruella De Vil, Ursula the Sea Witch, and Maleficent mugs. For just a second, he felt those aches again—the ache of knowing that it was over. There would be no more trips to Disney World like that. There would be no more sitting around at the end of the day, talking about their plans for the day after tomorrow.

You've got to move on. You just have got to. You can't pretend that she's going to ever want to make it better. You can't make it work. It was a lie. A lie that felt good for a while.

His head throbbed. Headache coming on.

He filled Cruella with cream, Ursula with sugar, and then made what he called a coffee cocktail for Laury—a mugful of milk with a touch of sugar and just a drop of coffee. He set the mugs on a tray, shooing Laury ahead of him as he left the cramped kitchen and returned to the living room.

"I just don't want her calling. That's all," Amy said, accepting the mug less than gracefully; she nearly spilled it across her sweater. "You always filled it too full."

"It's not her," Jake said, glancing back at Laury.

"I'm telling you, it is."

"How would you know?"

Amy looked sharply at him, then at Laury. She whispered, "We don't have to fight about it."

"I know," Jake said, hanging his head slightly. Feeling like he was the dog. Sipped his coffee. "Where's Daniel?"

"He's working." Her whole face seemed clouded over with some confusion. *She must've been confused the entire time we were married*, he thought.

"If she calls again, I'll just call the police."

"It's not her. And besides, whoever it is, just block the call."

"It's my phone," Amy said. She set her mug down on her knees, balancing it carefully.

"Look," Jake said, "she's dead. All right?"

"Who's dead?" Laury asked, chomping down on the cookie. Her fingers soon dusted with powdered sugar, a big milk mustache covered her upper lip. Her mother made a wiping gesture under her own nose until Laury got the idea. She took her napkin and wiped at her lip.

Jake reached over and scruffed Laury's hair. "Hey, Berry. An old friend of mine died." He returned his gaze to Amy. "I hadn't spoken with her since I was a kid."

"Oh," Laury gave a knowing look to her mother. "Her. The lady."

Amy's eyebrows creased slightly, and she reached behind her back to adjust the pillows against the chair.

"I guess I'm giving you a headache," Jake said, glumly. "As per usual."

"No," she said, smiling, and for once, the smile seemed genuine. "It's my lower back. It's giving me some problems."

"That because . . ." Laury began, dropping cookie crumbs all around her.

"Laura, remember what we talked about," Amy warned.

"That's because Mommy's going to give me a little brother. Finally," Laury said. She went over to her mother and pressed her head against her mother's stomach. "It's only maybe two months old. His name is going to be Jackson. And he's already giving Mommy lots of aches and pains."

Amy smiled. "I wanted to tell you myself. I was going to wait—"

"No, aw, Amy, congratulations." Jake raised his mug in a toast. He wasn't sure what he felt. He remembered talking with her about having more children. He remembered her objections. He remembered thinking it was okay that they didn't have more kids, they could spoil Laury, they would have more time to themselves, and it was what Amy wanted, anyway. He wasn't sure how he felt. He tried not to think of Daniel and Amy together with their new baby. For some reason, it bothered him. He looked at his daughter and tried to muster some nice thoughts. Now Laury will have a kid brother or sister. That was good. Sure, that was good.

When Laury went to use the bathroom, Amy said, "That woman has called every night. Sometimes twice a night. If someone's told you she's dead then that person is lying. That's all. I am getting sick of Naomi Faulkner and her late-night calls."

"She has to be dead." Jake tried to laugh. He tried as hard as he could, but something in his voice weakened. His laugh fell flat against the room. He felt phony laughing at something that he didn't find the least bit amusing.

Something within him did not believe—anymore—that Naomi was dead.

Amy glanced out the window. "The rain's stopping. You two should get going. The park will be nice."

"The park!" Laury cried out running from the back hall. "Yeah, and I want a big hot dog!"

2

After leaving the apartment and going for a long walk in a damp and only slightly rainy Central Park, Laury grabbed her father's hand tightly and squeezed it a few times. "I have to go," she said.

"But you just went before we got here," he protested mildly.

"I know, but I still have to go. I musta drank too much milk," she whispered, embarrassed by having to mention it twice. "Mommy lets me go in the bushes."

"In the bushes?" Jake laughed. "She does? Mommy?"

Laury nodded. "If it's a 'mergency and number one."

"Let's go to Starbucks or maybe we can find a diner where—"

"Daddy, I can't wait," she whispered her urgency.

"Okay, Berry, let's find one. A nice fat bush."

"I can do it. Don't follow. I can," she said, her mood turning haughty. He watched her dash between roller bladers across the road to a low hedge. Slowly, he walked across the road, following her.

On the other side, he called to his daughter. He stood there, expecting to hear her call back in her cheery voice, or an annoyed tone, but there was nothing but the shouts of others and the sound of traffic beyond the park. He gave her another half minute, knowing how privacy had become increasingly important to her.

When she hadn't come out on his next call to her, he ran into the bushes, with every fear returning to him of Manhattan and what could happen to a little girl all by herself for several minutes—

He envisioned a crazed killer stabbing her or strangling her or kidnapping her or just hurting her. Even the slightest hurt, the most minor cut, he would never forgive himself if—

Instead, he found her farther among the trees and brambles of weeds and grasses, kneeling over a dead squirrel, crying. Her sobbing was nearly silent, but the tears had already soaked into her shirt.

"Poor baby squirrel," she said, when her father put his arm around her. "It's dead just like that woman you knew. The one who keeps calling Mommy. The one who told me that you made her go to the bad place."

Chapter Twenty-four

Namey

1

Jake whistled down a cab out by the park, and laughed when Laury said she wanted to pay the tip when they got to the end of the line. That's what she called where he lived, "the end of the line."

"That's what Mommy calls it," Laury insisted, reading her father's face.

"Oh, does she," her father said, sliding into the backseat of the taxicab. Laury scooted over next to him and checked—as she always did—to make sure the driver had turned on the meter. Then, she grabbed her father's umbrella and claimed it for herself. She laid it down on the seat beside her. Laury was much better organized than either of her parents.

"Hudson and Horatio," Jake told the driver, and when they'd pulled out into traffic, he asked his daughter, "What woman did you mean, Berry? Back in the park. When you saw the dead squirrel?"

"The one with the funny name."

"Like Bozo?"

"No, Daddy," she said, laughing. "It's almost like Namey. Namey is her name."

"And I made her go to a bad place?"

"That's what she said. That's what she told me anyway."

"You spoke to her?" All right, he could admit it to himself. He felt a chill inside his bones. He felt as if he'd been buried in ice, suddenly, with each word his daughter spoke. *Namey. Naomi. A bad place.*

Laury nodded.

"When?"

"Maybe two days ago. Maybe. She was nice."

"What else did she say?"

"Just things."

"It's important to me, Laury. Try to remember."

Laury scrunched up her eyebrows. "She said that she's always been watching me to make sure I don't get hurt, and she says things like you are her best friend and like that. She must be my guardian angel."

"What about the bad place?"

"Oh. That. That's what made me sad. I put down the phone when she started talking about it."

"I'm sorry, Berry."

"I know all about hell, Daddy. Matt told me about it in school. He said that some people go there."

It was the first time he'd ever heard his daughter use that word, *hell,* and it only bothered him because he knew he was no longer around to watch her grow up. Not in the way that he had once been there. *So, a school playmate had told her about hell already. Whaddayaknow.*

"I doubt that. How could I make someone go to the bad place?"

"She said you pushed her. She said you pushed her into the train, and it ran over her."

"Laury?"

Laury raised her hands, shrugging, imitating her mother. "Well I know it's not true, Daddy. I mean, how could she call me if it was true? But just the same," and her saying that "just the same" was her mother, all over. "It made me sad. It made me think about dead things."

"I'm sorry, Berry," he said, wrapping his arms around her. "I'm sure she was joking."

"If she's joking, she's weird."

"Absolutely," he said, kissing her forehead. "She's weird all right."

"Daddy?"

"Yeah, sweetie?"

"You gonna marry her?"

2

The house on Rose Street was a perfectly nice brownstone—Maddy Sparke had visited it many times as a child when her great-aunt had lived there.

Over the years it had been kept up well so that she had, the previous year, fully expected to sell it for a few million dollars. Her other option might be to divide it into condos and sell off at least five of them depending upon whether or not the basement could be converted into an apartment. All of Rose Street had been kept up over the years, so that the street had a sense of timelessness to it.

Even in the sixties, the houses had not been divided into apartments for the most part. It was a safe street at all hours owing to the street lamps along the sidewalk and the fact that a police station was just one block over. It didn't hurt that the families who had held on to their properties had all—until recently—known one another and taken some pride in the street. It had once been a grand old street; its wrought-irons gates, sculptured stone, and small but abundant gardens making it one of the undiscovered beauties of the Village for anyone who took a wrong turn down the side street. It was very nearly tucked away.

In the past decade, of course, the inevitable had occurred: houses were divided into condos and some actually came down in favor of a new apartment complex, but Maddy's place had remained the largest house on the street with the widest garden in back.

Since the excavation had begun, all of this had changed. Maddy had watched jackhammers dig through the kitchen floor as well as several husky men scoop out the earth around the garden, but surely this would be replaced.

Yet, she knew the worst was to come as she turned down Rose Street. Maddy Sparke knew that the discovery of the bodies beneath the house was just the beginning.

3

The first sight that greeted her were the police barricades at either end of Rose Street, apparently to discourage traffic from slowly moving by the now-infamous house and its minions. *Yes*, she thought, *they are minions—minions of Hell:* Those gawkers and onlookers who stood outside the house. On the front steps, a gathering of what looked like aging hippies (with signs that read, PAGANS FOR PROTECTION OF OUR HERITAGE) were lecturing to a group of cloaked young women (more signs, WICCANS OF GREATER MANHATTAN, CHELSEA CHAPTER and HATE CRIMES ARE AGAINST ALL), while what looked like a miniature contingent from Wall Street—all suits and sticks up their rears—added to the mess of humanity. And then, there were the cops. Lots of cops. And the two TV crews, their vans parked down the block on the other side of the barricades.

Maddy's first impulse was to walk the other way.

Her second was to scream.

Weeping copiously did not seem to be the best option.

Besides, the sky was doing that well enough,

intermittently. She glanced up to the gray clouds and let the light rain wash over her face. It felt good. It helped untie the knots of tension she'd begun to feel—the rain was cool.

Maddy did not want to find out all the terrible things they'd been doing to her house, but she could not help herself.

She stepped forward, and found a nice police officer who was covered with sweat as he tried to keep various miscreants from running through the police tape and into the open door of the house.

"Sir," she said, and then shouted it since the Pagans on the porch had begun to chant.

"Please, we're very busy here," the cop said, weary from the day.

"I am the owner of this house," she said, and she barely had to raise her voice above a whisper when suddenly a woman with a slightly nasal but overly self-confident voice spoke up behind her back.

"Are you Madison Sparke?"

Maddy whirled around, and came face-to-face with a coat hanger of a woman in a business suit, with short-cropped blond hair, pink lips, and teeth like a barracuda. A light blinded her for a second. Then, Maddy saw the cameraman, and the female reporter from hell thrust a microphone in her face.

"Wendy Whalen, Action News," she said. "Miss Sparke—"

She spat profanity like it was tobacco juice in the woman's face. Maddy felt her rage begin to do a fast disco number in her brain. "This is my property and—"

"Miss Sparke, when did you first discover the bodies beneath your home?"

"It's not my home, it's my property, and I have nothing to say to you or any other television stooge," she said. But like a whirlwind revelation from heaven, Maddy found that she did indeed have a lot to say, and she began to say it.

4

To one reporter, she said, "Where's the goddamn mayor? That's what I want to know! Where is he? A small businesswoman is being stepped on because a bunch of three-hundred-year-old bones are found in her backyard and now it's going to be turned into a goddamn national landmark? I know what this is about; this is about stomping on the little person. This is about ignoring the—" Then someone from the crowd yelled, "What about the rights of the dead?"

"They don't got no rights," Maddy shouted back. "They're dead. Holy mother of Jesus what kind of outfit is that, no, I have nothing—nothing—against you doing your magic but I do have something against all this. These are bones. We can move them to a graveyard and then you can set your bonfire over there, but not until—"

To another reporter, "I am completely shocked. That's right. I am utterly shocked. Shocked is what I am. This property is my security and right now that security has been ripped out from under me and—" Maddy grabbed the microphone and moved in closer to the camera, "Mr. Andreas Weasel Harris and you thugs at the Museum of Early Manhattan, if you think for one minute that you can create this circus to scare me away and make me give up what my family has owned for—"

With another reporter, she calmed a bit. "I completely support Wiccans and any persecuted group. But let me put it plain: human bones were found here. That's all. The guess is that they are a few hundred years old. There was a plantation on this site, and I'm sure there were graveyards just like anywhere. This was probably just a family plot. There's no evidence of witch trials, and unfortunately some rather immoral character from a certain museum has suggested that this is some sort of witch holocaust spot when in fact—and I mean no disrespect to witches—but first, we know there are no witches and second, we know that New Yorkers would never have hanged no witches even in the 1600s because New Yorkers even then didn't give a good goddamn."

When she had finished, she managed to finagle a police escort through the small crowd that had thinned considerably in the rain. The cop guided her up the steps and into the house that she had been hoping would dig her out of the financial hole. She glanced back at the people outside, briefly—her only thought was that she wished she could get one of the Wiccans to lay a hell of a curse on Andreas Harris.

The inside of the house made her wish she'd said stronger words to the reporters.

The place looked as if a giant two-year-old had gone and thrown a tantrum. The beautiful old oak paneling was scratched; the walls covered with ashy handprints; the staircase that wound to the second floor had been chipped at by souvenir hunters.

She tried to keep her eyes in front of her. She tried not to weep.

But when she reached the back garden, all she could think about were her parents and how they had taken such good care of their properties. How they had trusted her to do the same. How she had messed up too much of life—and now life was messing with her.

The yard looked more like a bowl of soup than a garden.

Deep holes in the earth, flooded over from broken pipes . . . the flowers and vines all torn or stamped into the mud . . . excavation markers from one end of the garden to the other.

It looked like one giant grave.

It is a grave, she thought. *It's a mass grave, and for some reason it remained undiscovered until now.*

On the back wall, vandals had spray-painted: THOU SHALT NOT SUFFER A WITCH TO LIVE

Beneath this: SERPENT IS LOOSE

5

A few workmen stood under a tarp, drinking beer and laughing among themselves, and even the cops seemed to be shaking their heads in bemusement over the graffiti and the mess.

But Maddy alone felt the world dissolve around her.

Her dream of getting back on her feet again, of turning her finances around, of making her parents proud.

All gone.

She turned and went to the filthy kitchen, tiles uprooted along the shelf. She opened the fridge, hoping one of the workmen might have left behind a Coke or Sprite, and instead was greeted by two six-packs of Budweiser.

Maddy Sparke had not had a beer in years. She had avoided alcohol. She had fallen out of love, and then out of like, with it.

But you always return to your first love.

She grabbed one of the cans, popped the top, and took a sip.

And then another.

It was like meeting an old friend again, an ex-lover, and realizing that love had never really died.

6

Laury decided she wanted Vietnamese for dinner. "Soup," she insisted. "I want soup, and I want it from a Vietnamese restaurant. It's the best food." She kcpt her umbrella up almost as a matter of defiance, for the rain was light.

Jake wanted Mexican.

"I say Benny's Burritos," Jake said, putting his hands on his hips defiantly.

"And I say Szechuan. Or Vietnamese." Laury, who had trouble pronouncing certain words had no trouble with takeout. Laury always took decisions of dining very seriously. "I had Mexican last night."

"And I had Chinese last night. And besides, it's not like you can't have the same kind of food two nights in a row. People do it all the time," Jake added. They stood at the corner of Bleeker and Christopher after having grabbed some movies at the local video store, and now it was just a matter of where to pig out. They'd spent most of the afternoon avoiding rain by going into shops around the Village and Soho, interrupted by a side trip to Washington Square to listen to some guitar players when the rain stopped for a brief period. Then they had combed some of the antique stores in Soho to buy a new lamp, only Laury could not settle on which one Jake should have, and Jake felt they were all overpriced and a little bit ugly anyway. "Sears is more my style," he had said.

"Mommy says Kmart is more your style," Laury responded, not understanding that her mother managed to say mean things without ever sounding like it.

"Hey, I like Kmart. My, my, Mommy's a bit of a snob, isn't she?"

"She's a bit of one," Laury said, almost too wisely. "But I like Kmart, too, Daddy. Don't worry. I like all the things you like."

So later, he used it in the war over what was for supper.

"You said you like all the things I like, Berry. Remember?"

"Puh-lease."

"I don't want Chinese."

"I said Vietnamese. Little Saigon makes good tamarind shrimp noodles. That's what I want," she said.

"Did you know when I was your age, I would've been thrilled with McDonald's?" Jake grabbed her hand, and they kept walking up the street.

"I like McDonald's okay, but tonight I want Vietnamese." Laury opened and closed her umbrella almost as a way to ward off going to McDonald's. For some reason, she was the only child on the planet who wasn't hooked on Big Macs and McNuggets.

"Am I spoiling you? If I am, tell me. I don't want a spoiled little New Yorker for a daughter."

"Please, Daddy?" she squeezed his hand and then gave him that winning look he could never resist. "All right. Benny's is fine. I love Benny's, too. I want you to be happy."

Now, she'd won. "No, now I want Vietnamese soup for dinner. And maybe some good calamari. And tamarind shrimp noodles," he said, and she laughed.

Laury laughed less when they found out that her favorite Vietnamese restaurant was closed for repairs, and so they settled for a little Chinese takeout place where the food was just average but Laury liked to collect the little white boxes the rice came in. They got back to Jake's apartment, and Laury immediately grabbed the Nintendo 64 and turned it on.

"We'll play Mario Kart first and then Smash and then maybe after I beat you a gazillion times, we can watch a movie."

He smiled, watching her, the light playing off her hair, the way she could be both haughty and lovable—the way he wished that it could have worked out with Amy just because this little girl deserved both mom and dad in one place to be there as she grew up.

After a dozen battles and a half-dozen races (in which Laury as her Princess Peachy Nintendo character managed to beat the pants off his Donkey Kong character most of the time), he heard the yowling across the hall and practically jumped.

"What's that?" she asked.

"It's the cat. Christ, I forgot to feed her today. She's probably starved."

"You have a kitty? Daddy?" Then her eyes widened like it was the best surprise in the universe. "Is it for me?"

"Aw, honey, no, it's a neighbor's cat. A neighbor who's away."

"Like we took care of the Mitchell's wiener dog?"

"Yep. Just like that. Hang out. I'll be right back."

"Daddy, I want to see the kitty. Please?"

"Okay. Come on."

Laury fell in love with the cat right away.

Jake enjoyed watching his daughter cuddle and stroke the animal. It made it feel more like home. He fought back a tear, because he wished that life had turned out different. Not completely the opposite of what it was, but he wished he had loved Laury's mother more, and that they all could be at their old place, sitting around on a weekend night, making plans for the future, figuring out how they were going to make payments to Laury's school, wondering if any of their stocks would go up, wondering how their parents ever managed . . .

He let the wishful thinking go.

Jake went over to the kitchen counter and opened a can of Friskies and dumped its contents on a small plate. The cat leaped from Laury's arms and practically flew to the counter, where she greedily devoured the food.

"Why do cats like that stuff? I really think it's because it makes their breath stink," Jake said, and Laury giggled.

"Sometimes your breath stinks," she said.

She wandered around the small apartment, picking up things, putting them down, looking at books and clothes. "It's a lady who lives here."

"How'd you know?" Jake went and washed his hands in the sink—he had a smudge of cat food on his fingers from opening the can. Something was different in the apartment. He wasn't sure what it was. He looked over at the bed, and then at the window.

Someone had been here since the previous day when he'd fed the cat.

"I can tell. It's a lady's place. And that," she pointed to the wall mural. "That's someplace pretty."

"That's where I'm from." Jake went and sat on the bed, and looked around. Something had changed. Or something was moved. Or something was missing.

Someone else had been in the apartment.

Someone had been in Naomi's apartment.

Alan Cowper, Jake told himself. *Alan owns the apartment. It's his. Of course he has every right to come and go as he pleases in this apartment. Of course. It's his. She's dead. Don't even pretend she's somehow just going to reappear from around a corner and give you a hug and say, "Hey, let's take up where we left off." She's dead. There's a prankster making these calls. Maybe you can call the police about whoever called your daughter and said those things. But she's dead. Naomi is no more.*

"You're from that picture?" Laury teased.

"Carthage, Virginia. Down near the mountains."

"How come the lady who lives here drew a picture of where you're from?"

"She used to live there, too."

"It looks pretty," Laury said, walking over to look at the mountains and trees in the picture. "There's a church and everything. Daddy, how come you don't talk to your family?"

"Well, it's just the way life is sometimes."

"Would you want me to never talk to you someday?"

"That depends, Berry. If I treated you as if you didn't deserve my attention, then, I would think you'd be smart to avoid me. Or if I acted as if you being honest and fair with me was evil and wrong, then I wouldn't be surprised if we didn't hang out like we do now. But I'll never be like that, sweetie. Not ever."

"Good. But someday I want to see your home, Daddy. It looks so different from here. In this picture."

"Yeah. It's a nice picture, isn't it?"

Laury nodded. "She's in the picture."

"Laury?"

Laury turned back and beamed a smile as if she'd just discovered a great big secret. "The lady who lives here. She went to the picture to rest. That's why she's away."

Jake glanced at his watch. It was only six-thirty.

She's not dead. She's not dead. It throbbed in his mind like a migraine about to erupt. *She's calling my daughter. She's here in this apartment. Something's going on. She's not dead. She is not. What you're thinking is completely irrational, but are you really going to lie to yourself and stay up all night staring at the walls wondering about these phone calls to your ex-wife and daughter and the woman you saw in the subway and everything in your heart that tells you she's still alive?*

It took him less than ten minutes to make up his mind.

By then, he was set.

"Berry, want to go back to Mommy a day early?"

His daughter's eyes went wide. "No! You promised the whole weekend to me. Saturday and Sunday. The whole thing. You promised."

"All right. You're right. I did promise. I won't break it. But . . . want to go somewhere?"

"I love going places! Where?"

"Virginia."

"Where you grew up?"

"Yep."

"Yeah!"

"Tonight?"

"Is it far?"

"We can drive. You can sleep on the way down. We'll get a motel."

"With a swimming pool?"

"Sure."

"Won't Mommy worry?"

"We'll be back by tomorrow night. She won't even notice we're gone. We'll call her."

"Daddy," Laury said as if he were trying to pull her leg. "You don't own a car."

"I'll borrow one."

"Well," she said as if seriously considering this madness. "Why not?"

8

He kept asking himself that—*Why not?*—for the next hour while he finagled with his friend Kate from his Internet company for the use of her Toyota Camry. He promised to check the tires and to be careful with it, but he pressed on: It was an emergency in his mind—perhaps only a psychological emergency, but a drive out of the city would be good, and he'd be there in several hours (*Eight? Nine?* He had forgotten how far it might be) if he drove fast but safe. If luck were on his side.

A gallon of coffee would help, and maybe some potato chips and Skittles for the road.

And a little faith that things could turn out right. That maybe this would become the best thing he ever did.

All he wanted to do was visit her grave.

It seemed crazy.

But he had to.

He knew he would not be able to sleep another night until he saw the grave with the name Naomi Faulkner on it.

9

Too drunk to even wobble home, Maddy got six beers down her gullet and decided to spend the night in the house.

The minions of Hell (workmen, cops, fundamentalists protesting the Wiccans, Wiccans protesting past injustice, police trying to keep a little order, and other assorted Manhattanites) had finally moved on for the night. Maddy was feeling cynical toward the world: Like a dead dog's fleas, she thought, they'd scuttled and hopped off down the road when the TV cameras were gone and the dinner hour had passed.

"Screw all of youse," Maddy mumbled between sips of one last Bud, as she hopscotched up the stairs, then slid down a few steps, still maintaining a kind of balance. On the second floor of the house, she glanced from room to room and decided to take the parlor with its cozy round rug and pillow rather than risk the empty coldness of the master bedroom. She lay down, head and world spinning around her, and tried not to think of her bank balance or her credit card bills or the fact that when she thought of anything, she owed.

The tears tasted like Budweiser, and she kept pressing them from her eyes until her eyelids finally shut fast, and she knew she was falling asleep because suddenly none of it bothered her anymore.

A noise awoke her a few hours later, in the pitch-black of a house with no light. The sound grew louder—a wail, as if a child were calling out to its mother—

Maddy managed to stand, the room still spinning, and at the parlor window, she saw something she couldn't quite identify at first.

In the garden of holes, a woman stood in the muddy water nearly glowing as if someone had smashed fireflies along her skin and face.

Fire burned where her heart should've been.

Where her eyes should have been was a blue flickering, like fire, as well.

And where her mouth should have been were lips sewn together.

This phantom held up her arms as if in supplication—

The woman had no hands.

Jake's ex-wife, Amy, never liked to let go of Laury, never enjoyed watching Jake take her away for the entire weekend—perhaps it had gotten worse for her since she'd become pregnant again, perhaps she harbored some regret about not remaining with Jake. . . . *No, don't think that. That's foolish. What's done is done.*

She had spent the day half in and half out of the drizzle of rain, doing the boring errands she saved for Saturdays, especially those weekends when Daniel worked. She read some of her favorites, particularly the new Elizabeth Peters book, and then she took a nap, which was fatal since it would mean that she'd be up all night wondering what Laury and Jake had been doing.

By early evening, with two phone calls from Daniel telling her that he had still more papers to go over before Monday, and feeling truly bored as she watched the lights of the city blink and Central Park fade to shadows, she turned on the television and caught the tail end of a *Simpsons* rerun.

Flicking around the channels, she caught the local news, and it was full of fires in Jersey, a brief story on an animal shelter with adorable puppies, and right about the time she developed a craving for Ben & Jerry's Cherry Garcia ice cream and wondered if it was ridiculously lazy to call for it to be delivered, a story came on the local news that grabbed her interest.

She turned up the volume on her Sony Trinitron. A reporter was interviewing a woman with flaming red hair and a determined and even cruel look.

"I'll tell you what I think. I think it's crazy. My family has owned this property for decades and now you and your camera crews stomp around like it's a public park—and look at what's happened—the flowers are all killed, the water is pouring into the street. Get your—" And here, a bleep came up like a hiccup and then another and another. The camera panned to words painted on the far wall of the house, THOU SHALT NOT SUFFER A WITCH TO LIVE—police tape all around the front of the town house . . . Then a shot of the street with the cops and various onlookers . . . the crowd overwhelmed the camera.

Finally, the camera cut back to the newsroom where the reporter sat—an attractive blonde with pink lips in a blue power suit—across from the anchorman with his slicked hair and slick smile. She said, "As you can see, not everyone is 'bewitched' by this new discovery in Greenwich Village that witch trials happened right here in our backyard."

The anchor laughed. "And I guess that's one home owner who must feel like it's more a witch's curse than a blessing."

"Well," said the reporter, "city police officers and local Wiccan groups are doing what they can to protect the site, but vandals are definitely getting over the barricade at night and grabbing souvenirs."

Amy switched to a different channel, and felt

something that might've been her baby kicking inside her.

But it's too soon. It's your imagination.

When the phone rang, it was Daniel. He would be home in a half hour and he'd pick up the Cherry Garcia ice cream and maybe a movie at Blockbuster. Amy hung up the phone and looked at the pictures on the wall of Daniel as a boy. When the phone rang again (Daniel always seemed to ring twice whenever he called from work. The first time was to say he was coming home and would be there soon. The second was to say, "Baby, I've got another twenty minutes of work. I'll be there in an hour.") Before he could say anything, she volunteered, "I know, I know. An hour. Just make sure you bring a lot of ice cream."

But it wasn't Daniel on the line.

It was that woman.

That woman.

"He's taken her," she whispered.

"Leave me alone," Amy said, about to throw down the phone. But something began boiling within her blood. She wanted to tell this woman off. "And if you call my house again, I'm going to file a harassment report."

"He's taken your child. He's left the city. He will never return with her again. She's his. And soon," the woman said too calmly, "she will be mine."

Chapter Twenty-five

Carthage

1

He smelled it all the way out of New York: the rain.

Like it was pushing him toward something.

Jake had already begun to wonder if this were not some lunacy of his to drag his daughter down for a quick twenty- to thirty-hour round-trip just to see a little piece of land in the middle of a country nowhere. Their first meal on the road was at a Roy Rogers just before they hit the Delaware line.

Laury had never heard of Roy Rogers—the cowboy actor or the franchise—and easily devoured a burger and fries. She noticed all the signs on the road, and pointed them out to him,

238

until, hypnotized by the comfort of oncoming night, she began to quiet down.

Jake felt all right for the first four hours. He managed to keep his speed upwards of seventy miles per hour without a glimpse of cops. The car made funny noises, and he prayed it would not break down on him. Interstate 95 was slick with the day's rain all the way to Baltimore, and then in Washington, D.C., it was humid but the rain had been held back. Laury fell asleep, strapped in tight in the backseat, leaning against a pillow. He glanced in the rearview mirror now and then to see her face go in and out of shadow beneath the intermittent glaring lights along the interstate. Sometimes he looked in the rearview mirror, feeling as if someone were following him. Now and then, he'd see a car and wonder if he had seen it before.

You're crazy to get paranoid about this.
Ghosts. Ha.

Hours had passed. Night crossed over to late night and then early morning in darkness. From the road, it all looked the same. Smudge of light against smudge of shadow; trucks with headlights that nearly hurt to see in the mirror; the unreality of sitting in a metal box with windows, moving at sixty to seventy miles per hour over the earth.

Jake laughed when he saw a family of six in a prehistoric station wagon, all looking tense and unhappy on some trip, no doubt, to see more family, or returning from a vacation of discontent.

Virginia loomed. At least the mountains did—they were massive sleeping giants. It was a big gray-purple sheet curling gently in the night wind, shades of mist along the hills as he got on 81, stopping for more coffee for himself and an occasional juice or milk for his daughter. He stretched at the gas stations, and fearing that Virginia would bring out his worst feelings, he inhaled the air like cigarette smoke, wanting to take a big lungful in to help overcome his revulsion at having to return to Carthage. Bought a flashlight; bought a map just in case his memory would fail him; bought some Wrigley's Spearmint and Lifesavers; told the gas station attendant that people were still friendly in Virginia and wasn't that nice.

Then, back in the car. Back down the dark highway, ducking between trucks and the mountains and the feelings that threatened him. His mind was the battlefield, for he'd been good and compartmentalizing it all. The past had been past. The present was now. The future was what he worked for.

But now, the past was the future. The past was up ahead.

Please, let it be different. Please let Quik-E-Marts and 7-Elevens and Super A&Ps and Wal-Marts and Barnes & Nobles and Borders and Kmarts and Holiday Inn Expresses and Taco Bells and McDonalds and Blockbusters and Pier One Imports and Home Depots have paved over the dead past of Carthage. Please, let it be unre-

cognizable. Let it look like every other gas station stop off the main roads, let it not have that genteel charm of the living dead, let it not remind me of what I've remembered to forget . . . Let the accents have sped up, let the cherished traditions have fallen like ancient idols, let the spirit of mud and asphalt and the vesuvial eruption and flow of time have buried the wooden and the brick and the colonial. Let the two churches be foundations surrounded by swamp and let those who thrive be from other lands or—better—let the wasps and mosquitoes be memory eaters. Let nothing survive of what was. O, hear my prayer. For all whosoever have left the place that worked so hard to twist their souls and bodies and make them bow before chaotic minds, and whosoever has lifted up a battered spirit against the whole of them and carried her out of their sanctuary of hypocrisy into the misty light of Sunday mornings across time, and told her that whatever was past, was past, and whatever they had convinced her of was wrong—and more than wrong, evil in a way that most human beings cannot possibly be evil— whomsoever remembers those moments of redemption, let the god of that person have bulldozed like judgment and flattened the field of what was.

He laughed at his heartless thoughts. He felt cold inside when he saw the sign for the turnoff to Carthage. He crossed the narrow bridge over the railroad tracks, and stopped at the blinking yellow traffic light that hung on the gallows between two worlds: the world he had chosen, and the world he had come from.

Laury awoke crying. She was tired of the car ride, and she was ready for a motel room.

"Just a drive into town, and then we'll get over to Lexington to spend the night," he said, but this meant very little to her. Laury complained all the way through the potholed streets; she whined under her breath as he pointed out the house he'd been born in; and she quieted again when he came to the church, or what was left of it. It stood against his wishes, but it was in disrepair. Its planks were warped, and it was smaller than he had remembered. It needed paint.

The headlights brought a revelation: It was an ugly church.

He glanced in the backseat. Laury had fallen asleep again, too weary even to complain further. He parked by the church, grabbing his new toy—the flashlight—and got out in the darkness. There were no twinkling porch lights in Carthage, nor were there lights upon the mountainside. The moon and stars provided a shine like tinsel across the land, and he took in what he'd just passed through.

Carthage had not changed. The houses had not been destroyed or rebuilt. The streets had not shifted. It was Jake who had been destroyed and rebuilt and shifted and twisted and then unknotted. He had somehow survived it.

Roses were blooming.

A blood-red rose with thorns, someone whispered within his mind.

His prayers for a quicksand black hole beneath the town had not been answered.

2

Living in New York so long, he would not generally leave his daughter's side, even for a few seconds; but in this predawn town—for, yes, the hour pressed close to the next morning and the blue aura to the east meant that it would only be another hour or two—she was safe. "Safe as kittens," his mother would say. "Safe as Jesus's sheep," she'd say. "Safe as a lie in a boy's mouth," she'd say.

He left Laury sleeping in the car, all wrapped up in a blanket, and went over to the entrance to the small graveyard behind the church. He pushed at the wrought-iron gate. It squealed as it swung shut behind him. He glanced back at the Camry. She was safe there. He'd only be a minute. Then, they'd get a motel room and then, after sleep, they'd drive back up.

3

He wandered the graves, his flashlight's beam grazing the headstones and markers. Names he thought he had forgotten all came back to him, and with them, faces. McCormick, True, Campbell, Jackson, Sanford, Wilmot, Ownby . . . the names brought brief remembrances of his school friends and their families. . . . When he found the one he'd been looking for, he almost was ready to remember everything. Beneath a willow, a gorgeous marker, which surprised him, a marker that looked as if it had been bought for many thousands of dollars by an old man who had at last realized his sins. When Jake arrived at it, he fell to his knees and put his hands to the engraving because he did not believe yet that she could possibly be dead.

Naomi Faulkner
Beloved Daughter
Sister
"Though the lamb may stray, it shall at last
be called home by the Shepherd."

Jake reached into the earth as if feeling it would bring him closer to her. He lay down on a slope of moss, shining the flashlight on the words and the flat stone as if he could make it somehow reveal what he'd been wondering.

And, falling asleep there, he knew what he had been wondering all along.

How had she survived this awful place?

How had she survived Carthage and not survived a subway train?

4

The dream came like a night crawler in his brain, which he resisted because somehow he knew he needed to go get his daughter in the car and find a motel.

But then, he was in the car with Laury, and they were pulling into the Econolodge off the highway, checking in to Room 13, and Laury was already in the small cot at the foot of the bed, and he was already in the bathroom washing his face.

Oh, but this is a dream, he thought, *I need to*

*wake up because I'm really just lying down by a
grave early in the morning.*

But it was no dream at all, and he hadn't
grown up. He was still a boy in love with a girl
in a town that believed that all family secrets
were shameful, and all of nature was to be held
in the grip of those who could not live comfort-
ably in their human skins.

And there she was, weeping, running to him
in a way he had not anticipated. Her force made
him fall to the ground, for she was more than
her slender body, she was a tower of grief. He
held her tight while she confessed as if she were
in church, that church he had come to think of
as evil, as destructive, as insane, for country
people though they were, he knew that it was
not like other churches.

He knew children in school who laughed
about it, who told him his mother was insane
to go there, he heard some grownups from
other places whisper about it, about those people, about what they did.

And how could the dreaming Jake even understand this place, where he had come from,
what it had meant?

Even in the valley, Carthage had been considered backward, and a little scary. It had belonged to the previous century in many ways.
Its religion was old-time, its conservatism was
extreme, it believed that outsiders were immoral, it believed that salvation was more important than survival, it believed in things that
were not in *Time* magazine or on television or

in book excerpts when backwaters were given notice.

The Jake of New York had never even spoke of the Jake of Carthage, and of *those people*, and that man. He knew it was a place that sounded unreal even on the tongue.

But there, in the dream, he was holding Naomi as she invoked the secrets of the place.

And when it was all out of her, he was not as surprised as he knew he should've been. When he saw the bites on her arms, how they had healed. He could not believe what her father had put her through, what he had done to her.

The snakes.

It was her purity, that was why she wept. It was gone.

"No," he told her. "You still have it."

"I want it gone," she sobbed. "I want to be corrupt and evil and all the things he can't be."

And yes, Jake in dream memory admitted to himself.

Yes, you know he raped her.

Yes, you know he impregnated her.

Her own father.

Yes, you know she is just a girl, a child still, a child who has no way to live.

Yes, you know all the things that happen to young girls who are brutalized in a world of men without conscience.

But the snakes.

The church.

The way he used her purity; the way he used her body.

But this is a dream, my boy. You're not a young

teenager. *You're not even holding her, you're lying on her grave. She's dead and gone, and this phantom is here to remind you of what you escaped.*

"Please," she whispered, her tears against his cheek. "I need to kill myself. I need to just be gone. I need to not be here on earth anymore. Help me. Help me do it," she said, and the anger rose in him. It rose that any man should do this, that a man should lay with his daughter, that any man should destroy her with words of gods that pretended to do good but were demons from the caves of hell.

You are going to open that church and let the light of what really happened in, you are going to rape that man with the truth, you are going to lay those same snakes from the cages down upon him until their bites prove that his god is the god of dark places.

You are going to avenge this girl whom you love with all your heart and if they get you—

They will try—

If they get you, then you will have done one good thing in your life and maybe that's it. They already think you're a thief. They already think you're a liar. What will this hurt?

He carried her back to the church, hearing the rattling of tongues and the swords of the Holy Spirit smiting the congregation. He laid her upon the steps and opened the great arched door.

The rows were half filled with the ignorant of Carthage, and these included his own mother. Hands raised, calling their god (*it's not God. It can't be. God would not be like this. God never has been like this*) into them. A woman in a flow-ered dress stood by Naomi's father, both a doc-tor and a preacher, a man of science and god and darkness, and in the woman's hands, the snakes of redemption.

"The serpent!" her father shouted. "He comes to sting, but Death has got no sting! Satan can't hurt the righteous! Only you who have let Sin into your lives will feel the sting of the serpent!" His voice was a string of nothing, all echoing nothing, crashing against a shore of human nothing.

Jake ran to the front of them, and opened the cages before they could stop him, and dumped the snakes onto the floor and pointed at Na-omi's father. Jake opened his mouth wide to let the truth erupt, and the words all came to him. . . .

Blood-red rose with thorns, someone whis-pered, and he saw Naomi's arms scratched up, and the petals on her lap, and he knew what he had always known but had not faced: She had tried to kill herself more than once in her life.

In the dream of what had been, silence poured from his lips as he watched the snakes move like overflow of muddy water across the ankles of the people in the church. When Jake looked up, he saw the face of Jesus painted on the wall, and Jesus looked so sad and Jake knew, even in the dream, that whatever he did, the serpents were already loose in this land.

The words appeared like a cloud of wasps in the air: THE SERPENT IS LOOSE.

The words became the hills, and the wasps faded into a crisp blue sky.

Truth or lie, Carthage was not for him and never would be.

5

Jake awoke to sharp sunlight.

Laury stood over him, looking sleepy. "Daddy? I need a bed." She yawned out the words.

6

Jake's Journal

It was not yet 6:00 A.M. when Laury woke me. I'd slept on the earth of Naomi's grave for an hour, forgetting my daughter, bad father that I am, forgetting my responsibilities, all for an awful dream-memory.

My daughter and I slept that morning in a Motel 81 out by the interstate, in two small dusty beds that could not have been used since the last World War. When I awoke, I called Amy and left three messages on her machine saying that we'd taken a quick trip south, so I'd bring Laury back bright and early Monday morning. I awoke six hours later, feeling better rested than I had in my entire life. Laury slept like an angel—one that snores—until the early afternoon. After a breakfast at the local ham-biscuit dive, we drove the few miles back to Carthage, and I showed her the house in which I'd been born. I told her that people in towns like this one believed in things people in other places didn't believe. I even told her about the snakes, the poison, and all the sights she'd never seen in the Episcopal church in Manhattan that she and my wife attended. Then, without thinking, I turned down the wrong road and there, at the end of a cul-de-sac, stood the house in which Naomi had grown up.

It was ugly. Your basic rich man's home in a rural town. The newly painted exterior couldn't hide its humble beginnings as an eighteenth-century farmhouse in which the farm had become the town itself. Naomi's family had been there the very morning of the birth of Carthage. How many times had I gone to that house to set it on fire, knowing what I knew? The fear Naomi's father had always held was that the communists were going to bomb little Carthage to Kingdom Come. His bomb shelter in the back, which led into the narrow, twisting caves—the Treasure Cave—in the foothills was my only indication of the extent of his fear.

How I wanted to chase that man back into those caves until he no longer lived in the light of day.

I can write now all the things he did. What I knew.

He was a man of great learning. He had gone to the University (in a town like Carthage, where four out of every hundred men had attended college, this was impressive); he had received his medical degree from a small school somewhere to the south of the South. He had found Jesus in an uncle's church in West Virginia. He had forsaken medicine in favor of preaching. He had, like much of his family, begun to practice the test of faith through snake holding. The snakes had bitten him but he had not been hurt, although he had a swollen arm after that. When I knew him, he had been powerfully built, and even handsome for a man his age, although his teeth were always bad, and his eyes seemed yellow to me. His first wife, according to Naomi, who was her daughter, had been warm and loving and had balanced him in some way. But it was not enough—she had died under her husband's care when Naomi was six, and no one spoke openly about it, but those who knew felt that her husband had subjected her to the snakes. His second wife was a vicious little dog, a woman from a clan in the hills, who snapped at his heels as he slammed his god and his snakes into people. He had a son as well as two daughters, and the son stole things from people—although all anyone knew for sure was that he'd stolen the old man's prized trophy from his high school years, a marker of some championship. The son was disowned at that moment and left Carthage in the night. I suppose all of Faulkner's children left him in the night. When Naomi's brother committed suicide in a stolen Camaro in Richmond, a plastic bag wrapped around his neck, no one in Carthage was all that surprised.

Faulkner was the source of all that had been bad in this place.

As I sat in the car, engine idling, my daughter

sipping from a bottle of Evian in the backseat, I knew I could not leave Carthage without seeing that man.

We got out and walked up the steps. It was Sunday, so on some level I didn't believe he'd be home, but in that church.

However, I'd forgotten about time.

He had been an old man even then, when I was a child. He had been nearly sixty when I was fifteen, and he had, he told me when he met me at the tattered screen door, given up the ministry several years before.

In his seventies now, he looked like a man who had already died, both physically and spiritually. It made me happy, and this feeling was accompanied by a small measure of guilt. When a tragedy is staring you in the face, it's hard to hate it. Pity and distance are the only feelings.

He told me that I was not welcome there, and that I should leave. I wanted to say many things to him, but I already saw a mark of death upon him. He was dying. Some disease was eating at him. I hoped it would be painful. I guess if there's a hell, I'll go to it for thinking that. Part of me feels that everything we do has a price, and we always pay. Now, it was his time to pay. But I said nothing to him.

I turned and got back into the car with my daughter, and we left Carthage. We arrived back in New York late at night, Laury half-asleep and cranky and as pissed-off as only a little girl can be for having to use gas station bathrooms all day long. I guess it shouldn't have surprised me that I found Amy sitting inside my apartment with Daniel, the door open. Amy had gotten into my apartment with the spare key I'd left for Laury. I guess I deserved everything she screamed at me and all the crying—Daniel shaking his head slightly as if I should've told them all about the trip before I took it upon myself to, in his words, "kidnap your daughter." The words came like tongues of fire from Amy's lips, "that woman," "threatening phone calls," "you could've told me where," "custody doesn't have to be this easy," "who the hell do you think you are."

I was too tired to fight.

Amy told me that she would've called the police if Daniel hadn't calmed her down. Laury began crying and stomping her feet; I left my own apartment, door wide open. I went across the hall to Naomi's, to feed the cat while Amy followed me in, still shouting as if she had so much shout within her that needed to escape.

"Jake, who lives here?" she asked, and suddenly for the first time in fifteen minutes, she was quiet.

I turned back to her from the kitchen counter to see what had captured her attention.

There, across the painted wall of Carthage, someone had used bright red paint: JAKE, THE SERPENT IS LOOSE. NAOMI.

Moments later, I walked out into the night, into the Village, and now I wanted Naomi more than I had ever wanted her.

There might be a grave; there might even be

a conspiracy; there might be anything.

I was nearly convinced that Alan Cowper must have written those words, and I would not rest that night until I found him.

Chapter Twenty-six

Behold, the Serpent

1

Romeo gathered what he could of the secrets, living on the slugs and rats and moldy bread as he always had. The Serpent was there—he could feel it—but Romeo had been raised with serpents and had their smell. He could follow scents for miles, and had been surviving with these skills for as long as he could remember, for he had lived much of his life in darkness. Sound and smell were his vision. He was not one to shy away from wormholes, and his scrawny body could pass through pipes that nearly flooded. He knew fear differently than people in the Above.

But when he glimpsed the Forbidden City, he

thought that perhaps he had already died some-where, in some dark tunnel.

They had all seen the edges of the Forbidden City, as the tunnels that ran beneath the city hooked and fell. The City had been built upon village, and village upon village, and village upon swampy cavernous rock and thick woods—and sometimes it seemed as if all that was beneath was the purest reflection of what was above.

The smell of gas was the first warning of the Forbidden City—not the gas of the city or of exhaust, but the gas of the dead. Even the rats, when dying, went to the great nestlike chambers that looked as if they were the lowest level of the Below. The people who lived Below, too, took their dead to what was only the gateway to the Forbidden City, as if they knew that a cat-acomb was the only way to keep the Serpent satisfied and in its cage. To get down to the City, he had to dig first through the small animal bones, and then, as the bones grew, into the sea of bones, some still wet, some still with the hu-man meat upon them, and still he swam down through them.

The gas layered what little air he could breathe, but he held the secrets in his pouch.

They would protect him and become the keys to the Forbidden City.

This was not a journey that happened easily. Scabber had prepared him for many years to make this journey. Perhaps his birth had pre-pared him. Certainly, the time he'd been caught and sent to the foster home when he'd been twelve had destroyed something for him—it had created a need for light and sun that he had never before desired. But that had only lasted a few months, in the hellish world called Connecticut, before he had managed to get back to his beloved dark beneath.

The bones and flesh of the dead sea gave way to more wormholes, which he squeezed through, wondering how Scabber had ever come back once her legs had been destroyed.

And then, the wormholes gave away to tunnels—and light. It was a light of blue mist, and a strong, retching gas smell.

The gas of rotting bodies.

The light of their energy.

Soon, he could nearly stand in the tunnels. The spaces widened until their archways seemed to be as tall as the buildings of the Above. Packed rock gave way to mud. Romeo had heard of hell from Scabber. He wondered if this could be it.

A great wall of human skulls arose against clashes of mist and gas. It towered above him, with flows of clouds and yellowing veils of smoke.

But Scabber had told him of this, not of the wall, but of the gas, and how it played tricks with the mind, how what seemed to be was only a vision.

He tried to see through this vision, but could not.

Figures like women but with great wings dropped like eagles from the air, their talons outstretched, but then they shimmered into blue mist; the skull wall became a brilliant and flashing gold like a great cathedral. He saw faces in the wall, their mouths opening in silent cries. The gas was suffocating, and he brought out the small shriveled secret that would be one of the keys, and pressed it to his lips. He felt pressure as if he were underwater, and his ears began popping. His breath returned.

The vision of the Forbidden City broke apart for an instant, and Romeo sensed that the Serpent was there, with him, in a small, dark tunnel rather than in an enormous cathedral of Hell. A field of some crop arose—but no, they were scarecrows of the most infernal kind. He saw they were human beings crucified, six or seven deep and twenty across. The sky brightened a sulfurous yellow. An enormous disk burned orange behind the battlements, and Romeo knew that this was all a trick of the Serpent's. Still, he began shivering with fear as he heard someone calling his name with his true mother's voice.

He was no longer in the Below.

He was in the dream of the Serpent.

A rain of blood began. At first, in small drips and drops as the sky above clouded and mixed in reds and blues and grays. And then, it was a downpour. He found himself moving toward the great wall, among the dying on their crosses, as blue lightning flickered across the bleeding sky.

Maddy drank coffee for four hours after coming down off her Budweiser-induced high, and when dawn broke, she sat up and stared out at the back garden of the Rose Street house. She had seen a woman. She was sure of it. It had not been a shadow, it had not been a hallucination. She jittered with the caffeine, and finally fell asleep on the floor by the stairway— waking up to the sound of more protesters outside the door as the day progressed.

She dragged herself home, fed her pets, and then went to the one thing that she was sure would give her answers to what she was feeling.

The diary.

Maddy opened it and skimmed several pages. She knew that there was something more there. Some answer. She was sure that the woman she had seen, fire where her hands, eyes, and heart would've been was this N. Cross, this Naomi of hundreds of years before. Something deep within Maddy's own heart beat faster, and she realized: *I am on a great adventure. Me. I am on it. I am not worried about my bills or whether I had too many beers or even my baby (my child, my lost child, please don't hate me for forgetting you all these years since you died), but something more than the lousy total of my life with all its balance sheets and fears of future security.*

She felt it.

She wanted to know.

She believed in ghosts.

Diary of a Witch

. . . So it has come to this. My child will not be born, ever. The man who professes to be a witness to God's Wrath has stopped up my mouth with his evil.

I am to die in my eighth month, hanged for the crime of witchcraft on Greenwich Plantation. Hanged with others so that he—that Devil in man's form—may triumph on this terrible earth. I remember what the vision of the deity said to me the first night I saw him at the sabbat. He told me that either I or my child must die in sacrifice. Now, we both will die. My son within me will hang as I will hang.

It is all James Cotton. It is all his wicked evil. What he has done to me is beyond evil. He does not know that my sisters taught me well the art of words and writing. He does not know about this book of spells and memories. He believes the only tongue is within the jaw. This book will be my truth. It will live long after my child and I have gone to the promised place, or are reborn into new life.

I have been in this prison for six weeks. I have feared I was near death at times with the torture, but Goody Carrier has given me herbs to dull the pain. I barely remember when he forced the pincers into my mouth. I cannot recall the touch of the knife.

A tongue in one's mouth is not important when one is to die.

Goody Carrier told me that the pain was a sign that I was alive, and to not let it worry me but to allow it to dance within my mouth. The blood, she said, is our juice like a sweet ripe pomegranate bursting before we are reborn. The gallows, she told me, holding me as if I were her child, is our necklace of gold so that when we cross over into the next world, we shall be beautifully adorned.

The belief is yet weak in me, but the sisters have proven their powers with their healing arts and with the nights we spent flying above the island, across the land, into the wilderness, even while held in chains in gaol.

And my child? I ask with my mind. What of my child?

Blessed, they tell me, for my son will be a prince, and will grow strong to defeat the ignorance of the world. My witch-friends tell me I must not pray ill toward Cotton, the father of my child and the destroyer of his life. But I cannot. I cannot forgive the evil man who has brought me to this fate. My sisters tell me there is no evil but what is thought. They tell me that even the minister and his injustice is part of a larger plan, and to wish him evil is to bring the wish back thricefold. But I cannot be as kind as they. I know his darkness.

. . . oh gods and goddesses, my child is to be born. I keep him inside me. I lock my legs together, but he insists. He must not be born. I would rather he die within my womb than he meet the fate that life surely has in store for him.

For I see what that man means to do. I know what he intends. He is a serpent disguised as a minister. He is the evil that he himself sees in others.

He will bury my child alive with the remains of my body. He will put the boy screaming in the grave, in my arms.

By all my wisdom of night and the secrets, may my child not suffer long! Hear my call, oh sisters who surround us. Hear my plea, oh brothers of the woods.

I must not let the child live. I must not!

Forgive me, creators, for what I must do, for if I can change the destiny I see in my mind, not for myself, but for my child, then I will go to my own death with the smile of a martyr and not the cry of a demon. . . .

I know one day he will read this. James Cotton will find my diary. He will intend to throw it into the fire. But he will hesitate. He will open it and read of all the witches and of his child with me.

James Cotton, this is for you.

I am truly a witch, Reverend Cotton. And now, for what you have done to me, to our child, and to those who I call beloved in our faith, I curse you for eternity. Here is my curse, and have I witch power then you shall fear the night and the wings of the bat and the cat in the darkness and all winds that blow unnaturally warm on wintry evenings and all water that turns to blood in your hand.

Ye will not die, James Cotton, but shall live forever, a cursed thing of the dark passages of the earth, the very image of what you yourself believe is the Devil. You will create your own Hell, a place that would not exist without your mind. You shall be your own nightmare. A serpent to be trod beneath the feet of the world, and your days shall be chained in dark misery. By my tongue, which thou hast torn from my throat, I curse you. By my hands, which you have pressed into numb obedience, I lay the destiny upon you! With my eyes, which you claimed bewitched you with the magic of the Fiend, I will see you chained in your own darkness. By my heart, which you held in your hands and lied most wickedly against, will beat your torment until the Day of Judgment! Ye have burned our Forbidden Wood, but there is a Forbidden City arising this day, the day of my death, born beneath this earth, and in it ye shall dwell as a worm, and all shall know ye as devourer and serpent and as the most cursed man under all of the gods' creations!

Your Devil take ye, James Cotton!

Naomi Cross, witch, mother, and guardian of Cotton's damned soul. Forgive me, my son, for what I have allowed them to do to you before ever you breathed the air.

4

Maddy had tears in her eyes, and almost closed the diary, until she noticed that beyond the blank pages, someone had scrawled something in a completely different hand, using ink as red as blood:

263

With thine own blood I write this, Naomi Cross, witch and devil worshipper. I have read your Book of Evil, witch. I see your devil has taught you the art of writing in exchange for your soul. Let me tell you of your last day. Our son I lifted into the cold air and let him breathe but few breaths before I placed him beside you in your grave. Even the grave diggers would not abide with me as they lowered you and your Vile Sisters into the mud and rot at the edge of the ash of what is left of the Devil's Wood. Naomi Cross, you will burn in Hell, and if your eyes and hands and heart are the devil's instruments, then just as I have taken your tongue so as to silence you, so I shall take them from you. I live, Naomi. I live, and today I have watched you hang by the neck until dead. You and your bastard lie beneath unhallowed ground, and your souls burn in Hell. I place this book of the Devil and these papers within the holy font to entomb thy Evil Spirit and Power forever. The head shall be torn from the body just as the witch must be separated from the soul.

5

Maddy slammed the diary shut; dust came off in her hands. "How could he? That damn psychopath!"

Then, she got on the phone to Andreas Harris.

It wasn't until Sunday night when they finally met at the Rose Street house, after the protesters and the gawkers all moved on to their dinners and gatherings. Harris looked as nervous as a mink on a farm. She could tell that he still had that hungry greed for all things that would bring him fame and wealth and some sad degree of museum-quality immortality.

She had him by the balls.

"After your rudeness of the other day," he began, but she cut him off.

"Just shut up for a goddamn minute and listen up," Maddy said. "All right. I have what you want, and you have what I want. I'm no longer in it for the money. I'm no longer in it for the house. I'm in it because I think the witch is still here. You give me what I want, I give you and your museum this house and property free and clear, maybe as a tax deduction for me."

Andreas mumbled something, and then scratched at the back of his neck as if he felt a prickly heat. "And what is it you want from me, Ms. Sparke?"

And then, she told him.

Chapter Twenty-seven

Secrets Revealed

1

Jake's Journal

I found Alan Cowper—I practically rammed the door of his apartment down, I was so keyed up. Cowper's place was less than lavish, but still looked like a Hollywood version of a Manhattan apartment—at least to someone like me, who was used to tiny bedrooms and kitchenettes. Cowper's place made Amy and Daniel's Upper East Side flat seem small; his view of the Hudson River was all deep blues and sparkling lights. I suppose I should've called him first, but I knew that late on a Sunday night, he would not feel it very important to go out and rehash what he already knew about Naomi. But I needed more.

I gathered he had a houseguest that night—a woman—and I could not blame him for needing companionship, but somehow I felt this was unfaithful to Naomi's memory. She had only been gone since December. He had loved her. It seemed too soon for him to be sleeping with other women. It seemed wrong—but then, what did I know? I was a kid who went to a friggin' snake church in ass-backward boondockville. I almost laughed at myself for barging into his life.

"I want to know everything. And now," I told him after he'd put on his shorts and met me at the door.

"This can wait," he said. "Whatever it is. This can wait. It's late. You look exhausted. Surely this can wait." But somehow, he knew that it could not.

"I want to know what she never told me. I want to know what you know."

He nodded. "Wait downstairs. I'll be down in a few minutes. We'll get a drink. Christ, I wasn't going to be able to sleep anyway."

2

They ended up at the Gaslight, a legendary watering hole that was still packed even after midnight, found a corner table, ordered drinks. Alan lit up a cigarette almost immediately. "I haven't been sleeping well. I keep thinking of her. Her face. I see it in my mind. All the time."

"And your woman friend?" Jake asked, pouring the Rolling Rock into his glass. His face was pale; his eyes were encircled with weariness.

Alan Cowper cocked his head to the side, blowing smoke across the table. "I think of her. I still like sex sometimes, Jake. You should try it. Mourning can only go on so long. So, what can I add to what you already know?"

"Why did she spy on me?"

"She didn't. She wanted to know how you were. That's all, Jake. Nothing more." Alan paused, glancing at the other drinkers at nearby tables. A puff of smoke from between his lips. "What's happened? I doubt you'd drag me out of my bed just to hang out and make chit-chat."

"She's not dead."

Alan glared at Jake. "Of course she is. Christ, you brought me out here on a Sunday night to—"

"Someone else died in that subway station."

"Her grave is in Virginia."

"I was there. Today. She's not dead."

Alan inhaled the cigarette as if he were sucking on candy. Smoke poured from his nostrils a moment later. "She is."

"Did you see the body?"

Alan Cowper grinned. "If you're asking, did I see her pretty face and perfect teeth and beautiful eyes, then I assume you must not understand what happens when a train that weighs several tons comes down on a woman."

"You don't know if it was her. Not really."

"A suicide note. Her handbag. Her clothes.

Her shoes. We're not talking mistaken identity, unless some other woman wanted to kill herself and went to the trouble of throwing herself under a train having stolen the clothes off Naomi's back." Alan shook his head. "What is it you want?"

Jake took a breath. He had to say it. Had to. He couldn't keep it in. "I saw her. In the subway."

"You thought you saw her." Alan reached across the table and gave Jake's hand a pat. "You loved her once. So did I. She's gone. Unless, of course, you believe in ghosts."

Jake began to say something, but held back. He sipped his beer.

"You want to know about the child," Alan said, as if the words were heavy.

"You know about—"

"Of course she told me," Alan said, losing his composure. "What do you think, that you were the only man on the planet she ever confided in? That she would keep secrets from me just because you were the only boy she had cared for when she was a girl? Christ. She was right about you."

"Yeah? In what way."

"Your head's so far up your ass you don't even know."

"Thank you. Thank you." Jake nodded, feeling screwed from the moment he'd found out about Naomi's death.

"She lied to you. Yes, your beloved little Miss Perfect. Christ, she told me that's why she couldn't see you again. She didn't want to ruin it."

"What the hell are you talking about."

"She didn't miscarry. The kid wasn't stillborn. Why do you think she killed herself? Christ, you have no insight, do you? You're just Mr. Lovesick hoping that you can find the girl you loved and somehow make this fantasy work."

Jake stood up suddenly. The room spun. Sleeplessness and beer clutched at him. "Shut up! You're screwing with me, you have been this whole time. What lies? What lies?"

"For God's sake, Jake, sit your ass down." Alan Cowper stubbed out his cigarette in his brandy glass. He softened his voice. "About the child. About her father. About all you hold sacred about her."

"They're not lies," Jake said, quietly. "They're not." He sat back down in the chair. He felt tired and stupid and wondered if perhaps he just needed a decent night's sleep.

"It was her brother, not her father. She cared for her brother too much to tell you. Her brother. He killed himself because of it. She blamed her father, I suppose. She blamed him because he had made her out to be a little saint, and the brother wanted to destroy that. Psychologically, it was like a dog pissing on a tree, marking territory in a home where no one had boundaries or kept secrets long. Who could grow up healthy in that family? Christ. And she didn't miscarry. She gave birth, apparently barely showing. She told me she wanted to kill it. She wanted to get rid of it. Her father did something else to the child."

"It wasn't like that. It wasn't like that," Jake said, trying to block out the voice of this awful man. This liar. Jake began laughing, "You're joking. That's all. You're some sick son of a bitch, but you're . . . Jesus, I was there when she . . . she couldn't have had the baby. I was there. Where was it? Tell me that, where was it? Carthage is a small place. You hear a baby crying, the whole town knows. No secrets there."

"Her father raised her son. You yourself know how backward a place Carthage is. When I was there—at the burial—it made me shiver to think of what had gone on in that valley. I saw the church. I saw the people from that place. They're different there, aren't they? You got a long way from that ignorant dark place, Jake. So did Naomi. So did anyone who had half a brain and ten bucks in his pocket. How many ways do you think a man can torture a daughter? Or a grandchild? The entire bomb shelter, the one that led into the caves, with its own generator, with its own survivalist food and furniture and his crosses everywhere, and those caves—where he caught his snakes, where he punished her sometimes, punished all of them—"

While Alan Cowper spoke, it all came to Jake, and he knew it was true. It fit. That was the worst part.

It fit so damn neatly.

Naomi's retreats, her coldness at moments that seemed inappropriate, times when she just

271

wanted him away from her house so fast he had to run—as if she would die if he didn't leave quickly. The rumors in town that something was going on . . .

That cats were yowling, cats that Jake never saw. Naomi would take his hand and draw him away from the yard, taking him to the river, taking him away while he heard the cats yowling, and she'd say, "They get in Daddy's bomb shelter, and they play," or "they get in season, they're too loud, I hate them," and even then, Jake thought it was weird and too secretive—

But it wasn't cats yowling. It was a child crying. It was something so monstrous to keep secret that he didn't want to accept it.

It had all been there in front of his face. Under his nose. All of it. The child had been alive. Naomi had given birth. He had worried that she had killed the child. He had worried that the child might kill her when it was born. She had told him it was stillborn. But he had never really thought . . . never believed that the child had lived. . . .

"It happens, Jake. It's monstrous. A child is raised in shame, away from the eyes of the world. A town like Carthage. A religious fanatic like her father, a man who believes snakebites are salvation, easily could keep a child in a dark and lonely isolation, feeling that the boy was born in the image of the worst kind of sin and only through constant religious training—separate from humanity—could overcome the sin under which he was born."

Jake sat down again.

"The original messed-up family." Alan didn't let up. "Last year, something happened. Something got worse for her. Naomi was terrified that he would come find her. She was sure he already had."

"Her father?"

"No, Jake," Alan Cowper said. "Her son."

3

Jake felt the room spin around him as Alan continued speaking. He barely heard the words—Naomi, her son, the bomb shelter behind the Faulkners' home, the shelter that led into the narrow caves, the shelter in which feral cats lived. That's what Jake had been told, that's what people in town believed. The cats . . . not a baby crying . . . but cats . . . and the snakes her father used in the church . . . all caught in the caves, snakes and cats and darkness . . .

He almost laughed, then, and was about to signal for another beer, but thought it might be best to ask for water instead.

"I'm sure it's not the first time it has happened in the history of the planet. A girl is raped by her beloved brother; she blames her father; convinced you, the boy she loved. Why would it be hard to believe that she'd lie about something so devastating? She delivers a baby without anyone in town knowing the better of it, and the child is raised in some kind of secrecy. In places like our fair city, this is the stuff of a social worker's day. But in Carthage, there are no agencies to monitor how families rot from the inside." Alan nearly smiled. "And her son. She told me she saw him all the time. She saw her brother's face in a boy, she would tell me. She saw him panhandling. She saw him from a cab. She saw her own face in him. I knew it was delusion on her part. I knew that kid had died or run away years ago and would not be coming to New York to find his mother. I tried to talk sense to her. To make her see: How would he even know she was here? What would bring him here if he ran? Surely he'd go to one of a number of small towns there in the Blue Ridge or even as far as Washington, D.C., if he survived by hook or by crook . . . But she had her beliefs. She said that he spoke to her sometimes; she said that he said crazy things. I told her to start seeing a new psychiatrist. I tried to take her myself. But by then . . . by December, it was too late. I should've seen the signs. I guess you can't ever save anyone in this life except yourself."

Tears formed in his eyes. "I know you think I'm a bastard. I guess I am. I guess I tried to control her environment. I thought it would make her better. I thought she needed . . . structure. Christ. She ruined my life. She ruined me. All I think about is her." Then, he began laughing, and even when Jake walked out into the rain, furious with the past and the present, Alan's laughter followed him as he turned the corner and headed for the subway platform where Naomi had met her death.

Jake's Journal

I sat down on a bench in the subway, and fell asleep almost immediately, and yes, I dreamed of her. And yes, I told her I didn't care about the lies, but I wanted to hear it from her. And yes, she lied to me again with all the words she'd used when we were teenagers—even when I had heard the cats yowling and the snakes in a dark pit, and yes, I felt better believing the lie than knowing the truth.

Blood-red rose with thorns. That's what Naomi had been. But she had still been a rose. She had still been everything to me.

It was a dream of affirmation of all the lies I'd swallowed. All for her.

When I awoke, I noticed graffiti on the far wall of the subway tunnel—perhaps it had been there when I'd fallen asleep, perhaps not. The platform was empty, and I felt a chill go through me and a prickly heat at the back of my neck. The words were simple and plain: NAOMI LOVES JAKE TO DEATH.

Sloppily sprayed in red, large enough for me to read. Perhaps it was the hour of day—for it could not have been 4:00 A.M. yet—an invisible but perceptible fog hung in the air of the subway tunnel. I breathed that exhaust-filled dead air, and it was as if a hand held me down on the bench . . . as if a heavy body pressed against me, keeping me from standing.

275

When I finally overcame this feeling—for surely it was something within me, a combination of nerves, beer, and exhaustion—I got up. I walked to the edge of the platform. I read each word, one at a time and said them aloud to make sure I had not made some mistake.

"Naomi loves Jake to death," I whispered.

A wind came up from the tunnel. I glanced down it to see the twin lights of an oncoming train. Dreadlights, I had called them when Naomi and I were kids. We played on railroad tracks, wondering where the trains were headed, who rode them, what their lives must've been like. The dreadlights are coming, I'd tell her and she'd laugh and ask why dread? And I'd tell her because I dreaded them. They meant that people were going places and living lives that I wanted. She said she dreaded them, too.

She told me once she dreaded everything.

The train came into the station, slowing at the platform. Within the train, the lights were on. The train itself was empty. Its doors opened, and something made me catch my breath for an instant. It was a feeling against my back, as if someone were pressing me to get on the train. Of course, it was my imagination. Of course, it was nothing real, but had the platform been crowded, I would've turned and asked the man behind me not to shove.

The feeling passed. The train's doors closed. The train moved on its course. The tunnel was empty again, but for that lone subterranean wind.

And then, I saw her.

It had been a long day for Maddy Sparke, and she had to speak slowly to Harris or he would not understand a word of what he termed her "babbling."

"How many times do I need to say it? There's a ghost in my yard. It's the ghost of the woman who wrote the diary. And the key to why she's haunting me is in that book. He cut off her hands."

"Who?" Andreas Harris nearly laughed. "Whose hands got cut off by what?"

"This man Cotton. She had his child. He was a sociopath. He cut off her hands, cut out her eyes, her heart, and her tongue. He knew her power. He knew it. He buried her child alive with her body. This wasn't just a witch holocaust. This was a serial killer at work. This was a government-sanctioned cold-blooded murder. And we've opened it up."

"And you accept this?"

"Yes," Maddy said. "It's irrational, but it makes nothing other than sense to me."

"Sense?"

"Inside here," Maddy said, pounding her breast with her fist like a warrior making an oath of battle. "I know what this sounds like to you. I don't even care. But if you want this property for your cursed little museum, you're going to give me what I want."

"You want the heart. Good lord, you sound like a cannibal." He nodded, smiling. "And what will you do with it?"

Maddy looked at him solemnly, across the candlelit table. "I'm going to give it back to her. She needs it. And I need her hands, her tongue, and her eyes as well."

6

In the Forbidden City, there was no time.

Romeo had been there for years, that's how he felt, even though he understood it had only been a number of hours.

The rain was intermittent, for the yellow sky above had emptied of blood, like a wound pressed too long. The damned, crucified along the battlements, had long since stopped their moaning and calls to him as he passed between their crosses.

He knew now how Scabber prepared him for this moment: His arrival at the gates of what few of the living had ever survived.

But his childhood, as well, made him ready for this. The caverns of his upbringing, the chill darkness, living among the serpents that slithered over him, never biting him, treating him as one of their own.

He was not meant for the daylight, the Dark Father had told him just as he taught him language. "You are meant for darkness all your days," the Dark Father had said, but even then, with the Dark Father whispering the curses and god and the end of days, the Night Mother had held him and told him that she loved him.

Her embraces alone had told him, those times when she came to him. But she had stopped coming at a certain point. He had learned the ways of the caves, the twists and turns of the narrow paths. He had followed serpents to their secret springs and then had found the cracks of daylight.

When the Night Mother was gone—a woman whose face he had never seen, but whose scent he had never lost—Romeo had begun to travel at night among the caves between cities and towns and wilderness. Finally, Scabber had found him and had taught him his destiny in the Below.

Scabber had been the only mother to him since the age of nine, although when he'd been twelve, a man like the Dark Father had grabbed him and had sent him first to jail and then to a family of emptiness in that other hell called Connecticut.

Finally, he had run again in darkness, back to the only home he felt was the right one.

And she had prepared him for this day.

Scabber had taught him of the secrets.

She had been told, she said, by the woman who had raised her in the Below, as well. And that woman had been taught by a man, and that man had been told of all by a woman, all the way back to the dawn of the Forbidden City.

"Forbidden City's always been?" Romeo had asked her more than once.

"You forget," Scabber had said. "It was born from the first of us. She had a mind that was stronger than others. She had great powers. Her blood sanctified and cursed its birth."

"She was bad?"

"Not bad," Scabber told him. "She was who she was. She built the city from her mind, from the death of those she loved, to imprison the Serpent. But the Serpent gets loose sometimes. Last time, a terrible plague came through the Below and the Above. That was before even I was born. Someone put the Serpent back, but died doing it. Would you die to put the Serpent back?"

"No." Romeo had shivered, thinking of his own death. But that had been when he was a child.

Now, he knew that it didn't matter if he died or not.

The Serpent must be imprisoned. Or destroyed.

When he came to the open gates, feeling weary and hungry, he marveled at the inlaid gold and the jewels that sparkled across them. He knew it was an illusion. He knew there were no gates, no gems, and even the crucified were part of the prison of the Serpent. The citadel itself was a trick of gas and darkness.

Still, this was the place.

The Serpent was loose, but would always return to its lair when it needed rest.

Romeo would find it. He was determined.

He would fulfill the destiny to which he had been born.

He stepped within the gates. The gaseous odor was pungent and overwhelming. He forced himself to take deep breaths. His mind felt cloudy. Dizziness set in, and his knees felt as if they would buckle. Uncontrollably, he began weeping—not from emotion, but from some atmospheric change. Tears flowed across his face, blurring his vision. When he wiped them completely dry, the Forbidden City had shifted.

A man stood before him. Not the image of the Serpent, but a handsome man with long, dark hair, wearing a white shirt and brown breeches and muddy boots. "Ah, my little boy," the man said.

Romeo could smell the Serpent beneath his skin. The man grinned, his teeth carved into points, "You've come home to me."

Part Four

The Serpent and the City

Chapter Twenty-eight

Underworld

1

Jake's Journal

I saw what I thought was Naomi.

I was sure!

It was her; it had to be. Her hair, messy; her eyes, sleepless; her face, pale but sparkling with life. Life! Not death, not pain, not hurt. She had life in her. This woman. Naomi. Nyomi. Na-wombi. Her clothes were torn and filthy, as if she'd been living in gutters since December.

Could she have gone mad? I wondered. Could she have run from her life again, this time to occupy space in the unseen parts of the city— the squats, the abandoned tenements, the tunnels within tunnels that ran like rat nests beneath Manhattan? Could Naomi have run to the only semblance of cavern the city had to offer in some madness to reconnect with an imitation of the bomb-shelter cavern where her child had been raised?

All right, I see now this was insane of me to think, but standing in the subway station, seeing her, was its own kind of insanity. This was no see-through phantom—she was flesh and blood. She stood at the far end of the platform, peeking out at me from behind a blue column.

On unsteady feet, I walked toward her. Although I kept watch on her as I moved, by the time I reached platform's end, she was gone.

I glanced around in the eerily silent station.

There was really nowhere for her to have gone to other than the tunnel. The long, dark tunnel with the hint of light at various points along its curved walls. Living in the city, the tunnels were mysteries to me. Sometimes, on the E or A trains, I saw abandoned subway stations—closed off from the world above, no longer taking passengers anywhere, just empty platforms gathering dust and rats.

Somewhere along Fifth Avenue, in the early 1990s, a woman fell through a grate, with all her shopping bags—like Alice in Wonderland, she went down, down, down, and it became more and more curious for her.

When they finally found her, two days later, she had been crawling in sewage, through tunnels.

She insisted that she had found a secret city, that there was a hell underneath Manhattan, full of golden towers and blood. One among the search party, a reporter for either the *Times* or the *News* found a whole underground culture within the subway—and old unused train tunnels that opened into a labyrinth along with, and below, the current tunnels. People who scurried from the light; people who seemed to move in silent darkness. The vampire kids, too, those teens and runaways who lived beneath tenements, digging farther down to create nests, attacking people—believing that they were vampires.

All kinds lived in the city's shadows.

Who was to say that Naomi herself would not go there? That another woman, thought to be Naomi, was killed by a subway train, some unidentified woman?

My imagination could play with it further, could stretch this fable out until I believed that Naomi had planned her escape from the pressures of life to go below, where the goblins go, where girls who had given birth to incestuous children might go—the caverns and canyons of the magnificent American city of New York. She had put her purse or her clothes with the dead woman on the subway track. She had seen her moment of escape.

She knew darkness.

I would follow her.

I was prepared for a journey into the heart of the tunnels. I knew there was more to the subway than just the subway.

And I was willing to follow Naomi wherever she would lead me. Ghost or human, I needed to find out what she wanted from me now, and more than anything, I wanted to hold her just once more.

Then, I could let her go.

2

The man with the pointy teeth held his hand out for Romeo. "Take my hand, son. Come with me. I will show you my kingdom."

"Serpent," Romeo spat, and reached into his pouch for the key he'd brought. Surely, the key would keep the Serpent from harming him in the Forbidden City. This is what Scabber had told him, but Scabber had ventured to the City when the Serpent had been in chains. Someone had released the Serpent to run freely, and Romeo had no idea if there were truly a way to stop It.

But I have been foretold, Romeo thought. *I am the one to stop this. I know I am.*

He withdrew the small skull from his pouch and held it up to the dark-haired man.

The man looked at the skull, and his grin faded, replaced by a look of pure blankness. Then, the smile, like a dark sunrise, returned, and he began laughing. "Give it to me, boy. Give it up, it's mine, you see, it belongs to me." He came forward, moving like a blur of liquid until he was right beside Romeo, his hands on the skull. "Is it my baby, my child, you've brought him home? Oh, good boy, to bring my son to me. How often do I hear him bawling in the dark like cats in season? Crying out through the dark roads I travel?"

Romeo tugged the skull back, but the Serpent drew it from him. The man held the skull high in the air. "Wait," the man said, "this is no child. This is the skull of a girl of fifteen. This is the nightmare. This is that Devil Witch. The Devil taught her to write and read and think like the angels of Satan, but he never taught her the secret of eternal life."

The man's hands poured liquid out onto the red earth, and he dropped the skull. "Thou art the Devil, boy." The man spat at him, but still he laughed. "Bringing me the head of the woman I hanged and beheaded and whose eyes I stole, whose tongue I cut, whose hands I held, whose heart I locked away so that even she could not find it again."

Romeo had failed. Within him, fears that he had pressed back into his memory, fears of the very serpents who were his brothers, fears of the Night Father who came to him and preached against him, all arose.

The man before him sprouted new hands, but now they had long yellow fingernails—*no*, *claws*—and his eyes turned blood red.

"No cursed gate can hold me. No skull of the Devil Witch can keep me locked away. She gave me eternal life with her prayer, boy. She created this prison for me, but she did not know that one day they would find her headless body, they would find her eyes and tongue and heart and hands, and even this, her skull. But in doing so, they would remove the very locks that kept me weak and held me here. But soon, my child, the world shall be my prison. I, James Cotton, the Serpent of the Forbidden City, will leave this unhallowed darkness and feed freely upon all who live Above as I have upon your friends in this place."

Romeo's fear got the better of him, and he felt a trickle of pee run down his leg.

The landscape shifted, like smoke in wind, and the blood-rain wept from the sky, painting the world around him a dark red.

He saw the army behind the Serpent. The army of the dying, the tortured, those upon whom the Serpent had been feeding for centuries—piles of skull and bone, and men and women in the throes of an eternal torment. It was a shore of damnation, reminding Romeo of the words from the Night Father about the Quick and the Dead and about Hellfire and Purgatory.

He wanted to run out of this place, but to what tunnel? To what new darkness? He existed within the mind of the Serpent here—and only the keys, the secrets would help him. The skull now lay on the ground. How would it help him? What would turn the key?

"My boy, you will be my little prince here. So much better to rule with me, child, than to live the filthy life you've had." The Serpent held out his hand, the twisted fingernails glistening with blood. "Come with me, boy. Your destiny awaits. I will show you the glories of the world that have been denied too long to you. You were meant for more than the nasty existence you have led. I will love you as no father has ever loved a son. And you will inherit all that I am. Take my hand, now, son."

Romeo closed his eyes for a moment. In the darkness of sightlessness, he felt as if he were back in the caves of his childhood, with nests of serpents all around him. The smell was the same. The feelings of both fear and comfort returned to him.

Destiny.

It lurks.

The only thing he knew from his survival was that there was nothing to fear in the dark. Only in the light of day did the illusion blind anyone.

With eyes closed, he let James Cotton, the Serpent, take his hand in his claws.

And then, Romeo opened his eyes to the daylight world, not the massive city of the Above or the sulfurous Forbidden City, but a world of woods and swampy land, thatched rooftops and a gallows with six women hanging.

Chapter Twenty-nine

The Infernal Vision of the Serpent

1

It was hardly a town, and yet it was more than a farm—and what kind of farm was this?

Romeo had not known much of farms, except the glimpses he'd had of the Night Father's land, and this was different.

The Serpent's world was flat and seemed to go on for miles at the edge of a straggly woods. A huge river ran just beyond the common house, and swampy land surrounded the curve of stables and what might've passed for a black-smith's shop.

There were no boats in the river, neither was there wind in the air, which created a stillness and a forlorn echo, as if someone had once been here, in this world, but had moved on, taking all life from it.

Several small houses—barely more than raised mounds in the earth with wood and thatch to keep the elements out—sat to the south, and a great road ran by them.

The sky was whitish blue, and too bright for Romeo—he had to shield his eyes in order to see the women at the gibbet.

Wearing long, dark dresses, they seemed a row of marionettes as they hung there: An old woman; a woman of middle age who might've been the elder's daughter; beside them, a stout black woman whose body continued to spin slowly as if she'd only just strangled on the rope. Three more women rounded out the grisly sight—a frail and pallid woman with long bushy red hair whose face was chalk-white and whose eyes remained open in an eternal stare; a woman who was little more than a girl, about Romeo's age, one shoe dropped to the platform below, one still dangling from her toe; and finally, another woman of considerable weight, not more than nineteen or twenty years old.

"Did you enjoy my puppet show?" the Serpent said, his arms draped gently around Romeo's neck. "Sometimes, my lips move so you know it's not really these witches speaking. Sometimes, it seems to come right from them. Watch!"

Suddenly, the oldest of the three women opened her eyes and began singing a song that was all out of tune. *Tree oh tree who learned me*

*strife oh strife I am thy wife fire oh fire thou know
desire and burn this tree and take my life.*

And then, her jaw sagged, and her eyes
closed.

Romeo caught his breath. "Serpent tricks," he
said, coughing and tugging away from the man
who held him.

"You are in my world now, boy," the Serpent
said, clapping his hand. As he did so, a distant
blast of thunder sounded. "I am god of this
kingdom come. She," and here he pointed to the
young woman whose shoes were all but
dropped, "may hold the keys to my prison, but
I have found ways around my pretty goal
keeper. Watch this, boy. Watch!"

Romeo didn't want to look up at the dangling
women, but he could not help himself. The girl
began spinning on the rope, spinning like a top,
one foot pointed almost daintily downward, the
other kicking out as she went.

"Doesn't she dance beautifully? Very much
like a witch at her revels. Watch how her sweet
little neck breaks as the rope winds tighter
around her. Tighter and tighter it goes, and
soon even her tender flesh won't be able to keep
her skull attached to her throat!" The Serpent
cried out, and Romeo watched—transfixed—as
the girl spun, the rope winding around her
neck, her feet beginning to fly out, her arms
spinning around her, all of it a blur.

Finally, the spinning ended; the girl's body
slowed, and went lazily around, knocking into
the bodies on either side of her. Then, stillness.

Romeo turned to face the Serpent. The man.

The man who called himself James Cotton.

"Serpent," Romeo said. He drew the second Key from his pouch, something Scabber had given him for safekeeping, knowing this moment would arrive.

It was a small round box made of leather. Blackened with age, torn at its edges, the box had carvings on its underside and what appeared to be a prayer in tiny print on its lid.

Romeo opened it, having never been able to before—for the Keys and Secrets of the Forbidden City had no power outside its walls, nor could they been seen for what they were without entrance into the nightmarish citadel.

There, in the box: two human eyes, rounder than Romeo had ever thought they should be. Red with blood, dark with a last gaze.

2

Romeo held up the box for the Serpent.

The Serpent almost smiled. "Yes, I've seen those before. They were hers. They belonged to Naomi, and I plucked them like ripe grapes from her vine, and would that I had crushed them in my hands and drunk her wine before locking them into that box. One of the witches themselves told me how I must do it. I tortured her well to get their own magic to work against them. But she tricked me. The eyes, the skull, and the rest—it all served her purposes. To keep me in this place. But you see," the Serpent said, grinning broadly. "I do not mind this Eternity, for look, I watch her hang each day. See, how lovely she is? Before sundown, I shall pluck out her eyes and her heart again, and I will bury her babe alive with her carcass. I find it most entertaining."

Romeo took the eyes into the palms of his hands, letting the box fall to the muddy ground. He held up his hands, and felt a burning right at the base of his palm. The eyes had embedded themselves there, burrowing beneath the tender skin. A burning itch began to spread across his hands.

"Yes," the Serpent said, laughing. "She will take you over. She will get inside you. She is a witch, after all, boy. You believe your destiny is to be my undoing, you will somehow set free all those I've kept here, all the souls and spirits I hold in my grasp, their energies providing the power to my kingdom. You believe," he said, laughing harder as if this were the most hilarious joke he'd ever heard, his laugh like sleet against a tin roof, "you believe that you will find what you've searched for all your young and tragic life." The laughing ended. The Serpent's face darkened, and his eyes became small, as if he were weary. "Yes, you have her eyes, boy. You have the witch's sight in your hands. But will she show you your heart's desire?"

Romeo looked at the palms of his hands, at the eyes in them, and he saw his own face reflected there, and somewhere in the darkness of her eyes, he felt himself falling—

Into an endless night, but not night at all—

The caves of his birth, the feel of the snakes in their pit, crying out, not for the Night Father, but for the mother who never came to him when he wanted her; the woman who held him but a few times as he lived in the uninterrupted dark. She came to him like a ghost, and she left as one who had buried the dead.

"I have seen your mother, boy," the Serpent whispered within the blackness of the cave. "You have seen her, too. This is the firmament of destiny. I tell you, Romeo, whose name at birth was Nathaniel, this is the land of those who seek darkness. You have spent your young life searching for your destiny, and she is here. Your mother, boy. Look, with your witch's eyes . . . Look. I have brought her here for you."

3

The night faded into dawn. Romeo was again standing before the Serpent. He began to feel a chill at the back of his neck, and tightness in his throat. Scabber had not prepared him well enough to enter the Serpent's lair.

Standing next to the Serpent: a woman dressed in the same clothes that Romeo had seen her in before, seen briefly while she ran to catch a subway train, seen while Romeo tried to tell her that he saw the mark of the Serpent upon her, that the Devourer was waiting there in the dark tunnel for her, tried to get salvation for her, knowing that she was tied into his destiny somehow.

It had lurked that day for him. He had felt it. Now, here she was.

He even understood what he had recognized

297

in her. Why their destinies had been intertwined. Why she stood out in a crowd for him, and why he seemed to see her on the street whenever he escaped into the Above for food.

"Mama," he said, his voice sounding like a little child's wail.

The woman dropped to her knees and held her hands out. Something in his blood surged, as if every vein were about to pop, as if his bones wanted to pull away from the moorings of skin, as if his being would break free of the tyranny of thought and body.

Romeo went running to his mother's arms for the first time in his life.

4

When he got there, she had become as insubstantial as mist. He stood, his arms expecting to find hers. Instead, his hands met air.

Standing over him, the Serpent. "Do you see what the witch's eyes bring you? They are not keys, Romeo. They are locks. Shall I tell you how I devoured your mother as a lion takes down the antelope?"

Romeo felt a tingling in his hands. The eyes watched him.

The witch's eyes were part of him now.

"Shall I tell you," the Serpent continued, "how she thought I was there to rescue her? To pull her from the oncoming metal beast, but instead, I fed upon her beauty, upon her succulent flesh? And like you, she is here, a stone in the wall of my Forbidden City. She will remain here, as will you. And I thank you for bringing these to me again."

The Serpent grabbed Romeo's hands and dug his claws into the boy's palms. Romeo began bleating in pain as the sharp glass of the creature's nails tore at his flesh.

But words flashed in his mind, a woman's voice, someone whispered: *Blood-red rose with thorns.*

And he saw a little girl's hands, her wrists scarred with scratches.

Chapter Thirty

The Keys to the Kingdom

1

Andreas Harris did not want to go into the house on Rose Street, particularly not after dark, but Maddy Sparke had convinced him that they must act fast.

"I know my ghosts," she said as she unlocked the door. "My great-grandmother appeared to me just before my little boy died, and I know now it was a warning of some impending disaster. Then again," she added, "those were still the days when I was knocking back eight shots of Jim Beam per night, so I was seeing a lot of ghosts then."

In the foyer, she lit a candle; Andreas set down the cardboard box on a spindly chair.

"These are all you have," she said, hoping that he would admit to others.

"I told you already. We don't have eyes. For goodness' sake, human eyes could not possibly last through the centuries."

"Well, this did," Maddy said as she opened the box. She shone a flashlight down at the contents. "Two human hands, apparently perfectly preserved, and one, count it, one human tongue. Salted, no doubt. To say nothing of a very dried human heart with bone splinters driven into it. Not bad work for a serial killer like this James Cotton, long may he rot in Hell."

2

"And what did the blasted diary say to do with all this . . . gruesomeness?" Andreas asked as he lit three more candles along the hall.

"The diary was for him. She knew he would read it. She had the Sight, Harris. She was no dummy. She knew that he would read it and know his damnation was coming. She also knew, somehow, that he would take these . . . bits . . . of her and seal them up so that she could not be whole again. It was what she gave me. What she gave me without me even knowing that I had received it."

"The ghost gave you something?"

Maddy laughed. "You're frightened, Andreas. That's wonderful. Come along, I'll show you." Maddy grabbed up one of the gleaming votives, and marched toward what was left of the kitchen. Now a shambles, it seemed to be more basement than culinary spot. She set her candle down, and lifted up the prize.

Andreas looked at it in the feeble light. "The angel's head?"

"Yes, it's been here all along. The reason I saw her was because your men had dug her up—the body with the head missing. I remembered that you'd found the headless angel in a grave, and it got me to thinking—after I'd read the diary. He cut off her head after she died. He took the skull to keep her in her grave. So for some warped ritual, he buried the statue, and put its head in place of hers when he buried her and her child. Don't you see, Harris? She foresaw her own doom, it was clear enough in the diary. She knew her child would be buried alive. She knew all that he would do. She even knew that he would take this broken angel and place its head to rest over her body. But there was one thing that he was too dumb to notice. Perhaps he was too busy with his cackling evil. Perhaps, like all insane murderers, he failed to notice the simplest of things."

"You are certifiable, Ms. Sparke," Andreas said. "Tell me what the angel head can do."

"We'll see," she said. She dropped the angel head to the stone floor, and it chipped on its edge. Maddy lifted it and dropped it again; Andreas jumped each time and gave little shrieks, remembering the museum value of the bit of statue.

Then, the head cracked open.

Inside: a thin scroll.

Maddy squatted down to lift the scroll. "Just as I thought—the body of the statue was hollow. Why not the head? I read it in her diary. It was a clue for the future, Harris. She knew someone would one day find this and understand," Maddy said, grinning. "I read one passage where she practically told me. He had broken the statue in a rage, and she had picked up the pieces for him. She knew her doom would arrive, and so she sealed this," Maddy lifted up the scroll, "into the very thing that he would bury with her body."

Andreas Harris, perspiration on his face and scalp shining in the candlelight like a glaze of ice on a ski slope, whispered, "All right, all right. What's in it? What did she write?"

Maddy took the scroll to the edge of the steel counter, and rolled it out. She held a candle over it. "Well, this is completely crazy," she said, her eyes narrowing in the flickering light. She moved her lips as she silently read the scroll.

Andreas laughed. His farting laugh echoed through the house. "Everything we've done so far is completely crazy."

Maddy glanced over at him.

The candlelight seemed to spread a yellow-blue glow across her broad but pleasant face, and a different kind of beauty bled through in the light.

For a moment, he was sure that Maddy had turned deep blue, as if her body had gone cold and her breath had stopped. Her eyes rolled up in their sockets until there was nothing but the whites. Drool spilled from the edge of her lips.

In the flickering candlelight, her face tensed and then relaxed in a strange rictus, as if a wave of pain had washed through her.

Andreas Harris felt his mouth go dry; a chill ran the length of his spine. For a moment, he thought that he himself had gone mad. He felt as if Maddy Sparke were suddenly out of context—a woman who did not belong in this room with him.

"We . . . we . . . need to leave . . . this . . . alone," he muttered, shivering because a fear had begun to grip his throat, and he felt a tightening along his chest.

Something was wrong. Something in the air had curdled, and a sourness filled the room.

A stench.

Maddy's color returned to normal, and she glared at him. "Speak for yourself, thief of my tomb, or hold thy tongue."

Chapter Thirty-one

The Descent

1

Jake's Journal

I followed the twisting of the paths through the subway.

I kept pace with the ghostly creature that walked ahead, like a single candle flame, leading me through the darkness. The subway tunnel became cavernous in the dark with lights at either end, but in its center, its core, it was a lost world.

Naomi flickered and went out for a moment, but I saw that she led me farther: another tunnel opened to the left, and I scraped my way through the broken opening in the wall. Here, what seemed to be a shutdown subway platform from early in the century—the paint on the columns at platform's edge had faded, arches and fake buttresses grew overhead, or so I imagined as the light of my guide wavered as if in a spectral wind.

She was on the broken track. Then, she was on the platform. I called to her, but she didn't turn; I climbed up on the platform, and she was no longer where I arrived, but at the end of the platform.

Then, she was gone again. This game of hide-and-seek did not stop me from running toward where she had been—and seeing yet another cracked and crumbling opening into another tunnel, this one with more flickering light.

What seemed like hours may have in fact passed in minutes—for in the dark, with the flickering light of Naomi before me, always too distant to touch, always too close to lose sight of, I realized that I was being hypnotized, that her light itself was my induction into the hypnotic state. Other than my echoing footfalls, there was no sound, neither was there wind, and the air—dusty and still—was like the air of some ancient catacombs.

Soon, I followed her down pathways that grew narrower and by the time I reached what I thought was a wall, I was crouching as I went.

Narrow and more cramped, the openings opened onto more tunnels, and there I was—on my belly crawling like a snake. My insanity knew no bounds as I followed her.

Slowly, a misty blue light came up, a fog of an aura, as if I were coming to the outside world, and it had filled with brilliant steam.

Through the vapor's glow, I saw the bones.

2

At home in her own bed, Laury got up in the middle of the night, thirsty.

"Mommy?"

"Yes, baby."

"What time is it?"

"It's too early to get up. I know that much."

"I can't sleep."

"Nightmares?"

"Uh huh."

"Want to crawl up here under the covers?"

"No. I just wanted to see if it was time to get up."

"Want me to come tuck you in?"

"No, that's okay."

"Go back and lie down and close your eyes. Then just try and pretend you're in a nice place having a picnic with your friends and the sky is full of white, fluffy clouds."

"Okay. Mommy?"

"Sweetie?"

"I thought I saw a snake."

"In your dreams?"

"No. Maybe. I got up to get a drink of water, and I thought I saw a snake in kitchen."

"A real snake?"

"Maybe. Maybe I was dreaming."

"I doubt there are snakes up here. It's too far for them to crawl. You sure you don't want to sleep up here with Mommy?"

"No, I'm okay. Can snakes talk?"

"It must've been a dream, Laury. It's not even five A.M. If we keep talking, Daniel's going to wake up and get all grumpy. And Mommy's very, very sleepy."

"Okay. It was probably a dream, anyway. Snakes can't talk either, can they. I know they can't, not really. Good night, Mommy."

"Night, sweetheart."

3

Jake's Journal

I had entered a genuine catacomb.

I imagined that it was similar to what must exist under the most ancient of cities: stacks upon stacks of bones and skulls, some, little more than muddy ash; others, recently polished a gleaming white. They were so nearly perfect that I thought at first some very fine artist had created them. They were neatly piled, bound together by the cramped spaces and crevices in the walls.

Was the light—through the mist—daylight? How could this be?

I was so far down in the subterranean labyrinth beneath Manhattan that I knew intellectually there could be no natural light, yet the light—yellow-orange and ashy, like the embers of a thousand dying fires—seemed the sky of a smoky twilight.

Here I existed, beneath the city, in what should've been an endless night of pipe and steam and stone and mud. Instead, I had stepped into another landscape altogether.

Some sort of deranged artist had indeed created this.

Or perhaps I, myself, had stepped off the world of sanity into the realm of the limitless possibilities of the distorted human psyche.

Was I in Hell? I knew that was not possible, for if I held my breath a moment and looked at the sky, it shimmered, nearly fading. I saw a tangle of dark pipes and for a moment, watched a rat scurry across a different reality as if running through the image of the world I occupied. This was some illusory imagining; this was a movie projected onto the crypt of the city.

The city! What was it but a great tree, its roots here? Or a mountain, a volcano, a great aspiration upward to the sky, and here I existed, at the center of its pit! Perhaps I had gone mad. After all, what man would follow a ghost through the darkness of the subways? I had never been an adventurer in my life—the closest I had come to adventure had been moving to Manhattan.

I mention the smell—it was like the tomb itself, thick with some sweet gas—because it kept me alert, it seemed to thwart my fear, it kept me focused on my goal.

Naomi.

She moved through the rubble of the Dead as if she were its queen. Her feet crushed skull and vertebrae, and she only turned once. I saw it in her face, I saw now what I had not seen before.

She shimmered, just like the landscape, the giant monument to the bones—

Her face was like a perfect bowl of water, rippling.

And then, the sweet odor blew across my face, my scalp tingled, goose bumps raised on my neck and arms. A twisting in my stomach. The smell of . . .

Roses?

Muddy creek?

And almost as I recalled these smells, my vision blurred. I wiped my eyes, for whatever dust had settled upon them stung. When I looked about again, I stood at the edge of a muddy field. There she was, thirteen again. My Naomi, my only love, her dress bedraggled, tears in her eyes, the unruly but golden hair—sunlight like small white flowers along her scalp . . .

Ashes shining under her skin.

We were in Carthage, and she ran to me, and I felt all of thirteen also. My hands were those of a boy, and my heart was that of a boy. She ran to me, and I held her while she wept against my neck.

"What happened?" I asked, the dream having convinced me in seconds that our adult lives had not yet been imagined.

"Something terrible," Naomi said, pulling away from me. She clutched her stomach, telling me that her whole body hurt because something terrible had happened, over and over, and she begged me to go into the water of the creek with her. "I need to be baptized all over again," she said, weeping. I felt such fear in her that I went with her, fully clothed, into the deep part of the water.

And then, she was fifteen, and I had gone to find her—something within me knew to go to her.

Yes, I knew somehow this was a vision covering over my subterranean mystery, but I went with it, I wanted the vision more than the reality—

I ran to her house and went out back, to the bomb shelter, knowing that she often hid there. In moments, she came running up from its shadows. She slammed the heavy door that sealed the stone entrance. "Don't go down there. There are snakes, the snakes," she shouted frantically, and then I heard them—a dream that had never gone away—the cats yowling. But I saw in her eyes that the noise was not anything other than part of that "something terrible" that had happened when she'd been younger.

A crack of lightning flashed across Carthage, lighting its sky with fire. The woods were burning—we were adults again. The memories had faded, and we stood there while all around us trees burst into crackling flame. Women and men swung in slow circles from ropes—hanging—from the branches as the fire licked their shadow forms.

Naomi reached for me, pulling me close. "I need you, Jake, I need you," she whispered as she pressed her lips against my cheek. I felt aroused as I had not in years—aroused merely by her touch, the intimate way she kissed me. The world seemed to spin around us in waves of fire.

When I drew myself away from her, my mind reeling from the scent of gas in the air, it was not Naomi who held me.

4

Laury padded down the hallway to her bedroom, but now that she'd had a glass of water, she felt the need to use the bathroom. She made what her dad always called a pit stop, and then glanced over at the kitchen where she'd seen the snake. Of course, it had been a dream, she told herself.

"You're such a scaredy-cat." How could a snake be that large anyway? And how often did snakes look like that? It had been shiny and slick and oily, like a puddle in one of the potholes on the street. And what had it said? What had you thunk it said? she scolded herself. She thought it told her that her daddy wanted her. That was the nuts part. She knew that sometimes she walked in her sleep. Her daddy had caught her doing that one time. Maybe that's all it was.

So, brave child that she was, Laury Richmond headed back to the kitchen and was about to flick on the light when something grabbed her.

It wasn't a snake at all.

5

" 'Hold thy tongue?' " Andreas Harris repeated, laughing. "You gave me quite a scare." Still, he was shivering a bit, and Maddy was almost happy to see it.

She wanted to tell him what had been in the scroll—words she hadn't quite understood, although their meaning had become clear enough to her in the few moments after she'd read them.

It was a spell. It was a genuine witch's spell.

And it worked.

For there Maddy stood, in her body with her normal consciousness, and yet she was aware of the invader. *Parasite, more likely. Damn parasite.* She would've been upset, but it was not an entirely uncomfortable feeling. She would've liked to have expressed to Andreas just how wonderful it felt to actually not feel as if there was an enormous gulf between one human consciousness and another. But she couldn't seem to get her mouth to work right.

The Witch had her.

6

Fear not, the Witch told her, speaking within her mind.

This is my body, please just give it back.

I cannot. Ye have invited me within through my spell of binding. We are held fast together now.

Will you hurt me?

No, good woman. All hurt is past. Thou art my deliverer. To thee I have appeared. To thee I have been bound. But I have no flesh to act or move. Nor can I use mind to do what must be done.

313

Are you really the Naomi who was hanged as a witch?

Aye. Witch and mother and strong spirit of greater power than I would know at my hanging, but Death is the illusion of ignorance. I am in chains here, as are others.

Others?

Many have been taken by the Serpent for his hunger. It is souls that he devours. My curse upon him bound him, aye, but his darkness is stronger. I was wrong.

My mind did not understand what comes after the flesh. He has his Kingdom beneath the earth, and he grows more powerful with each spirit he keeps. So that my son could be reborn, I remained in the tomb, but had I eyes to see, I would've stopped that Serpent Cotton. He is a creature of cruel desires. He can seem a man, a serpent, a demon, a woman, a child, as he wills, for the Forbidden City is his mind, which my bones and my heart and my eyes and my hands and my tongue have locked him within, until you and your people stole what belonged to me. Maddy, the Serpent is loose. We must bind him. We must destroy him.

Maddy realized that the voice within her was very much her own—not an alien sound. One of her thoughts was that she had gone insane, and quick.

The Witch laughed. *You are indeed mad, thus the name Maddy. But be you mad or blessed, you must let me use your vessel. I have but a few hours within you.*

7

Maddy looked at Andreas, who had gone from laughing to shivering in a the corner by the stairs.

"I am Naomi Cross," she said aloud. "It is the hour of the Serpent's deliverance into Eternity. Give me my heart."

8

"Daddy?" Laury asked, almost giggling because he had really scared her.

"Yes, baby, it's your old man," he said, picking her up and butterfly-kissing her on the forehead.

The kitchen was dark, but she knew his smell well enough—it was soap and sweat and sometimes beer. This was Daddy, all right. "Let's go for a little adventure, Berry."

"Won't Mommy get mad you're here?"

"Naw, I already talked it over with her. She said it was okay. She was real mad at first, I guess. But you know Mommy. And you want us to get back together, don'tcha?"

Laury didn't answer but nodded, anyway.

"Well this'll help with that, Berry. C'mon." He hugged her close, and Laury felt a little sleepy still and thought that maybe she should tell her mother and Daniel that she was going out, especially after how mad her Mommy had been at her Daddy just last night.

She closed her eyes for just a second, and felt a chill when her father opened the door to the apartment. She opened her eyes quickly—her ears popped just like when she was on an airplane.

What she saw made her scream.

9

Laury began crying, but didn't mean to, and the woman who held tight to her whispered, "Don't worry, Berry, they won't bite, not if you believe."

Laury glanced down at the floor. It was covered with writhing snakes, and she wasn't in her apartment hallway at all. She was in some kind of cave strung with tiny white Christmas lights, and the snakes moved around the woman's legs and the woman began singing a little lullaby.

Please let this be a nightmare, Laury thought. *Please let it be a nightmare.* Because for just a second, when she looked at the pretty woman's face, she thought she saw the eyes of a boa constrictor, just like at the pet store—cold eyes, watching her just like she was a mouse.

"I want to see my mommy," Laury whined.

"I'll take you to see your daddy instead. How does that sound?"

"Where am I?"

"In a cave far away. Want me to tell you a story, Berry? Once upon a time, there was a little girl whose father had died. That's sad, isn't it? Her father had died, and her mother forgot about her because she was having another child. And in the night, a serpent came up through the sewer, up through the pipes, into her kitchen. And when the little girl went to get a glass of water, the serpent was waiting for her. He pretended to be her daddy, and he took her back down, down, down, down into his own darkness where he showed her many wondrous things. And then he wasn't a serpent anymore, or her daddy, but a woman who her daddy had once loved and who was now lost forever in a cave full of snakes, looking for her son, believing that he would be there. And this little girl would stay in the cave of snakes forever and ever, until the end of time," and while the woman told the story, Laury began shivering uncontrollably in her arms.

10

Jake's Journal

I looked into the eyes of someone who I can only call Other.

It was a creature that looked as if it had been patchworked together from various skins and bodies, the color of skin varying, the degree of rot—for it had used corpses to build itself, I had no doubt of that. The seams showed through between the flesh, and it seemed more scarecrow than human. Its eyes were empty holes of darkness; its scalp, burned and patched; faces along its body, rows of them, as if they'd been ripped from their original owners and pressed against this creature's chest and thighs while still blood-moist.

And then, the vision of the scarecrow was gone—

Naomi stood, watching me—like an overlay of beauty upon the real world of rotting flesh.

"What are you?" I asked. "What in God's name are you?"

Her smile was brief, flickering like a candle before going out. "I," the creature whispered, through the mouth of the woman I had loved all my life, "am the only god you will ever need."

Even though it looked like Naomi before me, I still sensed the patchwork scarecrow lurking beneath her skin. I stepped backward, watching her—watching the scene of the hanging bodies and burning woods behind her as well. The smell of sulfur and gas overpowered my senses, and I knew that in a moment I would black out.

I had not come all this way, to this hell, just to die. I had come for Naomi. Somehow, she was there. Somehow, even if some demonic phantom held her in its grasp, she was within this realm of the underworld.

And then, behind the image of Naomi, I saw what looked like the filthiest teenager I'd ever seen.

He stood there, looking at me with the same expression of astonishment on his face that I must've had. He didn't seem to shimmer as the other images of this place had, shimmer in their gaslike nature. He was solid; he was real. He was small and covered with what looked like mud, and except for the fact that I knew he wore a T-shirt and torn jeans, a large knapsack hanging from his shoulders, I could've sworn he looked like something right out of the Middle Ages—a beggar boy from outside the castle walls, come to pull the legendary sword from the stone. Despite my fears and terror in this unknown place, something about him actually made me smile for a second—I suppose I recognized him as "one of us," a human being, not a phantom from the past drawing me into its dark circle.

"Who the hell are you?" I asked him, ignoring the shimmering figure of Naomi.

11

Before abandoning Andreas Harris at her house—he had remained a shivering pile of sweat and gibbering after he'd delivered the heart to her—Maddy had managed one last joke on him.

She asked the Witch to predict that should he take the house from her for ill means, she would take his soul with her to Hell. Maddy thanked the Witch for that moment of fun; then she settled into the vehicle of body and let the ghost drive.

Maddy let the spirit take her, feeling the gentle warmth as the Witch directed her body to go down into the dig behind the Rose Street property. She cringed as she watched herself dig—with one hand yet, for in the other, she held the heart—down farther into the mud, like a badger, but she didn't fight it, and the Witch seemed to know exactly where the pipes broke around the mud; squeezed herself between

them, and down into what seemed to be an underground chamber the size of a large box. She
moved through it very nearly like a snake, and
the sensation was not unpleasant. Maddy felt a
kind of freedom within her own body, as if she
were a consciousness that could just watch her
body do things without feeling the pain or
smelling the no-doubt disgusting odors that
passed by her.

Where are we going? she asked the Witch.

*There is a hell beneath this city, from which
this city has grown. It is the roots of the tree.
Within it, the Serpent lives. But the Serpent has
been loose and will begin his journey up through
the roots, to the tree. I alone can bind him to his
cage.*

Within moments, Maddy felt as if she were
buried alive beneath the city. Then, minutes
later, a curious blue light grew along a long,
low-ceilinged corridor. She moved down it in a
blur—the Witch could make her body move in
ways she never had been able to. She wondered
if consciousness itself weren't too much of a
cage, that in fact the physical body was able to
do things that she herself could never believe
possible. . . .

If I could just harness this, she thought. *If I
could know that my own consciousness kept me
from doing things. That ordinary accepted-reality
is not the only reality . . .*

She saw the world of the underground melt,
with all its dark browns and blacks, and in its
place—like a new crop—a world of brilliant

reds and golds burst as if from a flame struck from a single match. Even the sun was there in the sky, and the muddy grass, and trees—great trees as she herself had never seen, bigger than the ones in Central Park—and a row of houses, and beyond them, a great blood-red river.

The Witch drew up the heart, and pulled the small bits of bones from it.

He bound my heart with splinters of other witch bones, to keep it from beating. But now, it will have its strength again.

And then, before Maddy could say anything in protest, the Witch tore open her blouse and pressed the heart down beneath Maddy's left breast.

12

Maddy would've screamed if she'd been able.

She wasn't so sure that letting this witch possess her had been such a good idea, for the heart felt like a small animal burrowing in her chest, digging down into the skin, a tick finding a good nest for sucking blood.

Maddy felt herself blacking out. She struggled to stay awake. She fought against what she felt, what she was almost positive meant her dying.

You're killing me, she thought, but the Witch was silent.

Maddy felt cold and weak, and just as she lost consciousness, she saw a large snake coiled before her.

13

The Witch knew this place.

The Forbidden City that she'd created for the man who had murdered her and others in the name of religion and law, and had buried her newborn with her in the grave. She had watched—her consciousness intact even after her death—as he had taken out her eyes and heart, cut her head from her body, and pressed the bawling baby into her lifeless arms. She had been with her child until his breath had stopped, praying all the while to the gods of her tribe to somehow rescue the baby, somehow keep her son safe. But a silence had returned that bewildered her.

She had remained in the grave, but with her mind, she'd spun the web with which to trap his soul as it left its body the day he died. She had learned the art of spinning visions, and so she spun with all her power a re-creation of the Forbidden Wood in a new world, beneath the graves of men—and her final curse to him brought his true self to that place. But she could not have foreseen, even with her abilities, that he would build a great citadel upon the dead, that above his cage, a great city would grow, the teeming masses, digging pathways in the earth so near the Serpent's lair that it could almost reach them, and sometimes draw them in, the lost souls of the city who wandered too far off the path.

He had built a greater Hell than even she had imagined he would. And now, borrowing this woman's body, she could see the handiwork of hers that he'd built upon.

It was magnificent in its own hellish design—the Forbidden Wood had burned, and in its place, a shining wall of gold and fire grew, and like sentries, the captured souls of the unfortunate arrayed its periphery, impaled or nailed to burned trees, poles, and wooden beams as if stolen from sailing ships.

He had created what he believed Hell was, here. He knew he was in Hell, and he had decided to be its Prince.

The Witch's heart beat slowly at first, then more rapidly, within her bosom. She passed the tormented visions, and pressed her body into the fiery gateway.

She stepped into the Forbidden City and whispered the six words she'd been taught that would give her power, even in the Serpent's Hell.

14

Do not forget the city above—Manhattan.

This is not the world of fairy tales or legend; this is the world of concrete and stone, and taxicabs after midnight and theater crowds and coffeehouse addicts and barflies and the lonely young woman who waits for the stranger who never arrives.

Beneath it all, the darkness of unknown Mystery.

The lair of the Serpent.

323

Romeo tried to say something to the man who stood just beyond the Serpent, but he knew his words were garbled. Instead, he drew the last Secret, the final Key to the Forbidden City, from his pouch.

He felt the burning along his scalp, and knew that if he didn't bind the Serpent soon, he would never escape the Forbidden City alive.

Chapter Thirty-two

The Key to a Secret

1

Behold, the Forbidden City.

It is both a vast cavern beneath the great city above, and a castle as there has been no castle since Babylon the Great—and upon its walls, the golden bones of the Dead. In its sky, the burning ash of the devoured. In the land, a growing crop of fire and corpse, and between them, the great ash pits of the past. The plagues of antiquity nurse along the city's walls—locusts fill the sky, and the great lake within its battlements is red as blood. It is as if a single consciousness has dreamed this city, that only a man who had believed powerfully in something so vast and dreadful could have conjured such a place.

The blood-red lake shimmers, as if a stone has been tossed upon its calm surface; the shimmering moves along the ash pits, between the bodies upon their crosses and pikes, up the reflecting wall of gold, even among the locust-encrusted air, until you can see through it to the forgotten walls of another fortress—the beneath that is under the Beneath, the subterranean way beneath the subway, the labyrinth beneath the pathways of the outer labyrinth.

Crushed skulls and gnawed-upon bones coat the absolute night with shape and impediment, but you can only see this truth for an instant, like a dream within a dream. You see it with your mind, as this world is dark as the deepest mine beneath the earth. Your eyes, are they opened or closed? How can you even know? For the world, you see, has no light other than the illusion of light.

And then, even in darkness, it wavers like the air above a desert road, and you see a swampland and beyond it, a vast forest, and the thatched rooftops of a settlement. Another shivering shimmer, and you watch as some creature holds your young daughter, but it is the love of your life holding her. It is Naomi, and you are in Virginia with her, the yowling of cats and the quiet of snakes all around.

And you know that it is not real, but everything in your heart tells you that this is the place you have longed for all your life.

The boy you've just called to doesn't answer, and you look back at your daughter, wondering if she is real or part of the insanity you've joined.

2

For Romeo, the joke welled up within him.

The thought in his head made him laugh out loud. If he didn't bind the Serpent soon, he would not leave the Forbidden City alive.

And the thought that went with that one: the last Key would also keep him from leaving the Forbidden City alive, as well.

Scabber had lost the use of her legs when she had returned from her trip into the Forbidden City. It had been the price she had paid to escape the Serpent. A price always had to be paid, Scabber had taught him.

Romeo withdrew the final Key to the Secret of the Forbidden City, the most important one.

The one that others, like Scabber, had failed to turn in the lock.

In his hand, a shard of glass.

He looked through the mists of illusion to the Serpent, and the little girl the Serpent held. A man stood there, also, beyond them, he thought he saw another figure approach, stepping over the trenches of bone and decaying flesh. But he could not wait for other phantoms to arrive. He had been born to this quest. Scabber must have known how it would end for him.

But it was all right, he felt. He had lived his life mostly in darkness, mostly among serpents, mostly feeling safer in the night than during the day.

Just the fact that the Serpent could create this nightmare in the Below led Romeo to believe that he should have no fear, for if this world were possible, then surely the night to come waited for him and was not to be feared.

He took the glass and with his right hand scraped it against his left wrist.

The final Key to the Secret of the Forbidden City, the Final Doorway to shut the Serpent down in its lair was the one thing that others before had failed: a blood sacrifice of the one who turned the Key.

3

Jake's Journal

She had Laury in her arms. Naomi had my daughter. I would've thought that this, too, was some vision as I lay dying or a phantom of my dream, but while Naomi shimmered into serpent and then unspeakable creature and then Naomi again but sometimes a man of grim aspect, Laury remained Laury, my Berry, my only child.

How she had been brought to this dark place, I didn't know. All I knew was that getting her from that place was more important a mission than saving my own skin or feeling the warmth of Naomi's breath on my cheek again.

This place was an illusion in darkness. Perhaps denied of light, we create from our minds our hells and heavens; and, perhaps, these were my own visions of those otherworlds; or, perhaps, I had entered someone else's mindscape. It was a vision of absolute madness rendered with absolute clarity.

A distant figure approached swiftly as if not walking or running, but moving like wind, and there we were, in a circle: Naomi holding tight to Laury who wept; the filthy boy who had something shiny in his hand; and now this intruder into our circle, a stocky woman with eyes that shone yellow and whose face, pale though it was, glowed with burning life.

I remember thinking: *The past is dead. Laury is the future. Naomi is not the only ghost; I, too, am a ghost. I haunt the past; I haunt myself.*

I went to Naomi, watching her unwavering eyes, looking for the creature within her.

There, I saw the face of a serpent, a large snake, coiled, my daughter wrapped within the body. I tugged at Laury, but she seemed in pain each time I pulled.

Naomi's grip was iron.

And then, the boy cried out as if in pain.

I turned, and saw what looked like fire pour from his arms.

4

"You have come, Witch," the Serpent said.

He crouched on the gallows, watching as the Witch opened her eyes, the noose around her neck became a snake, which slithered down her back to the platform. "You devil's slut, you can do nothing to me. You have given me my own creation here. I am not under your power. You cannot invoke your demons around me."

"I have no demons," she whispered. "I have only memory."

"Memory? What memory?"

"Come closer," the Witch said. "I will show you."

Within her own body, Maddy Sparke watched with some fear as if she had stepped into a dream and found the texture of reality.

5

Romeo knelt down on the icy ground, tears coming to his eyes, darkness growing around him.

It was his own death coming in thunderclaps toward him. His blood flowed, and he began to feel a chill within. He knew why Scabber had been unable to do this, and others before her. It was hard to let go of life, even in the darkness of the Forbidden City, it was hard to willingly do what you would let no other attempt.

He closed his eyes and tried within his mind to see his real mother, the one he had only felt and heard, when he had been a young child. He needed—the way he had as a baby—some small comfort among the serpents, some feeling of human warmth.

The ice began to fill his stomach and then his chest. His heartbeat slowed; he tasted copper in the back of his throat.

Jake's Journal

The image of Naomi began to waver, like a candle flame, and then Laury pushed at her, at the creature who held her—and did I see there, beneath the layers of illusion, a serpent like the kind described in ancient and arcane texts, as if someone had learned from the Bible and other writings what Leviathan lurked beneath the seas and had re-created It for himself here?

The creature's coils loosened, and I grabbed Laury up from It. I held my child tight to my chest; she buried her head there, tears soaking my shirt.

Then, I saw the boy. He had collapsed to the ground, and fire poured like liquid from his veins.

The sky flickered with flashes of lightning and drumbeats of thunder.

The boy was dying. It was not fire pouring from him, but his own blood.

I wanted to run from that place, but where would I go? How would I return to the world?

And I could not leave him dying, whoever he was.

Carrying my daughter, I went to him. I set Laury down beside us, and I tore my shirt open, wrapping the strips of cloth around the boy's wrists, bandaging them.

His pulse was weak.

His eyes opened and closed, lazily. "No," he gasped. "No, Key, Key, open, open."

I pressed my hands against his wrists to stop the flow of blood.

"No," the boy whispered weakly. "Please no, Key, Secret, Serpent."

7

Romeo groaned as the man wrapped his wrists.

What was this stranger doing? Why would he want to stop the turn of the Key? The Serpent could not stop the turn of the Key, why was this man doing it?

No! Romeo tried to shout. *Don't stop the blood! The Key must turn, the Serpent must be destroyed, and the Forbidden City must burn!*

But he was too weak. His blood no longer flowed.

All was lost, Romeo knew. If he'd had the strength, he would've told the stranger that. And all of them here would be playthings for the Serpent: the little girl, the man, and Romeo.

The other stranger, the woman who stood before the Serpent like a charmer before the cobra, glanced at him for a moment as if she understood.

Romeo knew: He was not the one meant to destroy the Forbidden City and cast the Serpent into Eternal Darkness. He had no quest here. He was not special. He was not chosen by Destiny.

He was just another who would be devoured by the Serpent.

The Serpent had won, finally. Everything that

Romeo had believed about life and the darkness had been for nothing.

He closed his eyes and fought against the man who bound his wrists with cloth as if he were fighting against the jaws of the Serpent itself.

The Serpent would devour all that came to it.

And then, within his mind, he saw something that seemed both beautiful and sad: *A red rose, with petals falling, pierced with thorns.*

Chapter Thirty-three

The Blood of Memory

1

Come into my memory, the Witch said. Standing before Maddy was this man whose face seemed to melt across itself—his skull peering through the molten flesh—as he came closer to her, so close that Maddy was terrified that this creature would try and kiss her.

Come see the world as I remember it last, the Witch whispered.

Maddy felt something tickling at her feet. She tried to look down to see what it was, but the Witch's consciousness kept her eyes focused on the man-creature as it drew near.

Then, she felt the coils wrapping slowly around her ankles and legs, crawling up her thighs, along her belly, tightening as they went.

It was an enormous but unseen snake, that's exactly what it felt like to her. *It's going to kill us*, she thought, hoping the Witch could hear her.

Drink the blood of memory, the Witch whispered and what Maddy saw next made her fight against the spirit that held her.

The Witch and the Serpent and Maddy all saw it rise around them, like a curtain of brilliant dawn being drawn against the night: A great primeval forest burst from the earth, the outer trees slender, nearly reedlike, but the greater trees darkening the woods until everything seemed like trees and thicket and fern.

2

Surrounding them, several men, women, and children. All were naked, with enormous rope burns at their throats. They moved in a slow circle around the Witch and the Serpent.

Do not be afraid, the Witch whispered to Maddy. *This is my tribe that this Serpent had tortured and murdered. No harm will come to us here.*

The Serpent reared back. Flashes of lightning burst from the Witch's hands, becoming like chains wrapping around the great snake.

The world seemed to burn with blue fire.

3

Jake grabbed Romeo, his strength reviving as he held both Laury and the boy. Romeo turned to watch the blue fire as it grew in a column, enfolding the Serpent.

He saw the circle of witches as they surrounded the Serpent.

"Sacrifice," he whispered weakly, but Jake forced him to his feet, practically dragging the boy alongside him.

"We need to get out of here," Jake shouted as the sound of locusts filled the air. "Show me the way."

Romeo closed his eyes, feeling as if he would fall down again.

But even with his eyes shut, he knew his way out of the Forbidden City.

4

The invisible coils fell from Maddy's body. The creature that had held her became more distinct—its aspect was both terrifying and pitiful. It was a man whose skin had been sewn together with patches of the skins of others, while part of the skull—at the scalp and then near the left eye—showed through, and bits of bone cut through other sections of flesh drawn too tight.

The creature opened its mouth in some agony—from its throat came a screech such as Maddy had never before heard.

Then, the circle of the dead fell upon what was beginning to look like a fairly handsome young man with long, shiny dark hair, dressed in black like a minister.

An old woman fitted a noose of twisted cloth about his neck, while children grabbed his hands, gnawing at them; the men of the circle dragged him away, toward a gallows that grew like a new tree along a path among the woods.

Maddy felt the Witch within her sigh.

He is bound again, the Witch said. *He is lost within the demons of his own past. Nightmares of his creation, his world.*

It was over.

Maddy was sure.

It had to be over.

Surely the Witch had done what she had come here to do.

5

The Witch spoke aloud to the Serpent. "And now, you shall spend eternity here, with me to keep guard over you. My heart, my eyes, my tongue, my hands to hold you where you can do no one harm."

Maddy watched while the Witch drew her over to the gallows to watch the man hang. The circle of the dead all spun him, laughing at his torment, while he swirled and writhed, unable to break away.

We can leave now, Maddy said within her mind.

No, the Witch whispered, kindly. *If we were to leave, he would find a way to unbind from his torment and loose himself upon the world. He would be stronger for it. He would defeat me. A snake such as this one must be kept underfoot lest it rise up and strike.*

But I need to go home. Maddy nearly wept thinking it.

I have someone here for you, Maddy. If you stay with me, I can give you paradise.

I can't stay. This is evil. This is not how I want to live. I have properties, I have friends, I have . . .

And then, Maddy heard the sharp cry of a child.

6

The little boy came walking on unsure feet, toward her.

He had only begun to walk before he had gotten the measles, but his balance was better now. His hair was dark but with a reddish cast. His smile was cast in twilight.

Her son.

Her dead son.

What are you doing? Why are you tormenting me? Maddy pleaded with the Witch.

All you have to do is hold him, the Witch told her. *You will know that he is truly your child.*

My baby. Maddy wept, holding her arms out. *My little Matthew. Come to me. My baby.*

The toddler went to his mother's outstretched arms, and Maddy was no longer at the edge of a gallows on the rim of a great forest, but in some kind of paradise with her little boy. He sat on her lap, and she wept across his beautiful hair.

The Witch whispered within her, *You can be with him, and Eternity will seem like moments as you watch him grow.*

But it's just a magic trick, isn't it? Maddy asked, unable to see for her tears. *He died years ago. He can't be here. This is like the forest and gallows. It's just a trick.*

All that we are, the Witch said, *is a dream within a dream. I will give you your dream in exchange for your remaining here, with me, to guard the Serpent.*

I will die here? Maddy asked. *But I have friends, and I owe money, and I have plans for what I'm going to do. I need to go back home. I need to arrange things. I have more things to do in my life over the next thirty years than just—*

The Witch said, *You are already dead.*

Maddy gasped, clutching her child to her.

Then, the truth washed across her in a chilling wave, and she felt a curious calm.

7

"All right," Maddy whispered. "All right. For my son."

8

Diary of a Witch

Whosoever opens this book, be warned: This is both a book of curse and of blessing.

Whosoever reads these pages, forgive this young woman who first writ here, for she were a fool and a believer and a mother of a child she will never know. Though the name of Naomi Cross be cursed in the books of men, let it be known that in this book I writ, the Serpent shall be named and bound for as long as my slumber remains undisturbed. But should I be awakened from my sleep, then woe to him who reads this, for though I be dust, I shall come again through magick to bind him who has murdered me and my child, and I shall needs borrow thy soul. Blessed is the one who speaks the Spell within the Face of an Angel, for that soul shall pass into the realm of the next world without pain of death.

9

Maddy Sparke had never experienced this kind of warmth. Her life had felt brittle and broken like glass. Her fears had always involved her security, her need for money, her want for something she had not been able to name.

If she had worried so much for her life in the Above, she didn't seem to show it here. She knew that her form was being used to guard the Secrets that bound the Serpent, and that she was in some phantasm, some illusion . . . but it felt to her like no illusion.

She held her young son, sitting beneath the shade of a great oak tree, while above her, in the emerald twilight, witches swept the sky like angels.

Chapter Thirty-four

To the Above

1

Jake's Journal

And now I know that something good from Naomi remained, even in that Hell, even within that darkness. She had led me not to my death, but to her son, a boy who had lived in darkness all his life.

When we reached the outermost subway tunnel, we rested, and the boy told me in his broken tongue of all he knew of life, and the rest, I knew from my own memories of Naomi and our hometown.

What happens from here, I don't know. What happens with the trouble that will probably just begin today seems minor compared to the trouble that I encountered beneath this city—all of it is less important than knowing why Naomi had found me again in the first place.

She had wanted me to bring her son into the light of day.

It feels now like I was destined to find her child.

Destined to draw him back from the underworld in which she had placed him.

So, we emerged from the night into the dawn of the city, of Manhattan with its beautiful and restless noise, my daughter in my arms, sleeping peacefully, believing it all a dream. Naomi's son walked at my side, exhausted, his arms bandaged, his body covered in the filth of the underworld, but his eyes, bright and ready for the rising of the sun.

2

Destiny lurks, but when the time is ripe, it devours.

Don't imagine for a moment the silver towers of Manhattan, shining with sweat and heat. Forget the postcard images in your mind of the city, the looming skyscrapers, the brown and gray apartment buildings obscuring any trace of morning sunlight; lose your memory of the small grocery mart with its rows of oranges and apples and cheap flowers, and the great clock over the Persian rug shop, and the closed trattoria with ragged awning flapping, traces of soap on its windows.

Imagine instead a vast cavern of overgrown

brownstone and gleaming pumice, frozen in spray up to the sky; imagine the anthill and its inhabitants; imagine anything but the buildings along Eighth Avenue, the yellow taxicabs, the young man in sweatpants and hooded jacket jogging, the gray-suited bald man with glasses, shivering, a steaming coffee cup in hand; the handsome and the ugly; the beautiful and the damned; the masks and the faces they reveal; imagine everything and nothing as life moves ever upward, a history of misery shrouded within a mythology of brightness; and through it all, the Serpent turns.

And it lurks. And it will devour.

The message burns in the smoldering air. The citadel of stone could stand for a hundred more years, and still none will escape destiny as it waits, hungry.

Only you know it, because you are part of the Below, you are close to the pulse of how this island kingdom runs.

You are one of the few who can journey from the Below to the Above and back without fear. Your daughter is in your arms, and the woman you once loved intensely is dead, but her son is with you, leading you upward into daylight.

You may fear the future; you may worry about this boy who has lived a darker life than you could ever imagine; you may worry for the soul of one you loved. But these are all passing, like the dust in the air, like the playful cries of the children in the park, like the sounds of the horns of trucks as they press against the over-growth of morning traffic.

Douglas Clegg

What passes will not last.

What remains of it all is your absolute love for life, and for those who hold the keys to it; in your hands are the keys.

In your heart, the secret.

In your soul, the blood-red rose with thorns.

Today, the Serpent is bound.

THE END

THE HORROR DOESN'T STOP!

If *Naomi* sent chills up your spine, wait until you experience Douglas Clegg's newest masterpiece, *The Infinite*. Prepare yourself to visit a house unlike any other, a house where evil knows no bounds and where darkness goes on forever.

Turn the page for a sneak preview of *The Infinite*, coming in hardcover in September 2001 from Leisure Books.

1

His biggest mistake had been picking up the hitchhiker in the rain.

She was a pretty girl, from what he could see of her. She had a face that he would call heart-shaped, and maybe she had small eyes, but something about her whole demeanor gave off vibes. The needy kind, but not the clingy kind, that's what he would've said. She needed help. She was in need. She needed him, and that made her prettier to him, in a way.

Mark Carpenter felt bad for her. He'd been to visit his father in Kingston and had only come back in the middle of the night, in a storm no less, because he could not stand to sleep in the same house with that man, and decided that enough was enough. He had not been in a good mood since leaving his father's house. After crossing the bridge to the east side of the river, he'd taken an old familiar route back to his home in Watch Point. It had been nearly midnight when he'd somehow gotten lost—he blamed the storm and all the roiling thoughts about his father and some sense of failure he'd always had as a son—but then found his way back by way of the old route (they even called it the Old Road).

He was nearly in town again when the hitchhiker ran into the road. Or was standing there. He couldn't remember, later.

She was no more than sixteen. Maybe fourteen. It was hard to tell with girls these days (he'd say later). The way they grew up so fast. Her mascara ran down her face, and the top of her blouse was ripped back. She held the flap of the torn garment up, for modesty.

Something bad had happened. He was sure.

On these muddy roads, this time of night—in a nearly freezing March gale of a storm—she seemed to be a silver tear on the windshield as he pulled his Toyota Camry to the shoulder of the road.

The trees whipped the air in a frenzy. He hesitated getting out of the car. She ran over to the passenger side, and he leaned over and unlocked the door for her.

The first thing he said to her when she slid in beside him was "Not a fit night for man nor beast," in his best W. C. Fields. He wondered if he'd said it wrong, because it didn't sound funny or reassuring at all.

She was in tatters, from her stringy hair to the clothes on her back, but he tried not to look at her too much. He didn't want her to feel threatened by him. She seemed so scared already.

"You all right?" he asked. Rain beat down hard on the windshield. A field of some sort beyond the trees—he saw it in flashes of lightning.

"Something's after me," she said, desperation in her voice.

"Someone hurt you?" Still, he didn't feel comfortable looking directly at her.

All right, he could admit it to himself. He didn't want to be thought of as one of those men who pick up girls on the road. It didn't seem right. He had never picked up a hitchhiker before, but she had been standing there in the road, essentially in the middle of nowhere, close enough to the nearby town, but far enough away—particularly in the storm—that it seemed wrong to leave her.

He didn't like the whole situation, and considering that his wife already suspected he chased women, this wouldn't look good. Not that his wife would find out. He just didn't need to make this known.

"Where you going?"

"Anywhere. Just drive," she said. Her voice was ragged, like her blouse. He noticed—out of the corner of his eye—that there were smudges on her face. Dirt?

"Who hurt you?"

"No one. No one hurt me. Just drive. Please."

"All right. All right," he said. He pressed his foot on the accelerator, driving back onto the road.

"Can I tell you something?" she asked, that desperation strong in her voice. That need. "Can I trust you?"

It reminded him a bit of his daughter, this girl, and it bothered him that she might be in some unfortunate circumstance. Had someone hurt her? Had someone bothered her? He tried to push other, darker thoughts out of his head. "Yeah. Sure," he said.

"I mean, something really important. Something that hurts to tell."

"Yeah. Yes."

"The rain's nearly stopping."

"Is it?" he said, and wished he'd remained silent. Without realizing it, he'd slowed down.

"Keep driving. Please."

His hands tensed on the steering wheel. "You live in the village?"

"If I tell you this, you have to promise. Promise not to tell. Anyone."

"I'm Mark, by the way."

"Promise me you can keep this secret."

"All right," he said. He would've thought she was nuts, but there was such an ache in her voice that he believed her. He was a trusting sort. But he believed her and knew that something was wrong. Something bad had happened to this child, and he wanted to help her.

"Do you know the house outside town?"

"Which one?"

"The one that used to be a school."

"Oh. Of course. The fire. Those kids."

"I had a bet with my friends, and we went out to stay in it. Just for one night. Last night."

"That's dangerous. It's condemned."

"Are you going to listen?"

"Sorry."

"We went to stay in it. Three of us. We drank a little, and I was there with Nick. My boyfriend." She began whimpering like a puppy; she was sobbing. He glanced over at her, but the car slid in the road, and he had to return his gaze to the front.

The windshield wipers slashed at the rain.

"We stayed up late and wandered around. It was half ruins, but there's plenty still there. There's room after room. And everything was okay. Everything was okay."

"Did someone hurt you?" he blurted.

She ignored him. "Everything was okay. And then, sometime at night, I started feeling cold. Not just cold, but really cold. Like something was touching me with ice. I looked over for Nick, but he wasn't there. We had candles everywhere, and Joey—he was the other one who came along—was sitting in a corner of the room, shivering. When I asked him where Nick was, he said nothing. I felt ice all over my neck and down my back, and I got up. I nearly knocked a candle over, but I caught it in time. I was all wrapped up in a blanket. Joey kept shivering and wouldn't say anything. It was like he was somewhere else. And then I went looking for Nick, and I went out into the moonlight. This was last night. It was a full moon. A clear night. Nick was standing there, looking up at the moon, only he wouldn't look at me when I called to him. I kept saying, 'Nick, Nicky, why'd you go?' but he wouldn't look at me. And then, I touched him, only I couldn't. Something was wrong. It was like my hand went through him."

Mark smirked. "Like he was a ghost," he said, and then wished he hadn't.

"But this is the secret," she said, not missing a beat. "This is the secret."

"All right, all right, calm down. I'm listening."

He remembered it later—the hesitation. The beating of the rain and the rhythm of the windshield wipers. The lightning that briefly lit the road.

Finally, she whispered, "I am the ghost."

Mike pressed his foot on the brakes. Enough of this tomfoolery. This was some kind of prank, some kind of spring break joke. "All right, all right," he said.

But he was alone in the Toyota Camry.

When he told the police in Watch Point about it, the first cop he spoke with laughed, and the second said, "That's Nicky Verona, he and Joey Willis. Bad kids. Really bad kids." He wanted to add: but only bad in the small-time way, the shoplifting, the lies, the loitering, the drinking outside convenience stores kind of bad. The bad kids of a village the size of Watch Point.

Ne'er-do-wells.

It probably would've ended there, but the second cop, named Elliot Brooks, decided to call the Verona household to see whether Nicky was around. He was not. Had not been back since the night before. This wasn't unusual, Mrs. Verona said. Nicky was wild. Then Brooks called the Willis's. He found out Nicky and Joey went off on some camping trip for their first weekend of spring break.

Brooks decided to check out Harrow, the property on the edge of town, the site of a terrible fire the previous year, a fire that had destroyed some of the property. A tragedy on the grounds had closed down the school that had operated there for decades.

The body of a girl was found, in a small room with a leaky roof, surrounded by snuffed candles. Joey Willis still shivered in the corner, staring at the body, but Nicky Verona had already taken off for points unknown.

The girl, identified as a local teenager named Quincy Allen, a resident of nearby Hyde Park, had been missing for several days from her family's home (supposedly at a week-long get-together at a friend's in Albany). Strangely enough, she'd had a heart attack, and someone on the scene noted that given her eyes and the position of her hands, it appeared as if she'd been frightened to death, if this were at all possible.

The only thing Joey Willis had said that made any sense to the local police was:

"I told Nicky it was wrong to do it. I told him it was crazy to do it. But it wasn't him, was it?

It was that place. They surrounded us. They made it happen."

Mark Carpenter, who had picked up the hitchhiker, still did not believe any of this ghost business. He began drinking at night and told his wife that he could not have imagined all of it. "She was there! I saw her. She sat next to me!"

This was the story that Ivy Martin heard at a party in Manhattan, when someone knew that she had a connection in some way to the house.

It was one of those stories that seemed almost an urban legend: *A friend of my sister knows this guy named Mark Carpenter, and he was from this town called Watch Point, and one night, in the rain, he was driving down a lonesome road when he saw a hitchhiker in the middle of the road*. And then, the story ended with Mark Carpenter's verbal eruption of the truth of the story.

That "Mark Carpenter" chose to drive a Toyota Camry could add to the factual way the legend would sound: It was a specific car, and the driver had a name. Mark Carpenter. Even the girl: Quincy Allen. Quincy was an unusual name, but for the small villages and burgs along the Hudson Valley, up beyond Cold Spring, it wasn't that out of place. It sounded right.

Ivy had then called the police department at Watch Point, and indeed, there was an Officer Elliot Brooks. He seemed like a young man with a deep, sonorous voice, who told her that he did not wish to discuss the death of Quincy Allen. So Ivy knew that the legend had some truth. She knew that it was connected to Harrow.

She knew that she had to go and see the place, now.

She had been dreaming of Harrow for several months, ever since she'd seen the news about the fire at the school. Ever since she'd had the connection to it that she wished she could shake.

The rest fell into place. She made the calls. She argued with people. She checked with her financial planner. She decided to sell some stock.

She went on a trip up to Harrow.

Like the legend of Mark Carpenter and Quincy Allen, it was another rainy night, but spring was like that in New York.

2

Coincidence abounds.

That was Ivy Martin's first thought when she saw the street called Mercy, and then when she noticed that she wanted to stop in a town called Red Hook to ask directions, and in doing so, found herself sitting down— in the rain—at a small diner called the White Heron. Although there had been no heron in her dream, there had been a large white bird, and that was enough. A white bird and a red hook and even the word "Mercy" written across some stones.

She noticed the sign, too, just inside the White Heron Diner, just felt marker on white poster board:

"Fortune Smiles. Time Flies. Love Grows. Customers Tip."

Coincidence abounds, she thought. How often does this happen, this déjà vu from dream to reality, from the subconscious flow of images in a completely illogical dream to the hard world of life with its benches and diner booths and signs? She didn't know, but she felt this all added up in some significant way.

There had been a sign, too, in the recesses of her memory—the dream within a dream, the writing on the wall that said something about "Fortune" only she couldn't quite remember what it was.

"I had a dream like this," she said to the middle-aged woman who waited tables. The woman had a small tag pinned to her lapel: NANCY. She had her hair done up, with a small pink waitress cap tied around it. She was small and stocky and smelled of krullers. She wore white lipstick and pink fingernail polish, and she looked as if she'd stepped out of 1964.

"I was in it?" the waitress asked. Her voice was a husky baritone, probably from thirty years or more of chain-smoking while screaming out orders.

"No. Nobody was in it. Just things," she said, and then grinned slightly. "Dreams are crazy things."

"Everybody's got a dream," Nancy-the-waitress said. "And all of 'em's crazy. I dreamed I was gonna grow up and be Nancy Sinatra. That's why I'm called Nancy. You gotta try the egg cream. You try the egg cream, you're gonna climax." She said it brusquely, with humor, and it made Ivy smile. "It's that good, the chocolate egg cream."

"That sounds good. And the chicken salad." Ivy stretched her neck a bit to work out the stiffness from the tense drive.

"Chick salad, cream!" Nancy shouted to the old man behind the steel counter. He dropped his cigarette into his cup of coffee and snapped something back.

A couple two booths over were dropping quarters into the jukebox, and some crooner came on that Ivy could not identify. She leaned back into the booth, closing her eyes.

She saw him in the darkness of her mind.

"Fortune smiles," he said.

She opened her eyes again, to the diner.

Don't dream again. No point in it. You'll be there in another half hour.

She glanced out into the cloudy darkness, the rain obscuring the road. Now and then, a flash of lightning lit Route 9, but there was really nothing to see out there.

"Mudslides on some of the side streets," Nancy said when she brought over the tall glass of chocolate egg cream and the salad platter. "Don't forget. You drink that down, you're gonna climax."

You're annoying me now, Ivy wanted to say. She used to say things out loud, but had begun to censor herself over the past few months. It had gotten that bad. She'd begun to say what she thought, which, to her mind, was the end of sanity. Things slipped out at times that she regretted. She found herself thinking out loud and had to train herself to just keep her mouth shut. She no longer wanted to be polite when she didn't have to be. She no longer wanted to hold things back. She had begun telling people off—minor incidents with the postman, or the pharmacist, or her accountant. Nothing too damaging, but she had stopped keeping it all in. Now she had to change this. *You can't get along in the world and tell it off at the same time.*

Her imbalance between saying what she wanted and keeping it bottled up had begun since she had heard about the fire at the school.

3

Ivy knew she would go to the house as soon as she confirmed the legend of Mark Carpenter, Quincy Allen, and the ghost in the night. She had decided that she would go to the village, which was up the river another few miles from the White Heron Diner, and find out if what had been bothering her for so long might have a basis in fact.

Nights could be wicked in spring along the Hudson River. It was one of those brisk, shivery river nights, the rain spitting and cursing with thunder and lightning. Even then, she wanted to keep driving. She wanted to find the village and then the house. She had spent so much time thinking about it, even obsessing over it, ever since she'd heard about the fire and the deaths, and the boy she had met, briefly.

The boy she'd felt such a connection with. And now she had to see for herself what had happened to Harrow.

YOU COME WHEN I CALL YOU

DOUGLAS CLEGG

An epic tale of horror, spanning twenty years in the lives of four friends—witnesses to unearthly terror. The high desert town of Palmetto, California, has turned toxic after twenty years of nightmares. In Los Angeles, a woman is tormented by visions from a chilling past, and a man steps into a house of torture. On the steps of a church, a young woman has been sacrificed in a ritual of darkness. In New York, a cab driver dreams of demons while awake. And a man who calls himself the Desolation Angel has returned to draw his old friends back to their hometown—a town where, two decades earlier, three boys committed the most brutal of rituals, an act of such intense savagery that it has ripped apart their minds. And where, in a cavern in a place called No Man's Land, something has been waiting a long time for those who stole something more precious than life itself.

___4695-4 $5.99 US/$6.99 CAN

THE NIGHTMARE CHRONICLES

DOUGLAS CLEGG

It begins in an old tenement with a horrifying crime. It continues after midnight, when a young boy, held captive in a basement, is filled with unearthly visions of fantastic and frightening worlds. How could his kidnappers know that the ransom would be their own souls? For as the hours pass, the boy's nightmares invade his captors like parasites—and soon, they become real. Thirteen nightmares unfold: A young man searches for his dead wife among the crumbling buildings of Manhattan... A journalist seeks the ultimate evil in a plague-ridden outpost of India... Ancient rituals begin anew with the mystery of a teenage girl's disappearance... In a hospital for the criminally insane, there is only one doorway to salvation... But the night is not yet over, and the real nightmare has just begun. Thirteen chilling tales of terror from one of the masters of the horror story.

___4580-X $5.50 US/$6.50 CAN

DOUGLAS

HALLOWEEN
THE
MAN
CLEGG

The New England coastal town of Stonehaven has a history of nightmares—and dark secrets. When Stony Crawford becomes a pawn in a game of horror and darkness, he finds that he alone holds the key to the mystery of Stonehaven and to the power of the unspeakable creature trapped within a summer mansion.

___4439-0 $5.50 US/$6.50 CAN

T. M. WRIGHT
Sleepeasy

Harry Briggs led a fairly normal life. He had a good job, a nice house, and a beautiful wife named Barbara, with whom he was very much in love. Then he died. That's when Harry's story really begins. That's when he finds himself in a strange little town called Silver Lake. In Silver Lake nothing is normal. In Silver Lake Harry has become a detective, tough and silent, hot on the trail of a missing woman and a violent madman. But the town itself is an enigma. It's a shadowy twilight town, filled with ghostly figures that seem to be playing according to someone else's rules. Harry has unwittingly brought other things with him to this eerie realm. Things like uncertainty, fear . . . and death.

___4864-7 $5.99 US/$6.99 CAN

. . . and coming
May 2001
from. . .

Elizabeth Massie

Wire Mesh Mothers

It all starts with the best of intentions. Kate McDolen, an elementary school teacher, knows she has to protect little eight-year-old Mistie from parents who are making her life a living hell. So Kate packs her bags, quietly picks up Mistie after school one day and sets off with her toward what she thinks will be a new life. How can she know she is driving headlong into a nightmare?

The nightmare begins when Tony jumps into the passenger seat of Kate's car, waving a gun. Tony is a dangerous girl, more dangerous than anyone could dream. She doesn't admire anything except violence and cruelty, and she has very different plans in mind for Kate and little Mistie. The cross-country trip that follows will turn into a one-way journey to fear, desperation . . . and madness.

___4869-8 $5.99 US/$6.99 CAN

The Lost

Jack Ketchum

It was the summer of 1965. Ray, Tim and Jennifer were just three teenage friends hanging out in the campgrounds, drinking a little. But Tim and Jennifer didn't know what their friend Ray had in mind. And if they'd known they wouldn't have thought he was serious. Then they saw what he did to the two girls at the neighboring campsite—and knew he was dead serious.

Four years later, the Sixties are drawing to a close. No one ever charged Ray with the murders in the campgrounds, but there is one cop determined to make him pay. Ray figures he is in the clear. Tim and Jennifer think the worst is behind them, that the horrors are all in the past. They are wrong. The worst is yet to come.

___4876-0 $5.99 US/$6.99 CAN